DANDELIONS

WAXWOOD SERIES: BOOK 4

TAM MAY

Dreambook Press

Dandelions

Waxwood Series: Book 4

Tam May

Published by Dreambook Press.

Copyright © 2020 by Tam May. All rights reserved. This is a work of fiction. Any resemblance to actual persons living or dead, businesses, events or locales is purely coincidental. Reproduction in whole or part of this publication without express written consent is strictly prohibited.

Click or visit:
https://www.tammayauthor.com

Cover Design © 2021 by Essi/100 Covers

ISBN: 9780998338521 (Print)
ISBN: 9780998338538 (ebook)

Quotes in the text are as follows:

Chapter 7

Joshua 1:6-9, New International Version

Matthew 7:15, King James Version

Matthew 7:15, King James Version

Chapter 9

Barrett Browning, Elizabeth. "The Lady's Yes." *British Literature*. https://surveyofbritishliterature.wordpress.com/2018/03/21/elizabeth-barrett-brownings-the-ladys-yes/. Accessed 17 November 2020.

Luke 6:37, New International Version

Chapter 14

Kol Nidre, the Metsudah Machzor. *My Jewish Learning*. https://www.myjewishlearning.com/article/text-of-kol-nidre/. Accessed 17 November 2020.

Corinthians 12:26, English Standard Version.

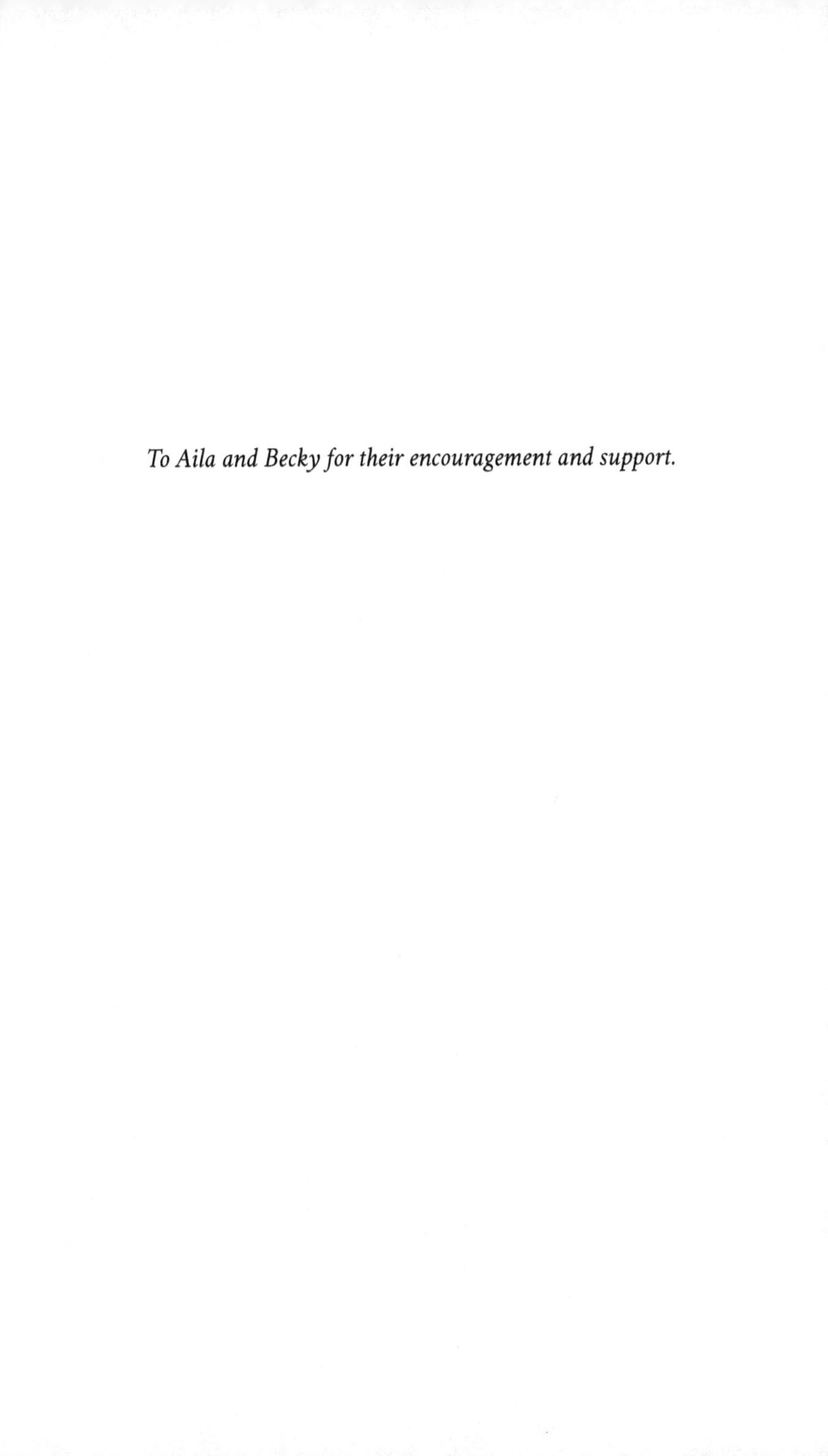

To Aila and Becky for their encouragement and support.

CHAPTER 1

Want more feisty Gilded Age heriones who go against conventions? Love intricate mysteries with humor and a fun cast of characters? Then you'll love my free offer at the end of this book! So don't forget to check that out when you get to the end. Happy reading!

Vivian looked at the man in front of her with the bushy eyebrows and a face that resembled a rag doll she had once seen when she was a child. "Mr. Bates, you ought not to take such advantage of a lady." There was no denying that, even in her worn tweed suit and faded blouse, her strawberry blond hair tucked underneath her, she was still a lady despite the past year's hardships.

She had also kept the cultivated finesse and helpless demeanor of a woman who was used to being pampered by men in the blue blood society where women were little better than lap dogs, which she put on for such occasions when she knew it would do some good. And it worked on Mr. Bates, for his beard quivered, and his eyes cast down with the shame of a man who had insulted a lady. "I assure you, Mrs. Caulfield, I have never taken advantages in my life, neither with a man nor a woman."

"I didn't say *woman*, Mr. Bates." Vivian eyed him. "I said *lady*."

Mr. Bates, a formidable opponent with bargaining, even with those far above his station, offered her a hard-seated chair when she came into his bookshop, but Vivian took the worn one with the stuffing nearly gone out the back. As she leaned forward and crossed her ankles, their definite shape appeared below her long skirt. She knew she presented the figure of a lady whom a man dominated by commercial self-interest could not outdo.

"Mrs. Caulfield, these books are rare antiques," the man insisted.

"They are nothing of the kind, sir," she said. "*The Fables of Phaedrus* was published a mere thirteen years ago."

"Well, really—"

"And the Lewis Carroll books are practically modern," she pointed out. "The *Wonderland* book has been with us since the end of the Civil War, and the *Looking Glass* book only six years after that."

He cocked one of his eyebrows, making the beaded dark eye disappear. "Your knowledge of modern literature astounds me, Mrs. Caulfield."

"I used to be a great reader," she said, not without a note of regret in her voice as she looked far off into the high book shelves that walled the shop on all sides.

"One has little time for books when one must earn one's living," Mr. Bates agreed with a sigh, throwing the same regretful look at the shelves.

Vivian put both hands on the pouch in her lap, making the man's gaze draw upon it. "I shall pay fifty cents for four copies of each of the books we discussed."

The disheveled beard and mustache hid his expression, but Vivian could tell from the grim tone in his voice that he was not pleased. "I sell to lending libraries at seventy-five."

"We're not another lending library, Mr. Bates," Vivian said firmly. "We don't take subscription prices for our bread and butter. These books are for women who desperately need to improve their reading."

"With all due respect, that would hardly concern me." His eyebrows evened, and the beaded expression hardened. "I will accept seventy and no less."

She leaned forward, casting a demure look in his direction, her eyes widening to just the right weight of helplessness. "You don't understand, sir. We are a charitable institution."

The buzz of the electric light hummed over his voice in the small bookshop. "Sixty."

"Fifty cents is all I can spare," she said, her look equally determined.

"Even the wholesalers wouldn't dare ask that," he grumbled.

"But you shall make an exception for a charitable institution for ladies, won't you, Mr. Bates?" She gave him a sweet smile.

"Charity begins in the home, does it not?" he asked.

"Precisely," said Vivian. "We occasionally allow ladies without one to bed down at the library. That makes it a home, doesn't it?"

He looked at her, a flicker of admiration in the grim smile. "You're quite a tradeswoman, Mrs. Caulfield. Lady like you, if you don't mind my saying so—"

"I do mind," Vivian said sharply.

He sighed and headed toward the back of the shop, calling over his shoulder, "You shall take the books with you, of course."

"I will do no such thing," she said. "I will take one copy of the *Phaedrus* with me, and the rest I will expect you to send promptly, just as any other library would."

"Sent!" He stared at her. "But, Mrs. Caulfield, you're in Waxwood!"

"You told me yourself you frequently send books to several of your clients living in those big houses up on the hills of Waxwood," Vivian pointed out. "Perhaps the Waxwood Women's

Lending Library isn't so fine, but I hope we may consider ourselves equally important clients."

"Clients who shall take the bread from my children's mouths if I don't take heed," he snarled.

"No, sir," she said firmly, leaning against her parasol as she rose. "Clients who will put noble ideas into your children's hearts when they learn their father has sold books at a special price to women who are helping other women gain a desperately needed education."

He leaned against the table with both elbows, peering up at her. "Seems to me you women have been using your education too well already with your banners and shouts outside City Hall and down Market Street, eh?"

"Not enough of us," Vivian said with a smile as she counted out the bills. "But the future will bring more."

"So they say, so they say," he muttered as his eyes turned like globes, taking the money in his hand and counting it again.

She stepped outside Post Street, breathing in the cool air. She couldn't help but think with amusement that Mr. Bates was probably one of those men who considered women only slightly superior to birds. Then she remembered the last time she had visited the man and his lamentations of a canary who had flown away while he was cleaning its cage in his shop. Recalling the damp-eyed fondness with which he had spoken of the yellow bird's sweet song, she knew nothing would coax Mr. Bates and his kind to speak of their wives with the same regard, had the wives been the ones to fly away rather than the canaries.

She looked at the watch hanging from her belt. At this hour, her mother would be at home.

She began walking toward Leavenworth, crossing Union Square to get away from the crowds. She came to the city frequently now for books and donations to the lending library, always walking to and from the train station now that there was no money for taxi cabs. More than once, Nettie offered to go in her stead, insisting it was hardly fair to send Vivian wandering around the city in the style to which she was no longer accustomed. But Vivian argued Nettie was the last person to wander the streets of in San Francisco.

"It used to be my city," she reminded her. "I know its streets, its rhythms, and its people. I still have connections, some of whom may help us." And, indeed, she had managed to get a donation for the library from more than one Nob Hill aristocrat. She found she enjoyed haggling with men like Mr. Bates, who thought their business savvy more than equal to a frumpy woman running a lending library and reading room without asking for a subscription from anyone.

Today, she welcomed the trudge up Leavenworth. She took the steps slowly, as her thoughts came quickly — the books she had just bought, the room at the lending library Nettie had said that morning could become sleeping quarters if they could only get hold of two or three cots, and her promise to make time to read with the two Mrs. Shiners, sisters-in-law who had just found an old Bible lying in the attack of their recently deceased father-in-law's house.

"We want to understand the Sunday sermons at church better," the women had said. "And talk about 'em too. Smart-like, you know." The older Mrs. Shiner had added, "Karen's man just got a job at the front office. He's takin' mail n'things, but the boss is a God-fearing man and likes to hear church talk 'mong his employees. He ain't much for book-learnin', so Karen figures if she knew how to talk 'bout them things, he might pick up on it."

Vivian couldn't help but grimace at her reflection in a shop window. Karen Shiner's husband, she knew, would avoid his wife's "book-learnin'" if he could help it. He would, she was sure, disapprove of her wasting a Sunday afternoon after church at the library, just like so many of the men.

The male population of the city had not greeted The Waxwood Women's Lending Library and Reading Room with many cheers when she and Nettie opened their doors in January. Not that anyone did a thing to stop them. Waxwood, her friend assured her, was not a town of violence. But the frowns on the faces of both men and women who passed by the small room, which had been a feed store a few doors down from Alda Quigg's office, said more than whatever words could come out of their lips. It was a wonder the women came at all. And yet, they did, not only from Waxwood, but from all over the county.

A cab pulled up to the curb, and two figures flounced out, their lilac perfume and bright pink and green dresses swirling across the pavement. Vivian slowed her steps as she saw the flax-colored waves underneath the picture hat, and the flushed cheeks of one of them belonged to Amber Griffith Stewart. Near her, a woman who looked much younger and had more of a scarecrow figure loomed, pressing her parasol from one gloved hand to the other, as if awaiting instructions. As she turned around, her eyes met Vivian's.

Before Vivian could move away, the girl rushed forward, her wide eyes matching the wideness of her mouth. "Why, Miss Alderdice!"

In a smooth voice, she said, "I go by my married name, Mrs. Caulfield, now. Just as you go by yours, Mrs. Leblanc." She had met Christina Sowberry, the sweet, if rather complacent young woman, the previous summer in Waxwood. Just before Christmas of last year, the girl had become Mrs. Monte Leblanc.

"Oh!" The girl seemed relieved. "Monte will be so pleased to hear you're married. We thought—"

"Vivian means her deceased husband's name," Amber said with her ferret smile. "If you don't mind my saying so, dear, it's about time you went by Miles' name. Odd that you never did."

"I could hardly feel like a Caulfield when we were only married ten months before he died, Amber," Vivian said. "Unlike you, I never considered my husband's name a given even before the ink on the marriage license was dry."

A flash of anger appeared on the woman's face, but her voice was pleasant as she said, "You're looking well, Vivian." Her sharp eyes swept from head to toe.

"You mean, I'm looking shabby, and that pleases you." Vivian cocked the rim of her hat a little toward her face, aware that she looked pale in the brilliant city sun. "You always needed a social interpreter, Amber."

"Perhaps you mean a truth-sayer," said the woman, eyeing her. "Still intending to take your freedom rather than have it given?"

Vivian felt her face grow hot. "How did you know about that?"

"Oh, Monte told us all about it," Amber said. "About you and he last summer."

"Did he?" She doubted Monte, from whom she had parted company on the best of terms, would have broadcast their rather odd summer together to Washington Street society. His father, on the other hand, loved to gossip as much as the ladies and often did so with little discretion.

"His father did, really," Mrs. Leblanc admitted, as if reading Vivian's mind. "He thought it rather amusing. The way you put it, I mean."

"I assure you it was anything but amusing." Vivian glanced at the window of a flower shop near them.

"You ought to have told us you were back from the Adirondacks," said Amber.

"Adirondacks?"

"Larissa gave us the impression you would be there for quite some time," the woman said.

"Oh, I see." Vivian felt anger bristling in her chest. "Mother told you I was in the Adirondacks."

"She said you found yourself a little peaceful cottage in the woods." Amber's ferret eyes cast their stone glance. "Recovering from your disappointment last summer."

Her words startled Vivian for a moment. "I had no disappointments last summer."

"I would hardly say that," said the woman with a little laugh. "Considering Christina is wearing Monte's ring and not you."

Vivian bit back a smile. So this is what her mother had told everyone. She felt her heart quicken. "You're quite wrong. I'm very happy for them both."

"Why, it was Miss Alderdice — Mrs. Caulfield — who suggested it!" Mrs. Leblanc fluttered.

Amber glared at her friend as if reprimanding her for daring to contradict, and continued, "I suppose you've taken up that cottage in Waxwood now?"

"Cottage in Waxwood?"

"Oh, the beach there has become quite fashionable now," said Amber. "George and I were thinking of buying one ourselves next year, just so we can have a rest now and then in the summer."

"Cottage." Vivian could hardly keep the smile off her face, thinking of the small, hollow flat in which she and Nettie lived on the commercial side of town. "I assume my mother told you that too."

"She mentioned something of the kind."

"I'm afraid I must correct some of your misconceptions, Amber." Vivian felt her chest tighten. "I was never in the Adirondacks, whether to recover from a romantic disappointment or anything else. And I don't live in a cottage in Waxwood."

"Oh?"

"I live on George Street," said Vivian. "In Waxwood's commercial district."

"Oh." Amber ground her lips. "Now I understand." Her eyes flicked again to Vivian's worn dress and hat.

"I've taken up with a friend there." Her voice grew stronger. "We run a business, and we also help working-class and poor women enhance their education."

"Then you've joined Mrs. Moore in her blue-stocking activities?" Amber asked. "I'm not surprised."

"I'm afraid Marvina and I no longer move in the same circles," Vivian remarked. "We're still friends, of course. But her work is about petitions and letters. Mine is more practical and immediate."

"You always were practical and immediate," said Amber icily.

"I wasn't really," Vivian said. "I was as frivolous as the rest of you. But when one has to earn every penny, one must be practical and immediate."

Amber glared at her. "Then it's very generous of you to find the time to visit us in our frivolous world here on Washington Street. Especially since Larissa told Mother you've become so engrossed in your romantic disappointment you haven't even written."

The eggshell pallor of her face contrasted the sudden flush on Vivian's. "I wouldn't have bothered any of you in your insulated enclave had Mother not summoned me."

"One cannot ignore a mother's summons, heaven knows." Amber linked her arm with Mrs. Leblanc's. "Come, dear, we mustn't keep Vivian from her important call."

"I'm sorry I've kept you from your important appointment," Vivian mumbled.

"We're helping Miss Dunstan with her trousseau," Mrs. Leblanc said in an eager voice. "She's getting married in a few months."

"You remember her, don't you, Vivian?" Amber asked. "Miss India Dunstan?"

"I met her briefly last year," said Vivian. "Congratulate her for me, will you?"

"You're so far removed from the likes of us, she would hardly remember you." Amber smirked.

"I'm still civilized enough to wish a young woman happiness," Vivian snapped.

"It's a perfect match, of course," Mrs. Leblanc blurted. "Monte says Mr. Firestone has the most precious jewelry shop on Union Street. He promised to take me there to buy me diamonds!" This sent a shine of cherry through her thin face.

"I doubt Vivian would be much interested in diamonds, Christina," said Amber. "She's made it quite clear her tastes are more plebeian nowadays. Or are they?" The ferret eyes glistened.

"My diamonds may be in the rough," Vivian said, "but they shine nonetheless."

Without answering, Amber shot into the flower shop, dragging Mrs. Leblanc behind her.

Vivian shook her head as she continued mounting Leavenworth with a less than steady gait. She had expected Larissa to come up with some excuse to explain why her daughter no longer lived among the people who had been, if not her friends, her acquaintances for most of her life. But she had hoped her mother had stopped spilling out half-truths that no one believed and hiding anything she thought Washington Street society would consider shocking or unconventional. She would have wanted nothing more than to see Larissa smash to pieces the box of Unmentionables that had held the family in a prison of the past for so long.

As she passed Clay Street, she saw a woman settled on the pavement with her back against the wall of an abandoned shop. Her dress was more ragged than Vivian's, and her stringy hair flew out from beneath a half-eaten hat. But her face and hands were not dirty, nor did she have the sour gaze Vivian had seen on so many city beggars. The woman was not quite begging, either. She sat cross-legged, her hands on her knees, staring straight ahead. The unblinking eyes made Vivian wonder if the woman had lost her sight and her home.

She stopped and dug into her pouch for a handful of coins. Bending down, she took the woman's hand and laid the coins carefully inside. "Here, ma'am. Buy yourself some pins for your hair. Better still," she pulled out a few bills, "buy yourself a new hat this winter."

"Bless ya, miss, bless ya," murmured the woman.

Vivian realized the beggar was younger than she had first thought. The city elements had not been kind to her skin, and a molten pallor covered the delicate wrists, which Vivian noticed as the woman's sleeves slipped down when she had taken her cupped hands.

She pressed Marvina's card into the woman's hand. "My friend can help you find shelter and food, miss." She added, "If you can get someone to read the card for you—"

The woman leaned forward and grabbed Vivian's hand, crushing her fingers in a savage way. "You're looking for forgiveness!"

"Forgiveness?" Vivian stared at the woman's face. She realized the half-closed eyes were staring straight at her with recognition.

"You shall find it," the woman promised. "In those who have caused you pain, you shall find it, but only if you do not deny them your own."

Vivian let her hand slip out. She backed away, feeling as if the woman's razor tone were cutting into her like scissors ripping through a lace pattern. Not that she felt the woman had cursed her. It was only the way she had said it with such certainty, like a prophetess, that frightened Vivian.

She ambled up Washington Street, and soon she could see the house — Alderdice Hall, on the haunches of the hill where her grandfather Malcolm Alderdice built it to prove that the Flesa buccaneer could outdo even the grandiosity of the Hopkins and Crocker mansions. Looking at it now, Vivian admitted that, compared to the flat she shared with Nettie, it was like a giant spider of a place with its turrets and towers and trim. How little she had thought about those wide-spaced rooms and high ceilings and hallways where one couldn't see the last room from the first when she had lived there! And yet, its coldness had chilled her bones, unlike Nettie's flat, which was always warm and bright, even when the curtains were closed.

Although she had never given back the key to the house, she knocked on the door as if she were a guest. Basset, the butler who had been with the family for generations, treated her as such. There was no warmth in the man's greeting, no recognition in the glinted gray eyes. He merely bowed as he took her gloves and parasol and asked her to wait while he saw whether "the mistress was still at home."

The way he let her stand in the hall, her hands folded in front of her, made her feel like an intruder. She lived in the house for twenty-six years and had come in response to her mother's message. And yet, she had to announce herself like someone waiting to find out if the master and mistress were at home!

She heard a tapping at the stairs and lifted her eyes to see Betty, the upstairs parlor maid, peeking down, the feather duster lifted like a sword in her hand. She gave Vivian a somewhat toothy smile and lifted her free hand in a wave. Betty had always liked her and admired her love of books, always venturing a question or two about the book Vivian was reading if she stumbled into a room where Vivian had settled herself with a novel. Vivian had always answered her by relating the plot, amused at the way the girl's eyes had bulged and her mouth had parted, as if she were a child listening to a ghost story.

For the first time since she entered the house, Vivian felt a wave of warmth surge through her. She made a mental note to send over a few of the books from the library for Betty through Mrs. Dale, the Alderdice Hall cook, who approved of "book-learning" for women.

The doors separating the hallway from the parlor slid open. Vivian expected to see Basset with his stony face, but it was her mother. Larissa's expression was pleasant and composed, her elegant features holding steady like a mask. It was the way she remembered her mother before Jake left. Larissa had now regained her equilibrium.

And yet, there was apprehension that pinched her sharp blue eyes as she came forward and took both Vivian's hands. "This is a pleasant surprise, dear."

"You wrote me, Mother," she reminded her. She wanted to lean forward to kiss Larissa on the cheek, but something in her mother's poise forbade it.

"Well, we weren't sure if you would come. We haven't heard from you in so long."

"I've been so busy," Vivian murmured. She followed Larissa into the parlor. "Where's Bennett?"

"At the club, dear," said her mother. "Where he always is this time of day. We weren't sure if you would come," she repeated.

Vivian reddened as she settled into the chair that had always been her favorite. "I would never ignore a summons from you."

"I hardly call it a summons," Larissa said sharply. "When I told you last year that I wouldn't return your letters unopened, I expected there to *be* letters. Not one Christmas card and no more."

Vivian looked down. "I told you, I've been busy."

"I see you've lost some of your ladylike manners." Her mother glanced down at the gloves. "You've also lost that annoying habit of fidgeting with your fingers."

"Sometimes one outgrows one's faults, Mother," Vivian replied, her voice equally sharp. "When one has a mind to."

There was the resigned silence that always followed her and her mother's sparring. No matter how stinging their words became, Vivian was aware of an underlying respect for one another's viewpoints between them.

She tried to lighten the mood. "I see it didn't take Bennett long to pick up the Washington Street habits."

"His habits were well established when we married," her

mother remarked. "I haven't tried to change a single one of them."

"I'm sure you didn't, since they coincide with yours," Vivian said slyly. "Isn't it lucky your third husband should have been Mrs. Marsden's relative and thus well acquainted with Washington Street practices?"

"I hardly see what that has to do with it." Larissa nodded at Annie, who had wandered in at the ring of her bell. "Tea, please, Annie."

"Yes, madame." The girl bowed, but her eyes flickered with warm recognition at Vivian as she went out of the room.

"On the contrary," Vivian said. "It has to do with everything."

Her mother regarded her with a simpering look. "Still speaking in circles, aren't you, Vivian?"

"Yes, that's one fault I haven't outgrown," Vivian admitted. "But you'll be glad to know I'm no longer your Dagger Girl. I've stopped probing, Mother."

"I'm glad to hear it." Her mother mumbled.

"I'm more sensible too," Vivian continued. "Compared to some of the peacocks here, I'm positively efficient."

"I thought you were looking rather tired," her mother said dryly.

"It's tiring to earn one's living, Mother."

"I thought you were doing charitable work."

"I am," said Vivian. "I'm also working with Nettie at the drugstore for our bread and butter."

"The hours are too long," said her mother.

"How could you know how long the hours are?" Vivian jumped. The cognizant look in Larissa's eyes made it clear. "You've had me followed!"

The parlor doors opened, and her mother turned her attention to Mrs. Dale, who set the tea tray down. As she did so, the simple woman's eyes cast upon Vivian. The dampness in them touched her as the cook said, "Good to see you again, miss, and if you ain't looking a sight for sore eyes!"

"It's good to see you too, Mrs. Dale." Vivian grasped the woman's hand.

"It ain't never been right, you being away, and Mister Jacob—"

"That will do, Mrs. Dale." Larissa's voice cut through the perfumed air. "Thank you for bringing the tray up yourself."

"Oh, madame, when Betty told me Miss Alderdice was home—"

"Mrs. Caulfield," Larissa corrected.

"Yes, madame, Mrs. Caulfield." The woman curtsied. "I just had to see her again."

"I'm glad you did," Vivian said kindly.

"You may go." Her mother's voice was now shaking. The woman withdrew, dabbing at her eyes with the edge of her apron.

"Well, at least the servants have missed me," Vivian remarked.

"Not only the servants, dear." The simple statement came from her mother's lips with the same even tone as she would use to welcome a Washington Street family back from vacation, but the glistening in her eyes told of something deeper.

"Is that why you wrote me?" Vivian asked. "Or is it because your spy told you I was disgracing the family?"

"My spy, as you call him, was your stepfather," Larissa snapped. "When he saw how upset I was at not hearing from you for six months, he took it upon himself to inquire after you." She set the teapot down. "I know you find it hard to believe, Vivian, but there are people in this world who worry about you."

Vivian felt the shame burn her cheeks as much as the teacup she took in her hands burned her fingertips. "I'm sorry. It was very kind of him to take an interest in my welfare for your sake." She sighed. "You've done well for yourself, Mother."

"The luck of the third adventure, I believe Miss Barrett Browning said." Her mother looked at her slyly.

"I hope so, considering the first and second time didn't yield much," Vivian murmured.

Her mother handed her the teacup with a cinnamon stick lying on the saucer instead of a spoon. Vivian had always loved her tea with cinnamon, but this was rarely served because her mother considered cinnamon too excitable for a young woman. "It yielded a little more than that."

Vivian knew her mother was referring to her as the result of first marriage and Jake the result of her second, and she covered her mother's hand. "Thank you for saying that."

"Bennett will be back for lunch, of course," said her mother. "You'll stay and have lunch with us, won't you?"

"I'm afraid I can't."

"But we haven't seen you in so long!" There was a ragged edge in her voice.

"Not as long as it ought to have been, according to Amber and Mrs. Leblanc." Vivian leaned back with a keen eye. "I met them coming up here."

"You ought to call her Christina, dear," said Larissa. "She's one of us now."

"But I'm not." Vivian gave her in a meaningful tone. "My station in life warrants a formal address of anyone I don't know personally. You remember I only met Miss Sowberry and her mother last year."

"Such nonsense!"

"It isn't, Mother," said Vivian. "I'm living a different life now, far away from Washington Street. Anyone walking down Leavenworth just now would have seen it. Me in my sensible suit and those two peacocks in their flouncing pastels and lace parasols."

"You sound as if you were jealous," said her mother with a shrewd look.

Vivian set the teacup down with a clang. "The only thing I'm jealous of is that they get more spending money from their henpecked husbands than Nettie and I can make in a year!"

"You may return here anytime you wish," said her mother in a soft voice.

"From my cottage on the fashionable side of Waxwood?" Vivian snorted. "I know you've been telling everybody that too."

"I had to tell them *something* when you didn't come back to San Francisco with me last summer," Larissa insisted. "And since they all expected you to marry Monte—"

"You let them believe I was recuperating from the disappointment of being cast off by the Canadian buccaneer and hiding myself in a cabin in the Adirondacks," Vivian finished. "We've never even been to the Adirondacks!"

"You hardly left me a choice, did you?" Larissa asked with an even smile.

"The truth is always a choice." Vivian glared at her. "You ignored that choice, as you always do. You left it up to me to tell those women the truth."

"Truth?"

"About what I'm doing," she said. "About who I am now."

"Vivian!"

"Well, it can hardly hurt you now, can it?" Vivian asked. "You're no longer Larissa Alderdice, the daughter of a Flesa upstart forced upon their society. If you ever were that."

"I was always that." Her mother stared at her.

"You're Mrs. Blackwell, wife of the respectable and retired owner of Blackwell, Fisk, & Moody, the most prominent brokerage firm in Los Angeles," Vivian continued. "Whatever they say can't touch you now."

"That won't stop them from saying it," said Larissa dryly. "It might make Bennett very uncomfortable."

"I thought you told him all about us," Vivian said, looking at her mother squarely. "All the woes I let out of Pandora's box last year and the years since Grandmother's death."

"A woman doesn't rub her past in the face of the man she loves," her mother insisted.

Vivian watched Larissa as she poured herself another cup of tea, then daintily took a lump of sugar from the bowl, dropped it into her cup, and while stirring, made a whirlpool in the brown liquid. She wanted to make some snide comment about love, for her mother's words from last year still echoed in her ears: *Love ruins a woman.* She didn't believe Larissa would allow herself to love anyone. Not now.

"At least you admit there is a past to rub in his face," she said instead.

"I admit no such thing."

The parlor doors opened, and the man in question poked his head in. When he saw Vivian, he smiled amiably. "I see you've decided to come see us after all." He opened the doors all the way and stepped in.

Vivian smiled, accepting his kiss on her cheek. She liked Bennett, whose robust figure and apple cheeks reminded her of a caricature of President McKinley, except his eyes and mouth were set in a less severe pose. But the slick hair and arched eagle eyebrows were the same.

"Help me persuade her to stay for lunch, dear," said her mother, tilting her head so he could kiss her cheek.

"Of course you must," he said with a smile, easing himself into the gold high-backed chair, the only one that fit him comfortably. "You've neglected us for far too long, Vivian. You can't fly off without a good chat, and we've much to discuss." He threw Larissa a glance.

"Mother and I have already had a good chat." Vivian rose. "I really must catch the train back to Waxwood."

"Larissa, did you talk about that other matter, ahem?" He made a pointed gesture at her mother with his arched eyes.

Larissa put her arm around Vivian's shoulders. "I wrote you for a reason, Vivian."

"Oh?" Vivian smoothed down the folds of her jacket.

Larissa tilted her head. "I hate to see you looking so dowdy, dear. Your clothes are still upstairs, you know. Your room is just the way you left it, in fact."

Vivian grimaced. "I can hardly serve sodas and shelve dusty books in satin and lace, can I?"

"You don't have to look like a factory girl either," her mother snapped.

"You look a bit worn, my dear," Bennett ventured.

"Nettie made me this suit." Vivian stiffened a little. "We went to a shop in Goldspur to see a woman. We had to buy something, so we bought this linen. I think it's rather becoming, in its businesslike way."

"One may wear businesslike clothes without looking limp," Bennett said and gave a hearty laugh.

"Nettie will be insulted when I tell her you said that," Vivian remarked, but she knew he was teasing.

"Then don't take your old clothes." Her mother's hand pressed her shoulder. "Buy your own."

"With what?" Vivian eyed her. "Do you know, Mother, a shirtwaist costs almost a dollar nowadays? One can buy a book for that, or a few boxes of fancy stationery—"

"And what of it?" Larissa interrupted. Bennett gave a slight cough.

Vivian, amused at the innocent look on her mother's face, realized how futile it was to talk to her about such things. "It's a question of priorities, Mother. A new shirtwaist is not a priority. More books and writing paper and pencils are."

"And why are they?" Larissa looked genuinely confused.

"Because the more of those we have, the more women we can help," said Vivian. "The more women we help, the quicker they can get better jobs and buy their own shirtwaists rather than go begging for them." She adjusted her pouch around her wrist. "And now that I've explained to you how the other half lives, I really *must* go."

"I asked you to come because I know you need clothes and

shoes and other necessities," Larissa said firmly. "Your old allowance is still waiting for you."

"Just like my old clothes?" Vivian asked warily. "And my old life too, perhaps?"

Bennett ventured, "Your mother's been most concerned about you, my dear."

"Yes, I know you've been asking after me," Vivian said. "But Nettie and I are getting by very well with what we earn from the drugstore. We're hardly paupers."

"You can't tell me you'd rather live as you do now rather than the way you did before," said Larissa. "When you were at home, that is." The last had a little tin ring of despair.

She pressed both her mother's hands. "You're very generous, Mother. But it's the library that could use the money."

"That doesn't interest me!"

Vivian dropped her mother's hands. "I see. Your generosity comes with conditions. I ought to have known."

"I only want to see you happy and not living in such squalid conditions!" The growl came out with even more despair.

Vivian kissed her mother's cold cheek. "I know your intentions are good. But I'm all right."

"You're being stubborn, you know," Bennett remarked lightly.

Vivian grinned as she headed for the doors. "I have my grandmother's mulish streak. Ask Mother to tell you about it sometime."

Larissa took a tight hold of her hand. "You won't let another six months lapse before you come and see us, will you, dear?"

"I'll try not to," she promised.

As she gathered her gloves and parasol from the hallway, with Basset's bowed figure presiding, she caught a glimpse of Betty at the top of the stairs. She lifted her hand and waved at her, and the girl grinned, waving back her feather duster so it flapped like a fine woman's fan. Vivian left the house, willing herself not to look back at it.

CHAPTER 2

The train station on Fourth Street was bustling with the lunchtime crowd when Vivian arrived. She saw a cluster of people around the locomotive standing on the tracks. It was clear there had been an accident.

Having no wish to see the gore, she edged toward the ticket window furthest away from the assemblage and bought her second-class ticket to Waxwood. She found herself a place on a bench near to where her train stopped and settled with the Phaedrus tales in her lap. Glancing up in intervals, she first saw two men in white wiggle through the crowd with a stretcher, then another man with the clear authority of a doctor. At last, the stretcher came away with a writhing figure underneath the blanket. She bit her lip when she realized the size of the person underneath was that of a child.

"These newfangled engines!" a man close to her remarked. "Ain't got but evil in 'em."

"You can't fight progress, Mac," said the woman sitting next to him.

"Fight, no," the man named Mac replied. "But get somethin' human in 'em, yes. Look here, I work ten hours a day at that meat grinder, and don't you go thinkin' I ain't got nightmares 'bout ending up in them blades one day—"

"Mac, please!" the woman shrieked, holding her hands to her ears.

"I'm sorry, Rita." He put his arm around her shoulders, no longer indignant. "Wouldn't upset you for nothin', you know that. And, anyway, there's the insurance in case—"

Vivian felt a lump in her throat. These were the people she had come to know in the last year, and the way they spoke of death, as if the Grim Reaper were always lurking about, ready to spring out at them with his hood and sickle, had shocked her at first. It was not long before she realized that, for them, it was a simple matter of equation. Their logic dictated that Providence rarely chose its victims among the wealthy.

The book slid off her lap. She tried to snatch it up before the rushed feet of those running to their train trampled all over it, but thin, knobby hands reached it before hers. The hands opened the book to the place where she had been reading and set it on her lap. She looked up to give the man her thanks and stared, as there was no mistaking the wheat-colored hair and elegant mustache, grown out a bit from the previous year.

"How do you do, Vivian?" Roger Howe tipped his hat back and took hold of her hand.

She had a hard time finding her voice to answer him. Seeing Roger again didn't stun her, but the view of the tall, red-headed man standing a little off to the side did.

"We seem to meet in crowds, don't we?" Roger smiled as he sat down next to her. "The last time was a picnic, wasn't it?"

"Yes." Though her hands were still shaking a little, Vivian had recovered most of her composure. "The Fourth of July picnic in the Waxwood city park, to be exact." She then gazed at the other man, who had not sat down. All the acrid loathing she thought she had driven from her heart in the two years since she met the man converged into one vile lump in her chest, and she gasped for a breath.

Roger, who had been watching her, stammered, "I was going to ask if you remembered my cousin, but I see you do."

"I will never forget him," she said in a stifled voice. "No matter how hard I try!"

Roger addressed the redhead, "Come, Harland, you remember Vivian, don't you?"

The man's head tilted at a strange angle, as if he were staring not at the ground or the train tracks but somewhere in between. His arms crossed, and his feet pointed outward. His silence and statuesque manner enraged her more. "We're more like old enemies, aren't we, Mr. Stevens?"

"Harland was never really anyone's friend," the young man agreed.

"If Mr. Stevens has forgotten his manners, I haven't." She put out her hand, feeling a sickness rise in her throat at the man's inattentiveness.

"My cousin doesn't move much these days," Roger said, a note of embarrassment in his voice. "He says nothing either, though he will occasionally write things down."

She suddenly noticed a notepad and pencil stub peeking out of Mr. Stevens' breast pocket. She tried to read the impassive face but met with stoic, manly features.

Roger looked more mature and more distinguished than he had the year before. His square jawline had filled out, and his eyes held the confidence of a man who knew his business. The arrogant boyishness she saw when she first met him had disappeared. If he was not yet a man of the world, he was well on his way. "The years have been kind to you, Roger," she said.

"Perhaps less so to you?" His keen eyes surveyed her frayed suit. "I beg your pardon if I sound rude."

"No, only honest," she said.

"Don't tell me the Alderdices have fallen on hard times." He laughed. "I won't believe it."

"No, the Alderdices are just the same," she said with a smile. "I'm not really one of them anymore. I go by Mrs. Caulfield."

"Oh?"

"My widowed name," she said. "Mother always thought it unsuitable for me when I was — well, that was another lifetime ago."

"I think we're all in another lifetime, aren't we?" His eyes swept toward his cousin. "Some have fared better than others."

The redhead neither moved nor ventured an answer where Vivian had expected a retort.

"May I guess you're taking the train to Waxwood just as we are?" Roger asked.

Vivian nodded. "I live there now."

"Do you?" The young man's eyes widened. "I never considered Waxwood more than a resort town."

She laughed. "There have always been residents there, you know."

"I suppose there have been," he admitted. "But why there?"

"A friend took me in," she said.

He hesitated, as if he thought better of what he was planning to say next. "I hope nothing is wrong, Vivian."

"If you mean, has my blue blood family disowned me, no," said Vivian, feeling a sharp pain in her chest. "Not that I have much of a family to disown me anymore."

Roger pressed her hand. "I think I know what you mean."

"I've no one to blame for it except perhaps myself," Vivian murmured. "But there it is."

After a pause where another wave of people rushed toward a steaming train, his voice became more cheerful. "You look quite in charge of yourself."

"I am," said Vivian. "I've been doing wonderful work this past year. Devoting oneself to others when they most need it does one no end of good."

"Indeed, it does," Roger agreed. "I sometimes envy you women. You do good deeds with your bare hands, so to speak. We men are expected to make a profit with ours. Those of us who must earn our living, that is." A tone of resentment entered the air, broken only by the shout of a man at a station master who refused to hold up the train for him.

Vivian eyed him. "Doesn't your work at Vanburgh & Gunn satisfy you?"

He smiled. "You remembered. They are a solid firm, to be sure, but I'm still only an assistant."

"I thought your uncle was going to insure you climbed quickly in the ranks," she teased.

"My uncle died six months ago."

Vivian's eyes flew up to Mr. Stevens. Not a brow had moved, and nothing in the face showed a flicker of emotion. "I'm sorry to hear that," she said delicately.

The man did not respond. A train pulled into the station, making its presence known with a shrieking whistle. Skirts flew and feathers in hats swung with the puffs of steam. The redhead remained unflinching.

"I believe that's our train," she said.

"Will you be joining us in the parlor car?" he asked.

She smiled ruefully. "I've no money for such luxuries anymore, Roger."

"Nor would I," he admitted. "Under normal conditions."

He helped her up, then stopped her from closing the book. He looked down at the pages. "'The Fox and the Stork.' I see you're enjoying Riley's work."

"You've read it?"

He smiled. "I'm no stranger to classic works."

Vivian noticed there was a slight flicker in Mr. Stevens' neck, a tiny movement, though she wondered if she had seen it at all, as the rest of the man remained anchored.

"An apt tale," Roger went on.

"Why do you say that?"

"Riley's stork is female," he said. "And a brilliant stork. She's quick to return the cruelty the fox has shown her." Roger's eyes slid toward his cousin. "I used to call Harland 'Red Fox' when I was a child."

"Because of the red hair?" Vivian asked.

"No, not the hair," he said. "The smile, I think."

"Perhaps if he met his stork, he wouldn't be a fox." She pressed her reticule in one hand while taking the book from Roger in the other.

"He met her, two years ago." Roger gave her a meaningful look.

"It's Jake who was his stork, not me," Vivian said.

"Is Jake still in Europe?" Roger asked as they walked toward the train.

The shrieking whistle from another train gave her time to answer. "Yes."

"I imagine he'll be home soon." Something in Roger's eyes reflected his watchful gaze.

"I imagine," she said vaguely. "He doesn't write often."

She was suddenly aware of the way her voice crumbled in the sudden wind of people pushing past her, and Mr. Stevens' head turned a little in her direction.

"Five minutes!" the station master near the Waxwood train called.

"Vivian." Roger looked uncertain. "Will you let me pay for a parlor car ticket for you?"

"I couldn't let you do that."

"I insist." His voice was stronger. "I think you could use the company, and so could I."

"You have your cousin for company," Vivian glanced at

Stevens. The dark eyes almost met hers.

"Harland isn't company," he said curtly. "Three hours is a long time to ride in silence."

"Yes, it is," she admitted.

"Then you'll allow me?"

Before she could say a word, he flagged a station master and arranged for the parlor car ticket. Vivian watched as he extracted a wad of bills from his pocket with the freedom of one who had been doing so all his life. "I thought you were only an assistant," she observed.

"I have legal power over Harland's assets," he said. "For the time being."

"I see." She turned to the redhead. "It seems you're the one I ought to thank for paying my fare, Mr. Stevens."

He did not answer or acknowledge she had spoken. She tucked the book under her arm, feeling the surge of rage swarm inside her like a hive of bees.

The parlor car was nearly empty, so they found a cozy corner with two plush seats. Roger led Mr. Stevens to the chair behind them and turned it toward the window. The redhead's dark eyes were like glass as they stared into the rolling scenery, his fingertips grasping his knees.

Roger settled in and studied her. "Tell me about why you stayed in Waxwood."

"It's no secret, really," Vivian said. "I liked the town from my first visit."

"When was that?"

"Eight years ago. It was only a small, sleepy town by the bay." She gave a rueful smile. "Not a trace of the lavishness that keeps the swells coming back."

"I should think it wouldn't have had much to offer then," said Roger.

"It didn't," she said, staring distractedly at the roundabout lying empty near the front of the car. "Not in the way of amusement."

"Then why go there?" he asked.

She gave him an even look. "Call it curiosity."

He grinned. "Your evasiveness makes me think it was some romantic intrigue."

"It was," she said. "But not my own."

"I see." He crossed his legs.

"Someone dear to me," she continued. "Forty years ago, in Waxwood, she was someone else." Her eyes stung. "So strange to think so many lies began with a packet of letters."

The car was silent for a while before she heard Roger's discreet cough. "I'm sorry. I should be very glad to challenge this romantic intriguer, whoever he was, to a duel for your sake."

She laughed. "That sounds a little too chivalrous!"

"I'm good with the sword," he insisted.

"You couldn't even if I wanted you to," she said. "He's a specter now. So is the partner of this intrigue. I've tried to stab her out with my dagger questions, but I lost."

"Eh?" He eyed her.

"My mother used to call me the dagger girl because I was always asking pointed questions," she said. "I realized too late one can cut out one's own heart with too many questions." She added, "Or that others can cut one's heart out with their answers. Even when that answer is silence." She stole a glance at Mr. Stevens, whose face had grown slack.

"Forgive me." Roger bowed. "I've been too inquisitive about things that are clearly painful for you to speak of."

"You have been rather curious," she said with a smile.

"Call it boredom, if you like," he said. "Long train rides have always made me restless." He took out a cigarette lighter and then, as if remembering himself, replaced it. "It seems strange you would return to the place where, as you said, so many lies began."

"My life began there too," she said. "I found out who I wasn't in Waxwood. I mean to find out who I am there as well."

She was grateful he did not ask her what she meant. She glanced out the window at the green and yellow valley they had entered, solid and dry-looking in the promise of the first months of summer. Their brittle pallor framed the face she saw reflected on the glass of a man with wide features and dark eyes.

She pivoted and realized Mr. Stevens was facing her. He leaned a little forward, looking more alert than he had at the station. His hands moved toward her lap, making her flinch. Then she realized he was reaching for the *Fables of Phaedrus* in her lap. His hands froze, and his eyes stared down at it.

"What is it, Harland?" Roger's voice was rough.

The dark eyes softened with interest. The domineering and somewhat charismatic man she remembered from two years before showed in the shadow of this weakened creature. She put the book in his hands, wondering what he would do next.

His fingers shook as he opened it and flipped through the pages slowly, his gaze as stiff as his face and lips. Though he was looking at the book, it was clear he wasn't reading it. Even Roger seemed taken by the determination on his cousin's face to find what he was looking for.

Mr. Stevens continued leafing through the pages with slow, walking fingers. Then he stopped and put the book back in her lap She saw he had turned to the story of the fox and the stork.

The young man sitting beside her spoke with some effort, "This is the first time he's shown any comprehension. The first time in months."

She looked at the redhead who had now gone back to the statuesque figure she had seen at the train station.

*S*he found Nettie waiting for her at the station. The woman's mouse-like features had eased now that she had come out of her six-year mourning. The crystal blue suit she wore gave her a lighter appearance, and her smile was more mischievousness, complementing her features better than the sneer Vivian remembered upon their first meeting.

"I thought you were waiting for that shipment of wallpaper," Vivian said as Roger helped her down the steps of the train.

"Odele said she would see to it," said Nettie with a smile. "I thought you might need some help with the books."

"Heavens, no." Vivian laughed. "I had Mr. Bates' promise to bring them to us. They should arrive in a day or two."

"You must have made a sinful promise to get him to do it," Nettie said with a smile. "I heard the man is as generous as a sieve."

"Mr. Bates and I are old friends," Vivian said. "I used to buy books from him—" Here, she gritted her teeth. "He's more apt to comply with the whims of a businesswoman who knows how to behave like a lady."

"I'm no lady, I grant you," Nettie admitted. "I never pretended to be."

"I'm no longer a lady either," Vivian said. "But I still remember how to put on a lady's face."

Roger, who had been busy settling his cousin and the baggage, threw out in his thin voice, "I object to that remark, Vivian. You've been nothing less than ladylike since the day I've known you."

"This is Mr. Roger Howe, Nettie," Vivian said. "We met at the station, and he kindly insisted I ride in the parlor car with him and his cousin."

"I know what the second-class car is like," he said briefly. "Rather scratchy seats and the sound of clicking knitting needles in one's ears when one is trying to get some sleep."

"You're not far wrong, Mr. Howe," said Nettie with a laugh. Then, her eyes caught the dark figure behind him.

"Nettie, I believe you already know Mr. Harland Stevens," said Vivian. "You saw him in a much less presentable state last year. He was the man who came into the drugstore that night asking for witch hazel---for the boy who ran into some hogweed in the woods."

"Yes," said Nettie. "I remember. I'm glad to see you, Mr. Stevens."

In the silence that followed, Roger said, "Vivian mentioned the excellent work you're doing. I'd like to hear more about it sometime."

Her friend nodded but continued to stare at the redhead who had taken the same posture as in the station in San Francisco — arms crossed, feet apart, staring at an unidentifiable point on the platform. "Your cousin had no money and insisted on working for the payment. He did very well stocking the heavier bottles, and he even fixed a shelf for me. He was very kind."

"No money, you say?" Roger's eyes were sharp. "That hardly sounds like Harland."

"It's true," Nettie said.

Roger looked at his cousin, a tightness in his jaw and his cheekbones angled. But when he turned to her, his face relaxed. "Perhaps we may see you while we're here, Vivian."

"You're staying at the Waxwoodian, I take it?" Vivian asked.

"We are," he said. "We've become rather a fondness for the place." He glanced back at his cousin.

Mr. Stevens came to life. He stared at Vivian's hands, still holding the book of Aesop's fables. His fingers reached out slowly, but rather than take the book as he had before, he withdrew the notepad and pencil from his pocket and wrote with his eyes still on the book. His hands held still when he finished writing, and Roger took the pad from him and gave it to Vivian. The words written there were *stork* and *fox*.

"He seems rather attached to that fable," Roger lamented.

"I don't believe I know it," said Nettie.

Vivian explained, "A fox invites a stork to dinner, but the stork can't eat the dinner because the dish is flat. The stork returns the invitation and puts dinner in a long jar so the fox can't get to it."

"And the moral?" her friend asked. "Aesop's fables always have morals, don't they?"

"If one does harm to others, one should expect harm in return."

A small cry escaped from Mr. Stevens' direction, and the fear in his eyes broke the monotonous stare. Roger glanced at the redhead, then settled with the sly look Vivian remembered from his college days. The young man tilted his hat to her and Nettie and sauntered down the platform with his cousin's arm under his.

~

She and Nettie went into the main road inundated with people during the end of the lunch hour. Though Vivian noticed the surge of growth during the previous years, Waxwood proper had settled into a comfortable pace separate from the resorts. Sometimes, she looked out the window of the flat she shared with Nettie and, seeing across the bay where the resort hotels stood glittering like washed marble statues, felt separated from them as if the past two years had never happened. Those were rare times, though.

"Mr. Stevens' state of mind disturbed you, didn't it?" Vivian asked.

"It didn't disturb you," her friend remarked.

"He looked like a savage the last time we saw him, all dirty and stringy," Vivian pointed out. "His cousin has made him a gentleman again."

"I can't think why he would go to the trouble," Nettie said. "I didn't get the impression there was much fondness between them."

"No, Roger isn't fond of his cousin," Vivian admitted. "He can be rather vicious, in fact. I remember Jake telling me that."

"And his refinement doesn't hide the fact that something or someone has crushed his spirit," Nettie observed.

Vivian thought of the clear features unhidden now by the beard, and the stiff collar and bowtie, the elegant vest and watch chain. Mr. Stevens had looked like the man she first met two years before. And yet, that man could dominate a room each time he entered it. This man, though the same man in size, seemed puny in comparison.

Nettie sighed. "Poor man."

"Poor man!" Vivian glared at her. "I'm glad of it."

"That's uncharitable of you, Viv," her friend chided.

"I prophesied he would end up like Dorian Gray, didn't I?" she asked. "And he has."

They dawdled as the scent of beef and potatoes came out of a restaurant.

"Did you see your mother?" Nettie asked. Vivian nodded. "And how is the Queen of Denial?"

"The marriage has done her good," Vivian said. "I won't say she's the belle of society, but she has regained her footing."

"Her new husband knows everything?" Nettie raised her eyebrows.

"Mother says he does, but I know how selective she is in her definition of 'everything,'" Vivian said shortly. "I imagine he's been told as little as possible. And I don't think he would ask questions, even if he suspected she wasn't telling the entire truth. He's a nice man, Bennett, but rather a milksop."

"You oughtn't to talk," remarked her friend. "The way you treated Mr. Stevens last year was hardly better than how your mother treats your stepfather. Sometimes, you have very little mercy, Viv."

Vivian stiffened. "He showed no mercy to Jake, did he?"

"Your brother is as strong as ever." Her friend stopped at the head of the stairs that led into their flat, fumbling in her pocket for the keys. "Mr. Stevens, as you've just seen, is little more than a crumpled heap. I would suggest the latter warrants more mercy than the former."

Vivian thought of the hollow face she had seen, the dark eyes like coals from an old fireplace. "Perhaps you wouldn't say that if it were your brother," she snapped.

After dinner, as her friend sat with a book under a circle of candlelight, Vivian wrote in her diary:

Seeing one's nemesis defeated by life is rather like finding out a murderer has escaped the hangman's rope by his own hand. The deed is done, but the end has not justified the means. Vengeance, justice, whatever one wishes to call it, is a vile thing, to be sure, but so is living with the poison in one's own heart all one's life, especially when that heart, once filled, is now empty and sealed shut like a tomb. That is what my heart feels like, and the man with the vacant eyes is partially responsible. So when Nettie asks me if I feel compassion for him, how can I answer without unleashing the serpent tongue of Medusa into the world?

A knock at the door made her jump. Nettie closed her book and rose. "Probably Olivia," she said, referring to a lady who roamed the streets in a stupor of wine and occasionally appeared at their door for the night.

But it was a messenger boy, and Vivian recognized the dark blue and gold of the Waxwoodian hotel uniform. The boy stood stiffly, declining Nettie's invitation to come in, and mumbled that he was to wait for an answer.

Nettie handed her the note with the resort crest. "It's from your new friend," she remarked.

The note was from Roger, though the writing was as delicate as a woman's:

Our meeting seems not to have been in vain, as I believe Fate put us in one another's path. Would you join me for tea at the hotel tomorrow? Shall we say eight o'clock? That ought to give you ample time to reach the hotel after dinner. I dare not ask you to dine with me, as I wish Harland to be in bed when we meet. I'm sure your friend will excuse me I do not invite her. There is a grave matter I wish to discuss with you, a grave matter. You're my last hope. Forgive me if I sound melodramatic, but it is the truth.

Tea in the parlor at eight. If you need me to send a boat, let me know. Please come.

Your friend, Roger

"Tea in the parlor at eight," she echoed.

She handed the note to Nettie. The woman read it with her usual cool manner. "Rather cryptic, don't you think?" She put it down on the table. "But intriguing."

Vivian turned to the boy. "You may tell Mr. Howe I will be at the hotel at eight tomorrow."

The boy bowed and withdrew.

"I wonder what it could be about," her friend lamented as she sat down to her book again.

Vivian shrugged, but a feeling of unease overcame her.

CHAPTER 3

The next evening, an early summer rain came across the town, but by the time Vivian set out to meet Roger, the air was clean and damp. She liked the main road at that hour, as many of the townspeople took their evening constitution. Couples strolled through the street or sat in the city park, taking in the cool breeze of the early summer months. Little boys jumped in the few puddles pooled on the street, ignoring their mother's threats of what would happen to them if they muddied their pants. Little girls skipped along the pavement, the ribbons in their hair flaring out. People stopped to talk to other people laughing over some silly joke.

Some days Vivian felt happy in this atmosphere of amiability, but tonight she felt envious. The Alderdices had never been the kind of family to join such a display, with her skipping along with an undone ribbon and Jake playing in the puddles. Her mother would have lectured Jake about how undignified and common the boys were to dirty themselves in the puddles, and Grandfather would have yanked his arm as if he were going to tear it from his shoulder. Larissa would have also complained about the dampness, while Grandmother might have remarked the daisies in the park weren't nearly as bursting as the ones they sold in at Podesta Baldocchi.

She reached the pier in time to board the waiting ferry that took people across the bay to the resort hotels. Mr. Blaine, the ferry driver she befriended last year, had retired last fall, and the younger man in his stead, unlike the old timer, was not inclined to talk to passengers. So she had a lonely ride as she studied the people in fine clothes with their bags piled up on one side. The season had not quite started, but more eager nomads who made a life of hopping from resort to resort had arrived, intent on being the kings and queens of the place before the rest of their brethren came. She couldn't help but remember when she rode the ferry across last year, Mrs. Bilton had remarked, with more ruefulness than amusement, "They will move the season back until summer begins in December!"

At first, she thought *The Waxwoodian* had not changed. The glass doors were as polished as ever, and the pomp of gold, yellow, and white reflected in the mirrors. And yet, the glass door squeaked as she went through it, and the furnishings looked shabbier. She noticed, too, the lobby was much emptier than it had been in previous years, even for so early in the season. The eyes of hotel staff sported a desperate look. Even the mural on the ceiling looked faded, and the gaze of the lady in the forest scene, whom Jake had thought was Titania, held the wariness of one eyeing an intruder. Vivian was little more than an intruder now.

The clerk at the desk motioned toward her. "Mr. Howe asked that you meet him in Private Room Number Three, ma'am."

"Private room?" Vivian stared.

"Yes, ma'am. Some rooms weren't being used—" She cleared her throat. "So we turned them into private rooms. We discovered guests sometimes preferred to meet there rather than in the lobby or courtyard."

"Yes, I'm sure." Vivian tried to sound dismissive. "Where might I find Private Room Number Three?"

"Take the stairs up one floor, left corridor, third door to the right."

"Thank you." Vivian paused a moment. "How did you know Mr. Howe left the message for me?"

"Oh, I remember you from last year, ma'am," said the girl, smiling. "Gets so it's easier to remember faces now."

"Because there are fewer faces to remember?" Vivian couldn't help but smile.

The girl blushed. "You always had a kind word for us at the desk." She then added, "It's good to have you back, ma'am, if you may permit me to say so."

"Yes, thank you," Vivian murmured as she wandered toward the stairs. She remembered hearing the chatter of a group of shop girls who came once a week to the library: *We always remember those who are kind to us.*

Private Room Number Three was more like a small sitting room than the meeting room she had pictured it. Roger sat on a winged-back chair, his legs crossed, tilted toward the French windows that overlooked the beach. He jumped up when she entered.

"A private room seems hardly necessary, Roger," she said as he kissed her hand. "There were few people in the lobby when I came in just now and even fewer in the courtyard."

"It seems as if the place is deserted," he agreed. "I looked around this afternoon and noticed the same thing with the other hotels."

"Perhaps the glory of the Waxwood resorts has become as much dust as the ideals of excess upon which they were built," Vivian remarked as she settled on the couch.

Roger laughed. "I thought this would be a more suitable place for us to meet. I noticed a party with people I saw you with last year." His tone lowered. "When I saw them in the parlor after dinner, I asked for a private room. I didn't think you would want to see them again."

"Your instincts were correct." Vivian laid her gloves neatly in her lap.

"If I may ask," he ventured, "are you evading anyone from your past?"

"Not deliberately," said Vivian. "I just prefer not to waste precious strength trying to explain myself to people who can't or won't understand."

He grimaced. "I spent most of my life among people who couldn't or wouldn't understand. Perhaps I should have been a better man if I hadn't cared so much." A few lines stretched across his face.

"It's a credit to you that you do care," she said gently as a waiter appeared with the tea tray, setting it down on the table and then withdrawing. "It's then that we must find the people who understand us."

"Ah, but it's not so easy," Roger said. "You were lucky. Some people are."

"And you believe you aren't?" Vivian asked.

"Shall we say I believe we make our own luck?" His voice was hard as he leaned forward. "May I pour the tea?"

"Let me."

He watched as she performed the duty. "I see you haven't lost your hosting talents, new life or no new life."

"There are habits one cannot get rid of," she said with a sigh as she handed him the tea, perfectly cooled and sweetened. "Now, what is so urgent that you must speak to me about?"

"Tell me about this new life of yours first."

"Are you really interested?"

"Very much so."

"I've been helping a friend fulfill her dream."

"That's been your excellent work?" he asked.

"It goes much deeper than that," she explained. "Nettie is a suffragist—"

"Ah!" The man's exclamation lent a sharp note to the atmosphere in the room.

"You don't approve?"

"I've no objection to women playing their part with men," he said. "It's a woman becoming president one day that disturbs me."

"Because you don't think we're up to the task?" She raised her eyebrow.

"Because you'll no doubt prove much better at it than we are!"

She couldn't help but laugh. "You'll be happy to hear that Nettie's interests lean more toward social reform than political domination."

"Oh, social reformers." He nodded. "Like Miss Jane Addams and her lot?"

Vivian nodded. "Except Nettie's ideas of education are more about learning than doing."

"I don't quite understand."

"She believes books educate a woman to work."

"Hence the women's library?" asked Roger, his chin in his hand.

"It was a struggle to get it going," Vivian admitted. "We sold everything we could get our hands on to rent out the small space we have."

"I can't imagine Waxwood rent prices would have offered much of a challenge," he said. "Not like San Francisco, where one must give their right arm just to afford a bed for the night. And what about the books?"

"We've five book cases."

"Five!"

She smiled. "I don't know how Nettie got hold of them."

"Best not to ask, I'm sure." He grinned.

"We've filled only three shelves so far," she said. "The books are proving more costly than the furniture."

"So it's a reading room as well?"

She nodded. "We have a few tables and chairs for the women to enjoy. And Nettie practically cleaned out all the old furniture her mother had left her for the space."

"All this with no help?" he inquired.

"We've had several women's organizations visit us," she said. "Even a few businesswomen who promised to do what they could." She gave him a shrewd look. "Is that why you're asking so many questions, Roger? Because you might know of where we could get help?"

"I might," he said vaguely. "You remind me of Harland's friend."

"I thought you said your cousin had no friends."

"An acquaintance," he said. "A woman not in the same class as you and Miss Grace. In terms of respectability, that is." He balanced the teacup on his knee. "And you're happy you've helped your friend achieve her dream?"

"I was looking to do *something*," she said.

He raised an eyebrow. "But not quite what your friend is doing?"

She looked at him sharply. "What do you mean?"

"You said you were helping to fulfill a friend's dream."

She fiddled with the lumps of sugar in the sugar bowl. "You're more astute than I gave you credit for, Roger."

He chuckled. "My past frivolity is a mark against me. My only excuse is I was doing what was expected of me. But that's not much of an excuse, is it?"

"No," said Vivian. "It's no excuse." She thought of how she had freed herself from the expectations that had weighed her down like the emerald necklace her grandmother had hated. But she paid a price for it.

"You have more ambitious ideas about women's education?" he persisted.

"I wouldn't quite say that," she said.

"You're bored with the library, then." He poured another cup of tea.

"Not bored exactly." She looked down at her hands. "I don't think I'm explaining myself very well."

He sat playing with his watch chain hanging from his lapel. "Tell me, Vivian. Do you help only women?"

"What do you mean?"

"I mean, do you help men too?"

Vivian pulled herself up, crossing her ankles so their bony shape would show through the skirt, the way her mother did when she was preparing for battle. "I gather your question is about one man in particular?"

"I had Harland in mind, yes," he admitted. "Was it so obvious?"

"You said in your note you wanted to meet me after Mr. Stevens was in bed," she pointed out. "It occurred to me this urgent matter of yours concerned him directly."

His hands grasped the arms of the chair. "Much has happened to my cousin since last summer, Vivian."

"I gathered that when you told me he rarely speaks or moves now." She nodded. "Surely, he's grieving his father's death."

"I don't know that he is," he said in a grave voice. "I told you last year he rarely saw any of us. He didn't seem concerned when we had to get Aunt Maggie a nurse companion." He looked down at a mark on the coffee table. "She's being taken care of now in a home in Sacramento."

Vivian's voice softened. "I remember you telling me she was ill."

"Harland watched the nurse lead her away as if he were watching a dog being led by its master," Roger said.

"I'm sorry," she said, pressing his hand. "I can't say I'm surprised, though."

He gave a strange, snapping chuckle. "Not that I pictured Harland going mad with grief over losing his father, but I expected some emotion."

"*Is* he mad, Roger?" She looked fully at him.

The young man rose and wandered over to the French windows. He leaned against the frame, looking out. "They say he must be, but I don't believe it."

He spoke with more emotion than she thought him capable of, and she could not see his face in the parting of a shadow. She poured a fresh cup of tea and held it out to him. "You might feel better drinking this. Or would you like a brandy?"

"Tea will do." Roger took the cup with steady hands. "I hardly know where to begin."

"Why not with this grave matter you referred to in your note?" she suggested.

He took his place in the chair again. "My uncle died in January. Harland hasn't spoken a word since."

"Hasn't spoken or won't speak?"

"I don't know," Roger said. "And it isn't just his speech. He barely moves unless you move him, and even then, he stays in that position until he's moved again. Do you know chess?" he suddenly asked.

"I never learned the game," she answered.

"Harland is like the pawn on a chessboard," said Roger. "One can move him forward but no more, and he can't move himself anywhere at all."

"He has no will of his own," Vivian ventured.

"An apt punishment," Roger said with a little snicker. "You and I know about his past puppet-mastering. Now he himself is the puppet."

"And you're his puppet master," Vivian said, looking hard at him.

He looked at the spot on the coffee table again. "What would you have me do, leave him to rot alone in the castle? We are, after all, family."

"I wasn't criticizing you, Roger," she said. "I think it's admirable."

He grimaced. "Don't make a martyr out of me, Vivian. I'm paying back a debt I owe to Uncle Joseph. He took me in when my mother died and my father couldn't care for me, and he did it willingly. I couldn't hardly abandon his son in this state, can I?"

"No, you couldn't," she agreed.

"I thought maybe I could help him," he said. "A familiar face, you know. But he won't respond to me." He peered at her. "You're the only one he's responded to so far."

"I would hardly call recognizing a fable in a book a response," she remarked.

"The specialist we went saw in the city before you met us said any spontaneous response is a hopeful sign." He leaned forward and took her hand. "You see now why I say you're our last hope."

"There must be doctors who can help him," Vivian lamented.

"We've been to doctors," he snorted. "They either declare him mad or are completely nonplussed. One recommended bloodletting, another salt baths, and another chloroform. The specialist we saw a few days ago made the most sense. He recommended Harland might gain his voice back with rest in the sea air."

"And it will do you good," Vivian observed. "All this has clearly made you overwrought, Roger."

He nodded. "Perhaps you're right. The sea may not clear the cobwebs from Harland's mind, but Mr. Vanburgh and Mr. Gunn gave me the time off to try. They've been very patient and understanding."

"You said they knew your uncle," Vivian reminded him. "I would think they would behave most favorably to your efforts to help his son."

"I can't continue to take advantage of their favor," Roger insisted. "This mayhem with Harland has affected my work." He peered at her again. "That's why I hoped you could help us. If Harland were to speak again, it would begin the road to independence from me."

"Perhaps his voice will come back with time." Vivian's fingers danced on the edge of the cushion. "A caretaker or nurse would release you of much of the burden, and I'm sure you could easily afford it." She saw him blush, as if he realized she had seen the wad of bills he had pulled out at the train station.

"I have a nurse during the hours I work, but she knows nothing about his condition. And it isn't the same, Vivian."

"No, it isn't the same." She tried not to think about how, even with the round of nurses her mother hired when Grandmother and Grandfather were ill, Larissa had exhausted herself caring for them. "Ill people like having someone who knows them well looking after them."

"You know him well, Vivian," he said. "Even better, perhaps, than I."

"There is nothing one can do with a grieving man until the grief has passed," she insisted.

"This specialist," Roger said. "He was definite about Harland's silence as something more than my uncle's death. He thinks my cousin has locked himself inside a room in his mind, and he can't or won't come out."

"One can always open the door when one finds the key," she murmured.

"That's it exactly!" Roger pressed her hand. "You can help my cousin find the key."

"Because he responded to my book?" Vivian eyed him. "If you were a lawyer, Roger, your arguments would fall as flat as wooden nickels."

The young man stiffened. "I know it's a lot to ask," he said. "Too much maybe."

The unspoken name on both their minds hung in the air. Vivian felt the tears well in her eyes. The soft blue curtains on the window billowed back to give way to the beetle black night and the line of sea in the distance. Even though she couldn't see it, the thought of the sea comforted her just then, maybe because she didn't associate it with Jake. The woods had been Jake's element.

"There was something in his eyes today," Roger spoke in a soft voice. "A spark of life, I should call it."

"As if he were standing at that door of the room he's locked himself in, wanting to get out," she murmured.

"I feel in my bones you could do something for him, Vivian," he said. "You told me you were looking to do *something*."

She rose and gathered her gloves and reticule. "That was a year ago, Roger. I've found my something."

"Helping people," he said. "That's why I thought—"

"Educating women," she interrupted.

"I see," he said. "Men are not part of the plan."

"Not that," said Vivian. "Between the drugstore and the library, I hardly have time to for much else."

He grabbed her arm. "You're not being entirely honest with me, are you, Vivian?"

She stiffened. "Those are my reasons."

"Perhaps they are," he said. "But I can't imagine you would refuse to aid a man in need because you can't or won't find the time."

She leaned against the couch. "You're right, Roger. I promised myself honesty would always come first, no matter how unpleasant it was. I wouldn't refuse to help a man in need. I'm refusing to help the man who destroyed my brother and my family."

He stared at her. "Surely—"

"He used my brother as his disciple," she continued in a crusted tone. "He abandoned him in such a cowardly manner that it brings sickness to my stomach to think about it. Seeing your cousin yesterday as he was, I felt nothing but satisfaction. I couldn't even feel pity for him."

"I can understand that, Vivian," he said. "But after all I've told you—"

She put on her gloves. "I still feel the same way. I loathe

Harland Stevens and have since the day I met him. I cannot be more honest than that."

"I'm sorry to hear it." His voice was low.

"Not a very ladylike way to feel, perhaps," she admitted, "but genuine. I haven't felt a genuine emotion for a year, Roger. For that, I am grateful to Mr. Stevens, but no more."

He rose. "Then your answer is no?"

"I'm sure you can find a good doctor in this area," she said. "If you care to have me ask—"

"We've seen too many doctors already," he said briskly as he took her arm. "I'm inclined to think a witch doctor could do us more good now."

"You must have faith he will get himself out of it eventually," said Vivian. "He has too much self-interest to lose himself completely."

"And in the meantime," Roger said. "We're to wait. But the years wear one down, Vivian."

"The years wear us all down," she said in a sad voice. "It's then we have to persevere the hardest."

She caught the distant look in his gray eyes as she glanced back from the hallway. He stood at the doorway, his hands on either side of the frame as if he were grasping them for support. He looked more foreboding than Lucifer himself.

∾

*V*ivian did not expect to see Roger or Mr. Stevens again, but a few days later, she was minding the library and carrying a dusty box in her arms when Roger's bright face beamed down at her as he lifted the box out of her hands. "My mother always taught me never to allow a lady to carry more than her position," he said.

"A very intelligent rule," Vivian said.

"You're not happy to see me, are you?" His keen eyes caught her look of annoyance.

"I'm not happy to see *him* again." Here, she nodded toward Mr. Stevens, who stood in the doorway in the same position she had seen him at the train station.

The young man set the box down and then guided his cousin into an empty chair. "I'm sorry, but I can't leave Harland alone for long. But as long as I am here, I can help you with these books." He tapped the box.

"Roger, why did you bring him here?"

"Harland won't disturb anything or anyone," Roger promised. "I told you, he's like a pawn on a chessboard."

"Seeing him is disturbing." Her voice sounded ragged in the stuffed room. "It's disturbing the ladies too." Two young women who had settled on the couch with their books were now staring at Mr. Stevens, their faces drawn in perturbation.

He lowered his voice. "I thought, if you saw him again, you might change your mind."

"He's no right to be here, nor do you." Her agitation was rising. "This is a library for women."

"You spoke so warmly of your women's library, I wanted to see it for myself." He cast his eyes about. "I suppose your friend persuaded you to help her when she gave you a place." To Vivian's blank look, he added, "As a favor, you know. Especially with your wealthy connections."

Vivian realized she should have been angry, but she only felt a wave of amusement as she went to the desk where two young ladies were waiting to check out their books. "What a suspicious man you are, Roger."

"Eh?" He stared at her.

"I suppose men in business subscribe to the idea that one never gets something for nothing." She recorded the women's books in the ledger, and when they had settled themselves with their books and the sandwiches they brought for lunch, she leaned forward with her elbows on the table. "I was the one who offered to come."

"Because you wanted to do *something*?" He looked at her with smiling eyes.

"Yes," she answered. "But it was more than that. Last year, I went to see a man who lived in the South of Market."

Roger whistled, his head leaning back with admiration. "That's quite a distance from your Nob Hill, Vivian. In more ways than one."

Vivian sat back, pressing her hands together. "The women there — the way they looked at me. It made me feel ashamed."

"Because you had what they all wanted?" Roger asked sharply. "I concluded long ago that there is an uneven distribution of luck in this world, and it's as useless to envy those who have it as it is for those who have it to be ashamed of it."

"I felt ashamed because *they* felt ashamed," said Vivian. "They thought I was judging them for their ragged clothes and dirty aprons. But my mind was entirely in another place."

"What has that to do with the library?" he asked.

She cocked her head. "There are two schools of thought amongst the progressives, Roger. To come to the aid of those in need and to help them aid themselves. Nettie belongs to the second school. Until the day I went to South of Market, I suppose I belonged to the first. I thought all it took was money."

Roger nodded. "You're right there. 'God helps those who help themselves,' as Benjamin Franklin told us."

"Nettie and I are helping these women help themselves," Vivian said. "Perhaps a few books doesn't seem like much, but it's a start."

"It's a charming place," he said graciously. "But I expected more — well—"

"Laces and flounces?" Vivian raised her eyebrow. "A library is not a boudoir."

His lips puckered a little. "I meant no offense, Vivian. I know how serious this is for you and for Miss Grace. It's why I've come."

Vivian rose and bent down toward the box. It contained the books she had negotiated with Mr. Bates for only a few days before.

"I saw a place this morning down the street that's twice the size of this one but has a cozier atmosphere, just as one would expect of a library."

Vivian's hand hovered over the books. "We've seen it too."

"You could have that place," he ventured. "And the books to fill it."

She slid the *Alice in Wonderland* books into a tight corner on the shelf. "I know what you're getting at."

He fingered the spine of a bronze-colored book. "Perhaps I am a little cynical."

She produced a small stepladder from the corner and placed the *Phaedrus* books on the top shelf. "And rather devious."

He studied her with a hard set of eyes. "I didn't tell you the rest of what the specialist in San Francisco said about his theory of Harland's condition."

"Which was?"

"That my cousin is suffering from fear. Or rather, the madness of fear."

"Fear." She slid her finger down the spine of the books in her hand.

"Harland's silent world is a world apart from fear," said Roger. "It isn't just grief, as you supposed."

"But you didn't tell me about this yesterday," she countered.

"I wanted to see what you would say first," he said shortly.

"And did the specialist also tell you what your cousin is so afraid of?" Vivian snapped.

"That's what I think you can find out," he said.

She slid the last of the books out of the box. "Not me, Roger. You. I told you before, I won't be any part of it."

"I'm no longer asking it as a favor of friendship and good will," he said. "I come with a business proposition."

She glared at him. "Business?"

"I could help you and Miss Grace," he said. "With the bigger space and the books."

She eyed him. "With a free hand on your cousin's money?"

He stiffened, and Vivian was sorry she had been so brutal. It was clear finances were a sore subject with him, but his voice was mild when he answered, "Why shouldn't Harland pay you for helping him, just as he would a doctor or a nurse?"

Vivian glanced at the redhead who had not moved from the moment Roger set him down. "When he is entirely unaware of it? Even I wouldn't propose to go so low."

"I told you before," said Roger. "Any financial decisions are out of his hands and in mine."

"What you really mean," Vivian said in a hard voice, "is you have the power to do with his money what you like."

"Not what I like," he corrected. "What I think is best. I shouldn't think paying a woman who has some hope of restoring Harland to his old self is a poor investment, do you?"

She blinked at the young man's face, seeing the lines form across his forehead. The seriousness in his eyes and the note of pleading in his voice touched her. He was no longer distant, as he had been a few days before.

"I'm sorry," she said. "I didn't mean to imply you're squandering your cousin's money. I believe that, whatever may have happened between you and your cousin in the past, you are genuinely concerned about him now."

"I'm glad you realize that."

She put the empty box near the doorway. "But my answer still stands."

He took hold of her arm. "You're very stubborn."

"Mulishly ornery." She met his keen eyes. "But that's not why I still refuse."

"Then?"

"My brother once warned me not to walk into other people's dark rooms," she said. "I didn't heed his advice, and I've never recovered from the scars. Now I've ceased walking into dark rooms, even my own."

He cocked his head. "Those are the words of a coward, Vivian."

"Perhaps I am a coward," she said with a rueful smile. "I realized last year if I didn't bury the dagger, my wounds will never heal."

"But these wouldn't be your wounds," he insisted. "If there would be any wounds, they would be Harland's."

"Despite what I said yesterday," she said. "I wouldn't wish such wounds, even on my worst enemy. And he *is* my worst enemy."

The door opened, and Olivia entered. Her lustrous hair tumbled down her back in chaotic tresses while a mass of tangled gold cords topped her head. They swung over her small face as she walked, the loose brown robe she wore floating behind her like the train of a bridal gown.

As Vivian approached her, she said in a croaking tone, "I have betrayed my father and my house."

Vivian took her arm. She wished Nettie were there. "Come sit down." She led Olivia toward a stuffed chair in the back of the library, though the two women had left long ago, and the only people in the place other than herself were Roger and Mr. Stevens.

Olivia caught sight of the immobile redhead and trailed in his direction. Even as Vivian tried to stop her, she took her place opposite him.

Vivian said quickly, "I have some chicken sandwiches and soup. You haven't eaten today, have you?"

The woman did not answer, nor did she look at her. Her eyes widened across her face as she stared openly at Mr. Stevens.

Vivian glanced back at Roger leaning against a bookcase with his hands in his pockets, trying to signal him to take Mr. Stevens away. But the young man's face showed curiosity and interest, like one watching a fight between two able-bodied men.

Olivia blinked and heaved a sigh. Vivian suddenly remembered the story of Goldilocks and the three bears. Mr. Stevens, with his wide frame and dark eyes, was Papa Bear in proportion to the gold-laden Olivia.

She darted toward the desk and removed the bag with her lunch. On her way back to the table, Roger whispered to her, "Is she mad?"

"Not mad," said Vivian. "Lost. Sometimes, she believes she is someone else."

"Poor woman," he breathed. "And who is she now?"

She glanced at the crown and robe. "Medea."

Roger laughed outright. "The Greek barbarian and the puppet. An apt combination."

"How can you be so cruel?" she snarled.

Olivia was now leaning toward Mr. Stevens. Her small hand lay next to his in the same flat position. "I betrayed my father for you, Jason. Do you remember?"

Vivian's throat felt dry as she set the food in front of Olivia. "Lunch, dear."

"I deceived my house for you," Olivia continued, her hand inching closer to his.

"Eat, dear, and then I'll take you to Nettie," Vivian continued. "She'll put you to bed." Her breath came out with difficulty because she saw how Mr. Stevens' countenance had grown even grayer, like a granite statue.

"Where am I to go now?" The woman's voice rose to a shrill as threads of silver hung over her thin cheekbones. "Tell me, where am I to go now?"

"Roger," Vivian murmured. "I think you and Mr. Stevens ought to leave."

"You were so brave with the snake-headed woman," said

Olivia, her eyes wide now. "So chivalrous with the Golden Fleece. But you are a coward at heart. A coward who cannot look at the woman you forsake!"

The thunder in her voice echoed through the room and, as if stabbed, Mr. Stevens' figure shot upward, his dark eyes alight.

"One's sins cannot go unpunished." The bloodshot whites of Olivia's eyes were visible now that they were so wide. "Betrayal can only lead to death."

"Roger!" Vivian hissed at him.

"You shall pay, Jason." Olivia leaned back, the triumph on her face so real, it made Vivian shudder. "I shall suffer the consequences, but so shall you. We shall both bear the loss."

A moment followed where nothing seemed to move, not even the wind through the window. Then, a crash echoed through the small room. Vivian looked around wildly, thinking someone had broken the back window. She rushed toward the back door, but looking into the small room they used for storage, there was nothing disturbed.

It was only when she returned to the library that she realized the crash had been Mr. Stevens. He had fallen to the floor in a dead faint, his enormous figure wound up like a spool, and Olivia was standing over him, her hands on her hips, her thin lips in a diabolical grin, and her eyes still wide open.

CHAPTER 4

*A*fter Roger got his cousin out of the library, Vivian took the shaking Olivia, who crumbled when she saw the redhead led out by Roger and two other men, to Nettie's drugstore. Her consciousness returned, the woman kept lamenting, "The man will die. He'll die because of me!" No matter how Vivian tried to reassure her, Olivia peered at her with frightened eyes, and her tiny figure shook against Vivian's arm.

Nettie took charge and calmed the woman with brandy and a small dose of sleeping powders. Afterward, Vivian sat in the kitchen with her friend and talked. Pan, the Scottish terrier she had brought down with her from Alderdice Hall, seemed to sense her troubled mood and lay silently at her feet, his chin resting against his front paws.

"If Mr. Stevens wouldn't have been there, it never would have happened," Vivian said with a sigh. The hum of the kitchen with its soothing lullaby made it her favorite room, though there really weren't what one might call "rooms" in Nettie's tiny flat. "Roger shouldn't have brought him."

"He was counting on your compassionate nature," Nettie said. "He's a sly one."

"He miscalculated," she said. "I have no compassion for Harland Stevens."

"So you say," Nettie said, a little wary.

"Whatever has happened to him is what he deserves." Vivian sipped at the tea Nettie had made. It tasted sharp, like pine needles.

"You can't be entirely hard-hearted about it," Nettie eyed her. "Or his presence wouldn't have alarmed you so."

"I'm disturbed about what it did to Olivia," said Vivian. "I really believe if there would have been a knife in the place, she would have plunged it into his chest."

"If she had, would you have claimed that too was only what Mr. Stevens deserved?" Nettie asked.

A shot of pain went into Vivian's chest. "You know me better than that. I wished no one ill, not even him."

"You won't help him either," said Nettie. "Not even for a chance to expand the library."

Vivian stared at her. The woman rose to put more wood in the stove. It was Friday, and, in a few hours, they would feed half the neighborhood with fish stew and the dark bread baking in the oven.

"How did you know about that?" A crack sparked in her, making her voice rough and angry. "Roger told you, didn't he?"

"He came into the drugstore before he went to the library." Nettie leaned against the back of a chair. "I suppose he wanted to extract my sympathy for his scheme."

"He is artful," Vivian remarked. "There has always been something a little sinister about him."

"He was sincere, though," said Nettie. "I think he's genuinely distressed about his cousin."

"More for his own sake than Mr. Stevens'."

"Perhaps," said her friend. "Do you intend to let the man go mad?"

"He's mad already," said Vivian. "From what Roger has told

me. A madness of fear." She looked at the glare on the sparkling tabletop.

"If that's the case, I suppose it's out of your hands." Nettie shrugged. "Still, I'm surprised at you giving in to your own fear."

She felt the sting of bitterness seep through her like blood in her veins. "Two years of heartache and loss have frightened me. No, not two years. Eight years, if one must be exact."

Nettie said gently, "We promised to let go of our specters, didn't we?"

"And we have," Vivian said firmly. "That's why I can't do anything for Mr. Stevens, even if I wanted to."

"But you don't want to?"

"Would you?" Vivian looked at her sharply. "If it had been your brother, would you have had the benevolence to help the man who destroyed him?"

"Not the benevolence, perhaps," Nettie admitted. "But the pity."

"Well, I've no pity!" Vivian rose and took up the bread knife, slicing into a loaf of brown bread sitting on the table, sawing through it as if it were wood.

Nettie watched her. "I don't believe that for a moment. And neither do you."

Vivian found her hand grasping the handle of the knife so hard that all the muscles in it ached.

~

A few hours later, Vivian forgot all about Olivia, who was still sleeping in Nettie's bed where they had left her. Scents of cooked carrots and trout simmered on the burner in the back of the store, making the air hearty and hot. People in ragged clothes and swarthy faces filled the tiny place, their features relaxed, many chatting garrulously with their neighbors. Pan threaded between the high legs, topping the volume of human voices with his sharp bark as he accepted the generous pats on the head and back.

Nettie attended to the stew while Vivian arranged the small bowls on the plates, laying the bread alongside and topping each slice with a few pats of butter. She cast her eyes across the room every time she handed someone their plate, proud of the mob forming the line outside, extending into the street. Many were people or relatives of people Nettie had known since she was a child. Vivian had learned she could call on any of them in a time of trouble, and they would give their hats or their hearts to her if she needed it.

A familiar face with a small, wrinkled smile appeared. "Good evening, Tillie." She tried to smile, but she was always cautious of the woman who had once been a maid to the Ross house and had known her grandmother forty years ago, as sometimes she spoke of the past and brought devastating memories with her.

"Evening, Mrs. Caulfield," said Tillie. "You're almost bursting tonight, aren't you? Can't hardly get a nose in."

"No, you can't," Vivian said.

"You ought to have heard the little one today," her voice rose in joviality. "She's ever so clever! Yesterday, I said, 'Say bye-bye to Grandpa,' and she waved!"

"She is clever." Vivian smiled.

Pan padded up to her, pawing at her leg and whimpering. Vivian laughed. "He wants some soup, I expect."

"Such a friendly little thing," said Tillie. "Miss Bertha had a dog almost like him."

Vivian stared at her. "Bertha Ross?"

"Hers was wheat-colored," she said. "Few of those Scotties about. She was keen enough on him when he arrived, but his nosing about her sewing basket made her nervous. And then when he chewed up a skirt she was making—" Tillie chuckled.

Vivian poured some soup in a small teacup and pushed it near the wall so Pan would follow.

"Amos and I are thinking of getting the little one a dog for her birthday," she said. "If you don't mind my asking, ma'am, where did you get him?"

Vivian's stomach tightened like a violin string. "A man on a farm was giving them away. I don't remember his name."

"A dog breeder?"

"Not exactly," said Vivian. "People left strays with him."

"Must be a kind man to keep all those strays and find them homes," Tillie said.

"Yes, he was." Vivian cleared her throat. "How old will Beatrice be?"

"Eleven months," said Tillie proudly as she accepted the plate. "She looks older, though. Cassie's a big woman, you know. Mrs. Caulfield," her voice lowered, "she and little Beatrice are waiting outside. They don't like coming in with so many people. Babies sometimes get so excitable from crowds. Could you—"

"Say no more, dear," Vivian said with a smile. She took a plate of stew and bread in each hand and followed Tillie, people moving aside for her. She chatted a few moments with Tillie's daughter-in-law and played a bit with the baby, who had keen eyes and a light grin. She watched as the women strolled down the street toward the alleyways where the working people lived.

"Grandmother, mother, daughter," she murmured. A lump carved in her throat as tears burned in her eyes. If her brother were there, perhaps he would have drawn a sweeping portrait of them. But what pain would such a sentimental portrait bring the daughter, years later, when, as a woman, she would look upon it and wonder whether there had ever really been a time when she was so small and innocent?

She spun around, intending to dive back into the crowd to preoccupy her thoughts with something more tangible, when she faced Roger.

Anger rose in her chest. "Has the summer bored you already so you must come among the poor to do your slumming?"

"We would never insult you by doing that, Vivian," he insisted. But his crisp tan suit looked as if it had just been ironed that morning, and his neatly combed hair and mustache were clearly out of place among the slouching figures of the men waiting outside, and they looked upon him with suspicion.

"You're being insufferable, Roger." She glanced back to see Mr. Stevens. "I don't think your cousin enjoys being dragged along to these calculated excursions of yours."

"Calculated?" The young man blinked. "I come as a friend."

"You seem to think the meaning of friendship is an exchange of favors." She entered the fold of people in the store, hoping to lose him, but she felt his breath close to the back of her neck.

"Miss Grace told me of your Fridays," he said. "Harland and I came to help."

"Help!" She whirled around. "What can you do? What can *he* do?"

Mr. Stevens followed his cousin, and his steps were so heavy they seemed to shake the entire floor.

"I have two able hands and powerful arms, don't I?" he asserted. They reached the back of the store where Nettie was moving one big pot out of the way to make room for a fresh one, and, as if to prove his point, he took it from her hands and placed it on a towel sitting on a crate.

"Yes, I suppose that is useful," Vivian admitted.

"Harland may not be of practical use," he said. "But I've always been told people who struggle for their living feel mighty satisfied when they see someone of the upper class in a pathetic state. Perhaps Harland can sit here and be of use that way."

"We do not put people on display, Mr. Howe," Nettie said in a curt tone, giving him one of her sneering looks. "But we will put your cousin here in the corner so the noise won't disturb him."

"Nothing disturbs him, Miss Grace," said Roger. "That's perhaps the trouble. He's found a place where no disturbance can reach him." His gaze slid toward Vivian. "I think you would agree that's no way to live one's life, is it?"

Vivian's gaze fell on the redhead, his feet still pointed outward, his face slacked, and his hands hanging down the sides of the chair as if they would fall off at any moment. She caught his eyes and detected a veiled fascination, as if the eyes alone absorbed what was going on around him.

In a quiet voice, she said, "If you wish to help us, Roger, we would be grateful. But I won't discuss that other matter with you any longer. I gave you my answer — twice. That should make my position sufficiently clear."

The young man seemed to take this with resignation, even bowing his head a little. But she had no illusions he was complacent.

Pan, having finished his soup, bounded out of the hidden corner and pranced up to Vivian, watching her with his soulful eyes.

"I see you still have your dog," Roger said. "I remember when we went to that farm and got him."

"The man was Mr. Stevens' friend, wasn't he?" Vivian asked.

Roger nodded. "Mr. Stoker. I met him only that once."

By this time, the horde had receded, and shades of dark blue appeared among the more temperate waves of daylight. Vivian wiped her hands on her apron, glancing around with a sigh. Her eyes again caught sight of the immobile Mr. Stevens. She was suddenly aware of her appearance — the stained apron, the edge of the calico skirt that looked almost shredded from use, and the tendrils of hair hanging around her temples and forehead.

Roger was leaning against the counter, a dish towel in his hand, circling the rim of a plate. "You really don't belong here, you know."

Vivian stiffened. "I know where I belong."

Pan appeared then, clearly wary of all the pettings from strangers. His short tail wagged as he peered up at Nettie, who had just taken up the last of the giant stew pots. She dug out what little fish had stuck to the bottom and dropped it on the floor in front of him.

Roger crouched down and scratched at the dog's ears. "He seems quite at home with this motley crew."

Vivian said in a distracted voice, "You needn't play up to my dog to make me more amenable to your offer."

Roger glanced at her. "I wouldn't pull such tricks, Vivian."

"I'm not at all sure you wouldn't." Her voice was crisp.

"You've given me your answer three times now," he said. "In your mulishly obstinate way."

She leaned with her arms folded against a counter. Pan gazed up at the man with the sorrow that always invaded his eyes whenever he sensed graveness. His tail swiped the air like a paintbrush.

She turned around so her back was now toward the redhead. Roger was speaking to Nettie as if in confidence, but she could hear his voice clearly.

"Can she be so cruel, Miss Grace?"

"Viv is merciless only when she's afraid," Nettie said shortly.

"We're all afraid of something, aren't we?" asked the blond man. "I thought she, more than anyone, would be the brave heart."

The bells hanging over the door rang, and Nettie glanced at Vivian with a slight groan. It wasn't uncommon for latecomers to arrive, and when there was no more stew left, Nettie ran up to the flat to gather whatever they had in the icebox for them.

The shades on the windows were half pulled down, and the people still lingering in the shop blocked much of the light. She could only see two dark figures advancing, the noise of swaying skirts brushing against the floor. Only when they reached the counter could she see their faces clearly.

"Ruth." She stiffened.

"It's been a long time, hasn't it?" The woman's smile was tight, with lines forming at the corners. Ruth Ross, the daughter of Tillie's former employer, Bertha Ross, looked more than a year older from when Vivian had seen her last.

The frail figure with the dark hair standing next to her was equally familiar to Vivian. "It's good of you to condescend to visit me, Verina."

"We wouldn't be here now," Verina laid her hands on the glass counter, "but we need your help."

Vivian regarded her with an icy glare. "Did you help me last year when I asked for it?" The words had their effect as the woman slunk a little behind the counter.

"That's hardly fair, Vivian," Ruth said.

"Is it fair to offer lies when one asks for the truth?"

Verina spoke in a soft tone. "You were kinder to me last year."

Vivian brought two folding chairs from the storage room. "Sit down."

Nettie took her cue and headed toward the stairway that led to the flat. "I believe we have roast beef upstairs, and there's plenty of bread still left."

Ruth's voice was rough. "We didn't come for that sort of help."

Nettie moved away from the stairs and stacked the dishes.

Vivian's eyes hardened. "Perhaps our kindness isn't to your taste, but you needn't reject it in such an uncivilized manner."

"Please," Verina said, her voice shaking. "We didn't come here to fight."

Vivian motioned for the two women to join her near the corner of the store, close to Mr. Stevens. Pan had now climbed into his lap, lying with his chin on his front paws and his eyes half closed.

"Whatever I've done in the past, neither of you have a right to treat my friend in such a way," Vivian hissed. She was aware Roger was nearby, and although he looked preoccupied with the display of cigars in one of the cases, his attention turned toward them.

"I'll apologize to her gladly," said Ruth in a brisk voice before she wandered off.

Verina reached out and took Vivian's hand. Though the grasp was a little cool, it was genuine. "I've no quarrel with you, Vivian. Not anymore."

"I've one with you," Vivian said, eyeing her. "I should think you know what it is."

The woman flinched. "I have no wish to relive the past."

"I'm pleased to hear it," Vivian said coldly. "Because neither do I."

"You made me an offer several years ago," the woman continued. "And you made it again last year. I wish to take you up on it."

"And what offer was that?"

"I need a job."

Vivian blinked. "The last I heard, you were working at a bakery in Goldspur and doing some correspondence courses in shorthand and typing." Verina stared at her. "You may have had no interest in me, but I had an interest in you."

The young woman glanced at the floor. "I lost my job at the bakery."

"I'm sorry to hear it."

"I don't think you are." Her eyes flashed.

"I don't lie, Verina," she said severely. "You should know that by now."

The woman now looked bruised. "You used to be more understanding, Vivian."

"You could have saved me a lot of pain last year if you had been honest," she said. "You chose silence."

"Perhaps I chose silence to save you the pain," Verina snapped back.

Vivian took a breath, regaining her composure. In a more amiable tone, she asked, "What are your plans?"

Verina stared straight ahead at the display window. "I thought I might go back to San Francisco."

"Start fresh elsewhere," Vivian agreed.

"Uncle Evan once said the city can be a lucky place." Verina's voice rose in the half empty store. "I could use a bit of luck."

The ice in Vivian's heart melted when she saw the melancholy that still hung vacant and unnerving on the woman's countenance. "Of course, I'll help all I can," she said kindly. "I'm afraid my connections aren't as strong as they used to be."

Roger, who had been standing close behind Verina, stepped forward. "Forgive me for intruding, Miss—" He glanced at her.

"Jones."

He gave her a charmed smile. "Miss Jones, did I hear you say you've done some office work?"

"I did."

"I assume you are good with figures?"

"That, and typing and shorthand," Verina said.

"Then I might know of a man who has a clerical position open," he said, his tone authoritative.

"You *might* know of one?" Verina glanced at him.

Vivian felt her entire face arching toward the young man, aware that his mind was moving like the parts of a watch. "What Roger means," she said in an icy tone, "is he might know of someone who could help you if I help him."

The young man's features caved with anger. In a quiet voice, he said, "He may have found someone by now, as he was desperate to have a woman as soon as possible and applied to an agency before I left the city. But if that position is no longer available, Miss Jones, I can find you another. I know of men in several companies in the city who are looking for skilled secretaries." He then added with a pointed glance toward Vivian, "There are no strings attached."

The heavy features on Verina's face eased. "I warn you, Mr.—"

"Howe."

"I warn you, Mr. Howe, I've lost positions on the mere fact that people don't seem to take to me." She squared her shoulders.

"I haven't had a pleasant time of it, and I suppose that doesn't make me the jolliest person in the office."

"In San Francisco, Miss Jones, no one cares if you're jolly," he said. "They only care if you do your job well."

"That I can promise you," Verina said with dignity.

"I'm sure of it." He slipped his hand into his pocket and pulled out a card. Vivian caught the Waxwoodian emblem on it. "Here's where I'm staying while I'm here. Call me there tomorrow, and I should have more information for you."

"Call," she murmured, fingering the card.

Roger seemed to catch on quickly. "Better still, come by. I shall be in the hotel parlor after seven o'clock."

"Thank you, Mr. Howe." Verina held out her hand. "You've been very gracious, considering you don't know me."

"One must take a chance being gracious now and then." He didn't look at Vivian, but she felt he was speaking to her. "And now, will you and your friend take something from Miss Grace?" He lowered his tone. "I don't like to say it, but I believe what you said before greatly offended her. Surely a meal from a friend can't be charity."

Vivian could see she was weighing her pride against her hunger. Finally, Verina gave him a tight smile. "You're right, of course, Mr. Howe. It was inconsiderate of us to refuse before. Miss Grace has always been generous to us."

They all gathered near the back of the store. Nettie accepted with sweetness both Verina and Ruth's apologies and scurried up the stairs to arrange some refreshment, with Ruth following, insisting on helping her. Verina wandered to a display case and admired the ornate jars. Mr. Stevens sat against the wall, Pan now asleep in his lap.

"Who is that?" she asked, staring at the man.

"My cousin," Roger said. "I'm afraid he's unresponsive."

"Oh?" Verina studied him. "Why is that?"

The question seemed both bold and innocent, and Roger's lips lifted with amusement. "No one knows."

"I've lived with people who would hardly speak a word to anyone for a period of time." Her tone softened. "My mother was an artist, you see. She could go for days without speaking when she was working on a sculpture. She said she had to be silent to hear the voices of her figures speak to her."

"I'm afraid no one speaks to Harland," said Roger. "He's mad with fear, the doctors say."

"What is he afraid of?" Verina asked, her eyes on the immobile man.

"The past, I imagine," said Roger shortly.

"You don't know that, Roger." Vivian's gut tightened.

"He went silent when his father died," the young man continued.

"I'm sure you're right," Verina murmured. She glanced at Vivian. "You ought to be interested, Vivian. Very interested."

"Mr. Stevens' illness is none of my concern," said Vivian in a curt voice.

Verina's eyes glowed like coals. "Aren't you the one who chases down memories until they become phantoms so vile, one ends up shut in with them?"

"They become vile only when one refuses to face them," Vivian snarled. "Only when one lies about them."

"I never lied about anything!" Verina's eyes glowered.

"Lying by omission," Vivian said. "What one doesn't say can be worse than what one does."

Verina turned to Roger. "Be careful of her, Mr. Howe. She'll destroy everything your cousin holds dear if you let her. She did it to me and to herself." The woman's eyes assaulted Vivian with an almost mocking gaze. "You're as alone as I am now."

Vivian half turned her back on them, though she felt no tears. The truth in the words made her feel as if she were being buried alive.

"Tell the truth, Vivian. If you had it to do all over again, would you?"

Vivian placed both her hands on the counter, feeling her blood run cold.

"I don't think you're being very fair to Vivian, Miss Jones," Roger said. "I have, in fact, asked Vivian several times to help me with my cousin, and she's refused."

"Then she's grown a conscience since I first met her!" Verina's voice cracked in the small store, now empty except for themselves. Nettie and Ruth had both returned, and Ruth held two plates in her hands. She edged toward Verina and put one on the counter, but the woman ignored it.

"Shall I tell you something, Mr. Howe?" Verina asked. "Something you may find objectionable?"

"I never find a woman's words objectionable," he assured her.

"I think your cousin is lucky."

Vivian glared at her. "How can you say such a thing?"

"He's lucky he's found a place of peace inside himself," said Verina. "He's fortunate that whatever ails him, he doesn't have to face it."

The horror of her words washed over Vivian like poison. "Get out!"

"If he is afraid of the past, as you say, Mr. Howe, you ought to let him stay right where he is." Verina's voice clipped with bitterness. "And don't let Vivian go near him!"

"Get out!" Vivian's shriek made the small room almost vibrate, making the others jump.

The bell over the door swung to and fro from a sudden breeze through the window, bringing a sad echo into the empty shop. A puff of sawdust seemed to come out of nowhere, as if a ghost had disappeared through a wall, leaving its essence behind.

Nettie untied her apron and folded it into a small, neat square. She put it on the counter and said in a quiet voice, "I think it's better if you left now, Miss Jones. You may take the plate with you."

Verina pulled her shawl tight around her shoulders, their blades piercing through the thin yarn. "You know I'm right, Vivian."

Vivian said in an unsteady voice, "You know you're wrong, Verina."

Ruth's eyes were half-closed, as if from wariness. As Verina advanced to the front of the store, she eased toward Vivian and said in a low voice, "I'm sorry this happened. I didn't think she was still bitter."

"Perhaps she still has reason to be," Vivian said in a steel voice.

When they had gone, Nettie turned to Roger. "I think you and your cousin had better leave too."

Pan, now awake, got up on his hind legs and leaned against the man's broad chest to lick his chin. Mr. Stevens did not twitch.

Vivian looked at the dog for a moment and then threw a glance at Roger. "What about your cocker spaniel?"

"Tessa?" He sighed. "She ran into the road and was trampled by horses, poor mite."

"I'm sorry to hear that."

Roger eyed his cousin. "Maestro's fate was even worse."

The mention of the dog's name caused Mr. Stevens' lips to twitch, though the impassive expression remained.

"Uncle Joseph and I never knew just what happened to him," Roger continued. "Some neighbors found him butchered in the woods near the castle."

His cousin's lower lip returned to its even line.

"This is a very distasteful conversation, Mr. Howe," Nettie scolded.

Roger scuttled toward Mr. Stevens and gently took the dog out of his lap, putting him on the counter. "You don't agree with what she said, do you, Vivian?"

"About your cousin being in a better place?" Vivian looked at the redheaded man. "Do you?"

The young man stiffened. "I won't believe it." He took his cousin's hand and helped him up. Mr. Stevens did not resist or object. As he took his arm, he said, "You told me you didn't want to walk into another person's dark room, and yet you lost your temper when Miss Jones suggested just that." Without waiting for an answer, he bowed at Nettie. "Forgive me for lingering. It gets so quiet at the hotel with only myself and my cousin."

He stared down at Pan, who had settled himself on the counter with his wistful eyes on his mistress. "Harland thought Tessa was just a toy to me, but she was really my companion. I know it sounds odd, Vivian, but I could talk to her—in private about the things I couldn't speak about with anyone else."

"Yes," Vivian said with a small smile. "Dogs are that way, aren't they?"

She watched them advance toward the door, two tall men, one towering above the other, both moving with the stride of those who carried with them the burdens of untouched years. Her chest pressed into her bones, and she grasped the edge of the counter, feeling a little dizzy. Pan leaned his head forward and licked her hand.

As she picked him up, she called out, "Another dog would lighten the load on your shoulders, wouldn't it?"

Roger turned around with a shrug. "It might."

"Is Mr. Stoker still giving away his dogs to good homes?"

Roger blinked. "I don't know."

"We could go there tomorrow and find out," she continued. "And take your cousin along with us. I remember how warmly he felt toward Mr. Stoker and his dogs. It might be good for him to see an old friend." She looked at the tall man, who had turned his head over his shoulder to mimic his cousin, though his dark eyes were like glass.

Roger's countenance relaxed. "Thank you, Vivian. Thank you

from both of us." He blinked into the light that had fallen on them from the gas lamp that stood just above the door. "I'll come at nine in the morning for you?"

"If you wish," she said. "Good night, Roger. Good night, Mr. Stevens." The redhead did not answer, nor did he turn his head as both men walked out of the store.

"Vivian, don't be a fool!" her friend hissed.

"What do you mean?"

"I don't trust that young man," said Nettie. "I'm afraid for you. You still loathe Mr. Stevens, don't you?"

"Perhaps I do," Vivian admitted. "But even an enemy deserves to find the key to his own prison."

"You may not help him find the key," Nettie said. "He might pull you into that prison instead."

Vivian held Pan up to her cheek. She felt the dog's wire fur rough against her skin.

CHAPTER 5

*V*ivian appreciated morning sounds outside the window of the tiny flat she shared with Nettie. Morning at Alderdice Hall had been filled with silence and the gray mist rising from the San Francisco fog before the morning sun burned it off into the blue sky. But on George Street, the morning was alive even while darkness still enveloped the small windows.

The produce truck for Foss & Sons Grocers woke her at five o'clock, and she could almost smell the ripeness of tomatoes and grassiness of lettuce tumbling inside the crates as it passed right under the window, especially in the compressing summer heat. She would remain in the bed and listen for other street sounds: the clatter of the cowbell on the milk truck, the tapping of hooves from the wagon filled with fishermen that always stopped outside the house next to theirs to pick up the few who lived there, and the shriek of a whistle from an automobile someone had built that seemed eager to wake the dead. The noises wrapped her in the feeling of being a part of something larger than she had ever been — the working world.

This morning, she slipped out of bed and dressed and, with

Pan on his leash and her diary under her arm, crept downstairs. The sun was settling in the sky, though still a watery ball against the faded blue sky. The noise had now disappeared, and the street was quiet again.

She walked toward the dark blue bay in the distance. When she came upon the main road, there were signs of life. Scents of fried eggs and blueberry muffins flew out open windows above the closed shops. A few merchants were opening their doors, and several gave her a nod as she passed. The condensed area gave a feeling of coziness she had never experienced during her early morning walks on the vastness of the San Francisco hills.

She crossed into the city park. As she undid the leash, letting Pan run loose on the green, she settled in the gazebo, the tender vines swinging from its entwined roof over her head like a woman's fan.

Taking out the diary and the pencil tucked inside her pocket, she wrote:

Nettie called me a fool yesterday. Perhaps I am. Perhaps I acted out of anger against Verina, like the arrogant boy who takes up the gun to prove his manhood. What is it I'm trying to prove? And yet, Mr. Stevens is a hollow shell, and he must be filled again. I was not filled until my Pandora's box was empty. So must his be.

She felt Pan's small body leaning against her legs, his whimper echoing in the silent park. She put the diary away and meandered back to the flat.

She entered to the scent of coffee and sizzling bacon. Pan pulled away from the leash and barked for his share. Vivian glanced down, suddenly aware the clothes she wore were of the sensible and durable type, not quite the fashion and not what Roger and Mr. Stevens would be used to. She remembered with some envy the days when she could buy dresses and suits of the highest couture without thinking twice about the cost.

Her friend took the frying pan off the heat, covering it so Pan wouldn't steal the rest of the bacon, and strolled over to the closet. She pulled out a box that revealed a skirt and blouse somewhat out of fashion but crisp and beautifully trimmed with Swiss lace. Without a word, she put it on Vivian's bed and returned to the stove.

The clothes fit Vivian well, and when she sat at the table to slice the tomatoes, a breakfast ritual Nettie had taught her, she draped a large towel over her shoulders like a bib to protect the fine lace. As the knife slivered through the red flesh, she said, without looking up, "Don't be angry, dear."

Nettie looked over her shoulder. "I'm not angry. I'm trying to make sense of it all."

"So am I," Vivian admitted. "I'm going with my heart and not my head."

"Sometimes one ought to ignore what one's heart says," said her friend.

Vivian finished the tomatoes and pushed the plate to the center of the table. "Have you ever done so, when a woman in need came to your door?"

"If it meant risking my own peace of mind, perhaps I would." Nettie set the table.

"I wasn't thinking of that," said Vivian. "I was thinking of how I no longer feel righteousness. as I did watching Mr. Stevens on the train."

"And that's a reason to help him?"

She gave her friend an arduous look. "You taught me to be charitable, Nettie. You also accused me of being merciless toward him, remember?"

"I didn't feel about it then as I feel now."

"Which is?"

"That it's all wrong!" An unsteady hand lifted the heavy coffee pot.

Vivian took it from her. "You'll spill it and burn yourself."

"Burn some sense into *you*, maybe," her friend grumbled.

"You sound like Bertha Ross." The wind chime she had bought as a gift when she came to live with Nettie cackled angrily as it swung back and forth in a gust of wind from the open window.

"Why is that?" Her friend eyed her.

"She thought everything about my grandmother was all wrong at her friend's funeral."

"And she was right, wasn't she?" Nettie voice was soft. "You went down that path and look what happened."

Vivian said firmly, "As Roger pointed out to me, it would be Mr. Stevens' wounds and not mine this time."

"That Mr. Howe ought to be a traveling salesman, not an architect!" Nettie snapped.

Vivian laughed as she buttered a slice of toast. "I don't think Roger would find that complimentary."

"He maneuvered you into it, Vivian," said Nettie. "His visit to the library and then last night, bringing his cousin along when he was in no fit state to be in such a crowd."

"You don't believe he's genuinely concerned about Mr. Stevens?"

"Do you?" her friend countered.

Vivian held her coffee cup with both hands, staring at the square of gray sky that peered from the window. "I'm not sure."

"You told me he despised Mr. Stevens."

"Perhaps he still does," she said. "A part of him, anyway. The worst thing that can happen to a person is to depend on someone who despises him."

Nettie put down her fork. "So now you're Mr. Stevens' protector?"

"I pity him," Vivian said. "Just as I pity Olivia and Mrs. Bowen and Martha and other women we've found in the gutters of Goldspur."

"He's one of your lost doves, is he?" Nettie snapped.

"We made a commitment to help people all we can," Vivian

sighed. "I think even you would agree, Mr. Stevens, in his present condition, needs help."

Nettie took her hand. "It's you I'm thinking of, Viv. You've been injured enough. I don't want to see it happen again."

Vivian blinked back the dampness in her eyes and kissed her friend's cheek. "If one survives the walk through the fire, one has an obligation to help others do the same. You should know that."

"Yes," Nettie breathed. "I know."

Not long after breakfast, Vivian waited outside the shop for Roger to appear. People hurrying past to their work or their shopping nodded at her, and a few stopped to say a word, recognizing her face from the drugstore or the library. On George Street, she was as constant and familiar as Nettie.

She heard a ghastly noise coming down the street and saw a beetle-like automobile hobbling along the gravel as it shook its way toward her. Roger was at the wheel with Mr. Stevens sitting in the seat behind him.

The blond man pulled up at the curb, jumping down to help her up on the cushioned seat next to him. He smiled at her bewilderment. "My latest acquisition, The Saco. I had it made especially in Chicago this spring."

"I see you take as much of an interest in these new contraptions as your cousin." Vivian settled into the high seat, the top of her hat brushing against its roof.

"Naturally, Harland wouldn't be able to steer a car in his condition." Roger glanced back at his immobile cousin.

"So you took it upon yourself to purchase this lavish four-seater." Vivian slid her eyes toward him as he started the motor again, its grating sound roaring in the quiet street.

He sat up in the straight-backed seat as he steered the car. "I adjusted quickly to a simple life, but Harland is used to luxuries such as this. I'm sure you remember what that's like."

Vivian's face grew hot as she looked ahead at the dirt road, a little more smoothed down by the recent surge of automobiles. "I sometimes marvel at all the useless things I thought were essential when I was living with my mother. Now, they seem like absurd frivolities."

He smiled. "As I man, I can't deny some of those absurd frivolities make for a very eye-catching lady."

She laughed. "I confess I had a moment of self-consciousness this morning, thinking my plain clothes were not up to your or Mr. Stevens' standards."

"I wouldn't know, and neither would he," said Roger. "We've been staying out of society here so far."

"One can hardly go to a party when one is in mourning," she said politely, remembering what he had told her about the death of his uncle.

"We curtailed our mourning for obvious reasons," Roger murmured.

"And you've no interest in what society might think if you and Mr. Stevens enjoyed your leisure," said Vivian with a nod.

"Harland was never really keen on that sort of leisure." He veered to a narrower road on the right. "Even as a young man, he went only where and when my uncle told him. Not that he was ever lacking for attention when he got there." Roger glanced at her with a sly look. "A man with such physical presence as Harland's easily impresses the ladies."

"Yes, he has that," Vivian admitted, turning her head to study Mr. Stevens. The man was dressed in a forest green suit that suited his auburn coloring and pale skin, and his dark eyes looked less stormy than she had ever seen them. He sat with his knees apart and his hands laced together in his lap, relaxing against the seat. She felt sure that, if he could, he would smile.

"How do you speak to him, Roger?" she asked suddenly.

"What do you mean?"

"Do you speak to him as you would normally?" she asked. "Or do you talk to him like a child? Do you tell him the truth, or do you keep things from him so he won't get upset?"

He grasped the tiller in both hands as he made a sharp turn. "Why should I keep anything from him?"

"I thought perhaps you were being careful in what you say to him," she said. "Did you tell him where we're going?"

"Certainly," he said. "Harland has always loved dogs. You ought to have seen his face when we got rid of all the dogs after my uncle died. He stood at the window and watched as the men led them into the wagon. You would have thought they were taking away his dearest friends."

A cool breeze darted through the pine trees lining the road, and Vivian shivered, drawing her jacket closer around her. "I don't doubt they were."

"Harland has never been one to make friends easily," Roger agreed. "He preferred to mentor young men like your brother."

"Odd that he never married," Vivian murmured.

"It's lucky he didn't," Roger declared. Then, as if sensing her discomfort, he added, "I mean, I don't think he would have enjoyed family life. He's always been the sort with itching feet."

The comment seemed a little out of place as she thought of the frozen man sitting behind her. She glanced back and saw that, although Mr. Stevens had not moved, his eyes were keen, and his hands, laced so naturally in his lap before, were now grasping one another.

"Roger," she said, "I think he recognizes this road."

As the car drove through the Stoker farm gate, the clamorous sound of dogs hollered close by. When Roger turned off the motor, the quiet breath of country air made the deep-throated barking echo even more.

Vivian now saw that, although the same impassive expression dominated Mr. Stevens' features, a milky glare came into his eyes. She glanced down at his hands and saw them tightly bound with the knuckles protruding through the pale skin.

She grabbed Roger's arm. "I think we ought to turn back."

"It was on your suggestion that we came here in the first place, Vivian," he pointed out.

"I think I was wrong," she said. "There's something frightening about the look on his face, as if he's about to jump out of his own skin."

"If Harland is responding, that's a good thing, isn't it?" Roger asked.

She saw his shiny face in the sunlight, as he had climbed down from the wagon. Though he was smiling, she suddenly felt a cold chill.

Rodney Stoker emerged from the house. He looked thinner than when she had seen him two years before, and the beard was longer, the ends of it blowing in the wind as he moved. But the gray eyes were still lively.

"Well, if it ain't old friends!" He threw his head back and yelled, "Mary! Mary, come on out here!"

Roger helped Vivian out of the wagon. The moment he saw the big man, Mr. Stoker's face lit up with emotion as he took his hand. "Been too long, Mr. Stevens, far too long."

Vivian expected a sign of recognition from the redhead, but the man took his usual stance, his head turned in an odd direction.

"Don't you rec'gnize me, Mr. Stevens?" the man continued, his half-toothed grin fading. "Many's a time you come to look at my dogs and visit with us. Needled Mary into baking you a cherry pie more'n once." The man laughed, sounding hollow and unsure.

"My cousin lost his father recently," Roger said in a low voice. "He hasn't been the same since. He's been ill."

The wiry man staggered back, as if a blow from an ax had hit him. His hand went to his forehead, his eyes brimming with a sorrow that touched Vivian. Even Roger looked humbled as he added in a soft tone, "I'm sorry to be so blunt, Mr. Stoker."

The man recovered as he said in a grave tone, "Wish I'd'a known 'bout it. I'd'a come—" Lines showed around the corners of his mouth. "Well, glad you're all here now." He dropped Stevens' hand and watched as it swung like a blade back and forth until it settled near his side.

Vivian cleared her throat. "I'm eager to meet your wife, Mr. Stoker. I remember you telling me she didn't get to see many women."

The man flicked his head toward the house. "Mary! Blast it, woman, where are ya?"

The door opened, and Mary emerged, looking none too happy about her husband's impatience. She had the worn look of an overworked farmer's wife, but her smile and step were as lively as her husband's.

"Sakes, Rodney, you gotta wake up the entire valley?" she snapped in a good-natured way. "Got the baby to put down, ain't I?" Her eyes rested on Vivian.

"Mary, you remember Mr. Stevens, don't you?"

"'Course I do," she scoffed. "Glad to see you, Mr. Stevens." She did not take his hand, and her fine green eyes surveyed the man's stoic posture.

"This here's his cousin, Mr. Howe," said Mr. Stoker. "And Miss Alderdice. I told you 'bout her a long time ago. She's the one who charmed the dogs." He winked at his wife.

"You have a good memory, Mr. Stoker," Vivian said with a smile.

"Friends of Mr. Stevens, I ain't likely to overlook," said the man. He leaned toward his wife and whispered in her ear. Her face became as grave as his a few moments before.

The woman stepped forward, shaking Roger's hand, and then she took Vivian's. "I was mighty sorry I didn't meet you last time, Miss Alderdice."

"She's Mrs. Caulfield now, ma'am," Roger said.

"Married?"

"Widowed," Vivian murmured.

"Ah, well, that's the way of it, ain't it?" sighed the woman.

"We came for a dog," Roger said. "From what we heard coming in, you still have plenty, Mr. Stoker."

"A dog?" The man studied him. "Didn't I give you one a year or so ago?"

"Yes, sir." Roger looked almost sheepish. "But my friend Mr. Adams took to Tessa, so I gave the dog to him as a present."

Vivian flashed him a look, remembering what he had told her of the cocker spaniel being trampled by horses.

Mr. Stoker's lips were even. "Don't know as I like that, son. Like knowing where my dogs are goin'."

Roger gave him his charmed smile. "I wouldn't have given Tessa to Mr. Adams if I thought he would mistreat her." Vivian felt more than saw a quick flicker on Mr. Stevens' face. "Mr. Adams is a partner at his father's dental offices and doing very well. A highly respectable person, sir. I assure you."

"You can't get more sober than a dentist, can you, Rodney?" his wife prompted.

"'Less you're a judge!" The man threw his head back and laughed. "I didn't mean I didn't trust you, son." He turned to Vivian. "And you, miss? You come lookin' for another Scottish terrier 'cause yours got the cold feet? 'Cause I got one."

"No, sir," Vivian said firmly. "One Pan is enough for me."

The man roared with laughter. "Well, I warned ya 'bout them terriers. Got the worst manners of any dog." His eyes fell on Mr. Stevens, but he directed his questions at Roger. "And the bull pup? Caught lotsa birds like his papa done?"

"He caught a few," Roger said. "In his day?"

"Eh, what, son?" Mr. Stoker gave him a quick look. "He's still a young'un, ain't he?"

"He would have been." The blond man gave an inaudible sigh. "If he hadn't been mauled."

Vivian again gave him a look. But Roger's figure was elegantly poised and his face as calm as if he had just told them there might be rain coming soon.

"Sorry to hear that," Mr. Stoker murmured, clearly disturbed. "I ain't hardly thought Mr. Stevens would allow—" He glanced at his friend, whose shoulders looked stiffer than they had been, almost as sharp as two hooks.

"Well, looks like we gonna have a few of them pups taken off our hands, Mary," Mr. Stoker said. "S'pose you make our friends here some coffee and round up some of them sugar cookies you made last night while I show 'em what we got in the pen."

"Be glad to," said the woman, smiling as she disappeared into the house.

As they followed him, Vivian noticed the fields were more overgrown, and the trees lopped sideways as if they had been through too many storms. She smelled the pine and lavender and felt the wind brushing her cheek like a kiss. "Are the dogs still skittish when they see a skirt and parasol, Mr. Stoker?" she asked jokingly.

"Well, ma'am, I'll tell you," he squinted in the sunlight, "we had many a lady come here since your visit, and I guess that sorta put Mary in a more amiable frame o'mind, where the dogs are concerned. So now, she comes and feeds 'em with me and plays with 'em sometimes, and so do our two eldest daughters. So the dogs are used to ladies now."

"I'm happy to hear it," Vivian murmured.

Mr. Stoker and Roger progressed through the yellow grass to the yard where the fence to the dog pen was now visible, but Mr. Stevens stopped. His arms hung at his sides, but his hands balled into fists. His head turned toward the fence.

"Are you all right, Mr. Stevens?" she asked gently.

"They won't hurt you, Vivian." Roger called. "Not after you charmed them the last time."

"It's not me," Vivian said. "It's your cousin."

Roger joined them and took Mr. Stevens' arm. "Come, Harland. Mr. Stoker has a pit bull pup he wants you to see."

"Roger, you don't understand," Vivian lowered her voice. "He's refusing to go on."

"He can't refuse anything!" The tone came out with a bark as vicious as the loud growl from a German shepherd that had now wandered near the fence in their direction.

"I don't think you realize—"

"It's you who don't realize, Vivian." His voice was curt. "Once Harland sees the dogs, he'll remember how fond he is of them. Come, Cousin." He took a firm grasp of the man's hand.

Mr. Stevens' pose melted, and he became like wax again. But a taciturn expression remained in his eyes.

As they neared the fence, a pug puppy teetered toward them, his wide eyes damp with anxiety, and his flat face tilted upward.

"You like them friendly dogs, as I recall, Mr. Howe." Mr. Stoker leaned one arm against the fence. "A pug's as friendly as they make 'em. Wonderful with kids."

"I have no kids," Roger said, a little embarrassed. He opened the gate to let the pug out, and the dog pranced in front of him, still looking up with soulful eyes.

"I live in a small flat in San Francisco," Roger said. "I need a house dog, sir."

"Oh, he's happy curlin' up all day, Mr. Howe," said Mr. Stoker with a laugh. "And love to eat, that one! Gotta make sure he don't get fat, y'know." With a keen eye on the redhead, he added, "Don't reckon Mr. Stevens would find much use for a dog like that."

"No," Roger said, giving the redhead a seething glance. "My cousin prefers more aggressive dogs."

There was an unpleasant silence as a squabble came from the henhouse, and two chickens came out with their wings fluttering and tails bobbing. A Yorkshire terrier burst forth, its gleaming white fur blown back as it barked at the chickens with the viciousness of a wolf.

"Quiet!" Mr. Stoker roared. The dog was silent, but only for a moment, then turned its attention to another dog sitting under a tree and unleashed its wrath once more. "Them Yorkies ain't the cushion dogs Victorian ladies think they are." He nodded at the dog. "Fool with 'em, and you'll get a nasty bite!"

Roger bent down toward the pug, petting its head. "I don't think I want a fierce dog, sir."

"Not like the Scotties?" Mrs. Stoker asked with a smile and turned to Vivian. "Rodney told me you got yourself one last time you were here."

Vivian caught the way Mr. Stevens' lips quivered when the Yorkshire terrier started its noisy attack. But the man had not moved his position. Without turning her eyes away from him, she answered, "Pan is my comfort, ma'am."

The woman nodded with approval. "Dogs are the best when a woman's alone. Better'n a man sometimes." She winked slyly at her husband, who sniffed back.

"Many's a time I felt he understood me better than anyone else," Vivian said. "I've always been very grateful that Mr. Stevens convinced me to come here that day." The redhead's chiseled features softened.

"I think I like the pug," Roger said. "Maybe he is a little like a lady's dog, but I fancy him sitting on the couch while I read at night with my pipe by the fire." He grinned at the dog and stroked its head with affection.

"Hate to break it to you, son," said Mr. Stoker. "But the dog's a 'she,' not a 'he.'" This made his wife chuckle.

Vivian glanced down at the animal. "She looks a little like my cousin Emma. Her eyes are always peering up at people like that."

"Is she a short lady?" Mrs. Stoker asked.

"No, ma'am," said Vivian. "Only a slow-nodding one."

Mr. Stoker and Roger both laughed, and the latter said jovially, "Then we must honor her by naming the pug Emma." He took the dog in his arms, and Emma promptly covered his face with lavish kisses with her pink tongue.

"See there, now?" Mr. Stoker winked. "I told ya — right friendly dog."

"What do you think of our new companion, Harland?" Roger turned to his cousin.

Mr. Stevens' head cocked a little, and his expression shifted, looking almost crooked with perplexity. A beagle wandered to the gate and peered into the distance as if it had spotted something uncertain. The redhead's lips parted.

Mr. Stoker bent down. "That's more to your liking, Mr. Stevens. Excellent small game hunters."

"Harland knows," Roger said. "We used to train beagles at the castle."

Mr. Stevens' hand moved to his shirt pocket, and Vivian felt her hands tighten on her parasol as he slid out the notepad and pencil. He scrawled on the page and held it out. Roger read the words aloud: *"Five. Fleece. Pinecones."*

"I know what he's trying to say," said the young man. "My aunt once told me she gave Harland his first dog when he was five years old. Harland named it Fleece."

The corners of the redhead's lips lifted, and Vivian wondered if he was trying to smile. "It wasn't a hunting dog," Roger continued. "It was a Spitz. Harland used to bring Fleece pinecones from the woods, and he would play with them."

"How sweet," Vivian said, smiling.

"It was a sweet dog," said Roger. "Uncle Joseph didn't like it, though. A year later, he got Harland his first beagle and taught him to hunt rabbits."

The older man lost the nostalgic look on his face and paled, his skin almost transparent in the sunlight.

"You haven't any Spitz dogs, have you, Mr. Stoker?" Roger asked.

"No, sir," he said. "Few lap dogs in my pen right now."

"What about the pit bull pup you told me about?" the young man asked.

"Got 'im just this morning from the feller that gave me the other one," the man said. "Last of the litter, he told me. Pup barely with his eyes open, but—"

"His pedigree is nothing to be ashamed of," Roger finished with a smile. "I remember you telling us the last time. I'm sure my cousin would be interested in seeing him."

"Roger." Vivian took his arm. "I think we ought to get back now."

The blond man did not answer but looked toward the fence, the rambunctious Emma still in his arms.

"Oh, not here, son," said the man. "We had to put it in the barn. Such a little mite, didn't want him spooked before someone got him."

"Can we see him?" Roger repeated.

"If he's as small as that, maybe we shouldn't." Vivian was thinking of something else. She remembered Maestro, with his skullcap head and damp eyes, and the way he had looked at Mr. Stevens.

"Lots of people about might scare the critter, Rodney," said Mrs. Stoker.

"Won't do it no harm to see people," Mr. Stoker insisted. "Mary, run in and get 'im, will ya?"

His wife gave him a look but obeyed and was back with the dog in her arms. Unlike his predecessor, this pup was all black with a patch of white around his eye. His ears were large and floppy, almost too large for his body, and the eyes looked as if they were half-shut.

"Puny thing," Mr. Stoker remarked. "But you never can tell how big they'll get. And how strong."

Roger mumbled, "Maestro grew up to be a gigantic dog."

Mr. Stoker glanced at the redhead. "Like to see him, Mr. Stevens? Be a real pleasure to give such a fine dog to a man like you. I know you'll treat him right."

Vivian heard small squeals and realized they were coming from Mr. Stevens. The stone features had cracked, and the man looked down at the pup in Mrs. Stoker's arms with fondness. His large hand rose, hovering over the dog's head as if blessing the animal. His lips twitched and opened, and the squeals came through, grating Vivian's nerves. But in a moment, the sounds turned into words.

"Frogs — Jake — good." His arms melted to his sides, and his features hardened again, and his eyes dimmed as if they had never moved.

Vivian's hand was now like a block of ice, the feeling gone out of it. She realized she was holding the handle of the parasol too tightly. She dropped it on the ground, and a rush of warmth entered her fingers.

Both the Stokers looked helplessly at Roger. His eyes were alert, and he said in a calm voice, "We don't keep hunting dogs anymore, Mr. Stoker. Thanks just the same."

"Well, I reckon — well, if you ever—" The man was clearly lost.

Roger continued, "My uncle was killed in a hunting accident, sir."

Mr. Stoker's lips tightened, and he signaled his wife, who diligently took the pup back to the barn. Vivian caught the dog glancing up at Mr. Stevens. Unlike Maestro, there was curiosity and affection rather than fear and apprehension on its face.

～

They rode back slowly, Emma dozing on the seat beside the redhead. There was silence between them for a while. Then, Roger ventured, "You think I did wrong in asking to see the pup."

"I'm glad you did," she said. "I think I know what's in that locked room in Mr. Stevens' mind."

"Oh?" The man glanced at her as they entered a stretch of bumpy road.

"He spoke when he saw the puppy," Vivian said. "He mentioned my brother's name."

"He remembered Maestro," Roger suggested. "He and Jake were together quite a lot with that dog the summer of 1898, weren't they?"

Though his eyes stayed on the road, they had just taken back into Waxwood, she felt as if he were really watching her. "I think the entire summer is in that locked room."

They entered the stable, and Roger stopped the car. "You mean your brother is in that room," he said in a quiet voice. "What do you propose, Vivian?"

She looked at the walkway between the horse stalls in front of them. "We should take Mr. Stevens back to that summer."

"How?"

She looked at him. "By taking him to places around here. Did you know I first met Mr. Stevens in the wax woods?"

"Indeed?" The young man glanced at her.

"The incident was a memorable one for Mr. Stevens," she said. "And not unpleasantly. Perhaps refreshing a pleasant memory, like the one he had with the beagle—"

"Might unlock the door?" Roger finished. "Yes, of course!"

She thought about the wax woods, which she had not seen in a year. Then it was a flirtation she was seeking, walking through the evergreen forest with the paw-like leaves hanging down over her and Monte LeBlanc's shoulder. And yet, it had turned into a haunting for her and made her run away.

"I don't want to go there again!" she screeched and slid out of the seat, her feet hitting the hard ground.

Roger scrambled out of the car, taking hold of her hands. "Please don't give up now, Vivian."

"You don't understand." The sting went to her eyes.

"You want Harland to repent what he did to your brother, don't you?" he asked.

She looked at the fresh face and unyielding eyes. "Do you think he wants to repent?"

He gave her a careful look. "I don't know. But there's no way to find out unless he goes back."

The panic in her eased. "Yes, you're right. He must go back."

"Then you'll go on?" When she didn't answer, he gave her arms a slight shake. "You'll go on?"

She looked at him. There was a seething glare in his eyes, perhaps from the sunlight coming through the pathway. She nodded.

CHAPTER 6

Vivian took the ferry to the Waxwoodian the next morning. She couldn't help but feel herself at home as she entered the lobby. The fragrance of eggs, bacon, ham, and hotcakes floated through the open dining room. A page boy jumped up from the velvet bench where he was waiting for orders and, saluting Vivian, said in a formal tone unbefitting his age, "Mr. Howe is in the dining room, miss — ma'am." He blinked as if he were reciting from memory. "He would be very pleased if you would join him there."

"How did he—"

"Oh, he said I was to tell you where he was whenever you came, ma'am," said the boy. "Him and me, we got an understanding." He seemed almost proud of this.

"Thank you," Vivian mumbled, but felt a twinge of annoyance at Roger's continual presumptuousness.

She felt belittled in the grandness of the dining room the moment she entered. The place had been as comfortable to her as the one in Alderdice Hall when she dined there with her mother last year. But now, they had redone it in neutral shades of brown to replace the green, red, and blue. The bland colors made the place look shadowy, though also, she admitted, more elegant and subdued.

She caught sight of the Tishers sitting in their usual center table, heading a large party. Faces glared out at her, shaped by her childhood memories: the Griffiths, the Breens, the Marsdens. She couldn't help but note with some amusement that the shy Mrs. Marsden, who had always spoken of her intention to yank her banker husband away from their usual summer at Fieldstone for the salt baths that were "so good for Matthew's bad back," had finally convinced her husband to come to Waxwood. Tears stung her eyes, forcing her to turn away. She had always thought them so parasitic and useless, and yet, their idleness was the very comfort she missed.

When she had composed herself enough to search for Roger, she found him at a table on the upper level. He smiled but didn't wave, as if he knew she was trying not to draw attention to herself. Mr. Stevens sat next to him, eating like a mechanical doll, yet as elegantly as she remembered. Emma's black-masked face popped up above the edge of the table, her lips opened wide as Roger slipped pieces of bacon in it.

Two other young men who looked to be Roger's age sat at the table. One of them, though his face was damp and smooth, was already showing gray hairs and a figure jointed like a man past his prime. The other had gathered features and was attacking his steak and eggs as if they were going to fight back.

"I hoped you would join us." Roger rose, taking her hand.

"It looks as if you expected it." She cast a wary eye upon the fifth place at the table, the place setting neatly arranged right down to the miniature cream pot and plate with sugar cubes next to the empty coffee cup.

"Roger goes all out when he has his mind made up," remarked the scraggly man.

"Mr. McDonaugh and Mr. Trent were just telling me how fondly they remember you from last year," he said.

Mr. McDonaugh gave her a pleasant smile. "We hope you remember us, Mrs. Caulfield."

"I do," Vivian said, holding her hand out. She could see both young men had settled into themselves and shed their rambunctious college boy ways as much as Roger had. "I remember my friend Mr. Leblanc playing croquet with you in the park at last year's Fourth of July celebration."

Mr. Trent eyed her. "You were rather hard on us, weren't you?"

"Was I?"

He laid down his fork and knife. "You accused us of almost letting your brother drown."

A spoon rolled to the table, leaving a few drops of coffee and cream on the starched white tablecloth. Vivian realized it came from Mr. Stevens.

"Isn't that right, Pete?" Mr. Trent seemed not to notice.

The other young man glared at him. "I'm sure Mrs. Caulfield meant no harm."

"I'm afraid I did," said Vivian, feeling her face redden.

"That's quite an accusation to make to anyone, Vivian." Roger said.

"I shouldn't have made it," she said. "I can't explain why now. But I apologize to you both."

Mr. McDonaugh bowed with acceptance. "You don't really think we would do such a thing, do you?"

"No, of course not." She fiddled with her napkin. "You know, I never found out who won the game."

"Game?" Roger asked.

"The croquet game."

Mr. Trent's challenging mood broke, and he laughed. "We did, of course. Me, Harrington, and your Mr. Leblanc. He proved a rather able-bodied player, your friend."

"I'm glad he was up to your skill," Vivian said, amused.

"We met Mr. McDonaugh and Mr. Trent by chance this morning," said Roger. "They're staying here."

"Quite a reunion, then." Vivian looked at the redhead and asked in a soft voice, "How are you, Mr. Stevens?"

Though the man did not look up from his plate, she thought she saw a quick flick of the fingers.

"We ought to all be on first names," Mr. McDonaugh declared. "We're old friends, after all."

"Yes, why don't we?" Roger asked. "It's time you were more personal with Harland."

"As I recall, your cousin prefers to be called Stevens." Vivian caught a flicker of the auburn eyebrow.

"That was a game he played," Roger said. "Just like all the other games." He shot a glance at both his friends, who looked away.

"All right," said Vivian. "You can call me Vivian, then."

"Splendid!" Mr. McDonaugh said. "We're Pete and Andy to you."

"And — Harland." Vivian looked at the redhead. "I rather like the name."

This time, Harland looked up and, although his gaze didn't quite meet hers, she felt he was trying to recognize her voice.

"As you can see, Harland is all right after our excursion yesterday," Roger said. "Emma finds him most appealing." He looked down at the puppy.

"I'm glad to hear it." Vivian poured coffee from a fresh pot, aware of the two young men on either side of her with alert eyes.

Roger watched her. "I've told Pete and Andy about Harland."

"Sad." Andy shook his head. "Sad situation."

"You keep your trap shut, Andy," Pete growled. He turned to Vivian with a kind smile. "We've always had the utmost reverence for Harland. He taught us quite a lot that summer of '98, though I doubt either of us would deny we couldn't fully appreciate it." His eyes slid toward his friend. The man grunted and attacked a second helping of steak and eggs.

Vivian heard the swish of a skirt, and, feeling her stomach tighten, she turned to gaze into the self-satisfied face of Fern Tisher.

"Hello, Vivian!" Her voice was bouncier and louder than Vivian would have liked.

"Hello, Fern." She kept her own tone subdued. "I see you're still gracing Waxwood with your presence."

"Oh, Ralph just had to see it for himself." She pulled the arm of the young man standing beside her. "You didn't know I was married now, did you?"

"No," Vivian said. "I didn't know." She felt a wave of sadness as she thought of all her mother hadn't told her.

"Yes, I'm Mrs. Gilmore now," said the young woman. "I hear you've gone back to your married name. Very sensible of you."

"That depends on how you look at it, Mrs. Gilmore," Roger said. "To Vivian, it's perhaps sensible, but to those men who might very well be searching for just such an intelligent and lovely lady, the name may mislead them to think she is no longer available."

Though Vivian knew he was trying to charm Fern, she glared in his direction. She had little desire to take the marriage vows again, and she resented the insinuation that, as she was now alone, she must still cast her eye toward eligible young men.

Fern, however, gave him one of her more coquettish smiles. "You pay her a great compliment, Mr.—"

"Howe," Roger said. He introduced the rest of the men around the table. Pete and Andy immediately cast an approving eye at Fern while Harland remained in his usual immobility. Fern, however, did not seem to sense anything unusual.

"Cecily and I were just talking about you the other day," she continued. "She's engaged to Silas Cremshaw, of the Boston banking family, you know."

"I didn't know that either," Vivian said stiffly. "I've been spending my time occupied by other things."

"That's exactly what we were talking about!" Fern leaned back a little. "We were both wondering what had become of you."

Vivian looked at her squarely. "I've been selling Feathers Vanishing Cream and sewing needles and strawberry sodas over a counter."

The statement seemed to have its effect on Fern, as the girl's eyes grew wide so that their robin's egg blue shone in the shadowed room, and her mouth slid open into a large "O." Vivian heard a chuckle escape from the general direction of the young men.

"Vivian is also helping unfortunate women improve their reading," Roger added. "She and her friend run a library."

"That doesn't surprise me," said Fern. "You know, Mr. Howe, we always feared for where Vivian's bookishness might lead her. I see now our fears were justified."

"This may surprise you, Fern," said Vivian, "but I'm quite contented exactly where I am. Sewing needles and dusty books and all."

"And your brother?" Fern asked, arching her eyebrows. "Is he contented to be where he is?"

A clang rang through the air, quiet now that the dining room emptied. Vivian saw Harland's coffee cup had tipped inside a saucer. As she reached forward with her napkin to catch the stream of coffee spilling over to the tablecloth, she glanced at the man's face. She detected a faint glimmer of distress in his straight lips.

Fern continued as if nothing had happened. "We've heard nothing about him for, oh, what is it now? A few years?"

"Fifteen months," Vivian murmured.

"And he's been in Europe all that time?" She glanced at her phlegmatic husband. "Jacob went to Paris to study art, dear."

"Indeed?" was all the young man could manage before he

turned with his hands in his pocket to survey the room as he had been doing for most of the conversation.

"He must study intensely," the girl continued. "Hardly a letter, I should think."

"Oh, I write him frequently," Vivian answered.

"It's good he keeps in touch," said Fern. "We're all eager to see him again, of course. Fifteen months is a long time to be away from one's world."

"Yes," Vivian said. "It is." She crumpled the napkin in her lap.

"Well, we must be off," said the girl in a dismissive tone. "You're always welcome to join us for afternoon tea. You remember where." And with a fish-eyed glance at Vivian, she strolled out of the room, her pigeon-shaped figure bobbing as her skirt swayed, almost pulling her husband along with her.

The moment she left, Emma released a flurry of growls, and several heads turned with annoyance. Roger silenced the puppy by offering her a sliver of ham, which she enthusiastically accepted.

Pete cleared his throat. "I believe Emma has expressed our sentiments too, Vivian."

"Damn prissy girl," Andy agreed.

"I suppose I'm out of practice," Vivian remarked. "I used to be better able to come back with quick insults in those little sparing games the ladies of leisure are so fond of playing."

"Well, it's better you ain't one now," Andy assured her.

"Yes, of course." Vivian looked down at the tablecloth, its peach color making a strange bright glare in contrast to the subdued brown of the rest of the room.

"Take no notice of her," said Roger in a brisk voice. "Join us at the casino for a bit of fun, why don't you?"

"They've dancing and champagne, even at this hour," Pete said cheerfully.

"I'm afraid it's all too grand for my tastes nowadays," Vivian said with a smile. "I'd rather take a walk in the woods." She eyed Roger.

"Oh, the woods are boring," Pete said with a yawn. "The first time, they're a sight, I'll admit, but afterward, a tree is just a tree."

"Unless you're Diana." Vivian glanced at Harland. "I was hoping to take a walk with Harland. I think the air would do him a world of good, don't you, Roger?"

The blond man rubbed his mustache as he held a glass of juice in his hand, though he hardly looked as if he intended to drink it. "I couldn't agree more."

"They say they discovered a pack of savages living there with a pit full of shotguns," Pete said. "The police had to run them out."

Vivian caught a twitch at the corner of the redhead's lips. She knew Roger saw it too, as he put down his cup and scoffed, "People come up with the most sensational ideas!"

"All the same, I hardly think it's the place for a young woman." Pete glanced at his friend. "And with your cousin the way he is, he wouldn't be much good if she should run into trouble,"

Vivian stiffened. "I can take care of myself very well. I can even take care of Harland if need be."

Roger gave a deep laugh. "Vivian is hardly one to quiver at the misgivings of men," he remarked. "However, Pete has a point. Perhaps we should all go."

Vivian folded her napkin. "I intend to take Harland alone."

There was a muffled silence around the table as all three men seemed intent on looking in any direction but hers. The waiter chose this time to shuffle up to their table and, addressing Roger, asked if there was anything they needed. Roger mumbled something, and the waiter nodded, shuffling back to his place near the wall.

Pete was the first to speak. "Do you think that's wise?"

"If he ain't talking, it's going to be mighty boring for you, Vivian." Andy sat back and wiped his lips with his hand.

"If you don't mind my saying so, it may also be a little indiscreet," Pete added. "A lone man and woman, walking in a lone wood—"

Vivian couldn't help but grimace. "There's no one who would concern themselves about my reputation anymore, Pete."

"All the same, I don't think it prudent," the young man grumbled.

Both men looked at their friend as if waiting for a confirmation. Roger was playing with his napkin, folding it into ripples like a fan. He now put it on the table so neatly that it looked like a reclining peacock. "I've no fear for Vivian or Harland. If she prefers to go with him alone, she has her reasons. Why don't you both head over to the York, and I'll join you in a moment?" He gave them a meaningful glance.

Roger's friends disengaged themselves from their chairs, bid polite farewells, and sauntered out of the dining room. When they were gone, she leaned forward and gazed at him. "I told you yesterday I intended to take Harland out to the woods!"

He blinked. "When I came to you for help, Vivian, I thought you would take me into your confidence."

She eyed him. "You've told me often enough what a burden Harland has been to you. I didn't think you would object to a day away from his company."

"I just want to be there," he murmured. "I want to be there when the door opens."

"Why should you be?" she asked. "It won't be a pleasant experience, Roger."

"All the same—"

She rose. "You seem to expect something."

"I don't know what you mean," he said in a stubborn voice. "If there is to be unpleasantness, you shouldn't have to go through it alone."

"All the more reason to spare you, at least." Her head became a little dizzy then as she thought of how many people had tried to spare her from her own unpleasant experiences—Verina, Ruth, Jake, even her own mother.

He pushed back his chair. "I only want to help you do what's best for Harland."

"You can," she said, smiling. "By letting me go into the woods alone with him. I assure you, no harm will come to either him or me."

He bent down toward his cousin. "You're going for a walk, old boy. Come on."

The redhead rose, stepping away from his chair with almost the same careless finesse Vivian remembered. If it hadn't been for the unmarked lines on his face and the way his eyes and mouth set as if carved in stone, she would hardly know that inside this impressively tall, suave man lay the bones of an unreachable child.

"What do I do?" she asked.

"Take his arm. He'll go wherever you go and do what you tell him to," said Roger. "He won't hurt you, Vivian."

"I know that," she snapped.

She took Harland's arm. It did not lie heavy against her hand as she expected. She led him out of the dining room, and although his steps were stilted, he followed her lead without resistance.

"We can leave through the courtyard," Roger said as he adjusted Emma's leash. "You haven't seen it yet, have you?"

"No," she said. "The first time I came back here since last year was when you and I met to discuss Harland."

Her steps faltered a little as they went through the lobby and down the hallway that led out the French doors, Emma toddling beside them, waving her head about as if fascinated by the activity going on around her.

Once they came out the French doors, she felt herself take a breath. The courtyard had changed. There was now a pavilion that dominated much of the grassy area with a red roof and ornately scrolled pillars. The flat roof allowed one to take in the sea's view, and the hedges that had bordered the courtyard had been removed, so the only thing that separated land and sand was the wooden planks of the boardwalk.

"You have a pleasant day for a walk." Roger shielded his eyes from the sun as he looked out to the sea.

"So do you," she said, smiling. "A pleasant day for catching up on old times."

He shrugged. "We're no longer boys, Vivian. We're men, with men's responsibilities. Pete is engaged to be married, and Andy has a sick mother he's looking after. The years bring their own tragedies to us all." He eyed his cousin.

"We shall have a pleasant walk, won't we, Harland?" She glanced at the redhead. They turned a little toward the sea, but his eyes remained cast down.

Roger grasped her hands. "I'll be in the men's lounge at the York. If we go elsewhere, I'll leave word at the desk."

"I won't need anything," she said with a smile.

As she watched him stroll down the boardwalk, his hands in his pockets, nodding at ladies as he passed, but without the leering eye of his college boy days, she felt again the wave of uncertainty engulf her like the sea wind. She was alone now with this large, silent man.

"Since you prefer everyone call you Stevens," she said, glancing at the redhead, "that's what I'll call you from now on."

Though the redhead did not speak, she saw his lips sway as if he were trying to answer her. She felt a surge of relief as she led him down the boardwalk.

As with the hotels, the place was empty. As it was Saturday, men had come down from their city jobs to spend the weekend with their families. She suddenly feared she might encounter people she had known the previous summers in Waxwood and couldn't help but wonder what they would think. Would they see her as a little plain in her shirtwaist and gray suit but nonetheless fashionable, and Stevens looking for all the world like the new century's gentleman with his stiff collar and tie tucked inside his closed vest? Would they guess their eyes were feasting upon a Washington Street blue blood nearly fallen from grace and a once vibrant, commanding man, now a hollow shell of silence and perhaps madness?

They came upon the York Hotel, and Stevens stopped. He did not move his head, but turned a little, his forehead wrinkled, searching for something. His hand moved to his pocket and, taking out the pad and pencil, he scribbled briefly and held it out to her. She read the word *Amarok*. "Someone you met here once?" She gestured toward The York.

The man did not answer. His head tipped back so that his eyes pointed forward.

"Perhaps you'll tell me later." She took his arm again.

She felt a slight pressure on her hand and knew for certain he heard her and understood. There was no madness in those dark eyes any more than there was disrepute in her position.

They crossed a stretch of yellow sand and reached the dark green hill leading into the wax woods. For a moment, she was afraid the trail she had always taken into the woods had disappeared by the police when they chased out the savages. But the red dust was still there, and the pines stood tall as if waiting for her.

"I always liked these woods." Her voice vibrated as they climbed. "I never knew why until I came walking here after — until I was alone. I know why now." She paused, glancing at the redhead's face. The features were still, but she felt his attention drawn to her. "Because they're outsiders too. The old people in town have a legend about the wax wood trees. Would you like to hear it?"

His chin bobbed. It was a slight motion, but a definite agreement.

"Some have lived in Waxwood since its settlement, when it

had no name at all. People referred to it only as 'Bayside 17' because it was the seventeenth settlement beside the bay." She heard a small grunt but wondered if it wasn't from some hidden bird in the trees as it sounded hardly human. She continued, "This hill was bald, they say. A hill of red dust. And then, one day, the wax wood trees appeared full grown, just as they are now."

They entered the tail end of the wax wood forest. The cup-shaped tops sheltered them from the strong morning sun, and the leaves swept their strange hand-like shapes in long loops in the wind. Vivian could feel them patting her hat and shoulders. "The leaves have grown," she remarked. "It wouldn't surprise me if, in a few years, we might not be able to walk here at all."

His arm loosened a little beneath her hand. She let go of his arm and stepped away, sensing he could walk on his own. He stood in the pose of feet apart and hands to his sides, but he was not looking down anymore.

"The old people say they were glad," she went on. "Of the wax wood trees, that is. When they found out the bark was like wax, the town elders wanted to chop them down. They thought evil spirits embedded the roots."

Stevens' hands slowly came together, almost as if in prayer.

"One woman told me when she and her friends were just girls, they once went into these woods right before sunset and saw a crown of light as if someone had lit a very large candle. Others saw it too, and that's when the town left the woods just as they were." She paused, blinking around. "I suppose they saw in it the symbol of Christ."

This idea seemed to agitate Stevens, as his eyebrows pierced together, and his eyes glanced downward. She took the man's large hand, feeling the smooth skin cool and dead against hers.

She led him further into the woods and reached the place with the carpet of clover and trio of wax wood trees amidst a wall of redwoods. This was the place her brother had once asked her to pose for his paintings. It had been alive then with salamanders and frogs, lending a wakefulness to the murkier places in the forest. But no live creatures scurried about now, and she felt frozen in a specific time and place.

She sat on a rock, glancing at Stevens. It was clear he remembered the place too, and not without fondness, for a smile almost crossed his lips.

"You recognize the place, don't you, Stevens?" she asked. "I was there." She pointed at a spot populated with bright green clover. "Jake drew me as a fairy in the woods. You said I was Diana with her crown of thorns."

His face relaxed then, the bone features molding into the pleasant countenance she remembered. He looked almost like the old Stevens.

She saw his jaw and neck tighten and realized he was trying to speak. She heard him say, his voice soft with the same mild tone, "Crown."

"Yes," she said, smiling. "Diana's crown of thorns. Not a very cheerful image." She chuckled.

More words escaped his lips, "Flowers. Crowns."

She realized his mind was not the blank slate Roger had made it out to be. "You remember that?" She held her breath. "You remember my brother said I used to weave flowers into crowns when I was a child? You said it was a charming idea, and you would like me to give you such a crown one day. You said if I did, you would reward me with a bow and arrow." She felt a strange warmth at the memory, though she had felt anything but warmth toward him at the time.

His arms moved as if unattached, and his hands rose slowly, shaping themselves into an invisible mold.

"I shall be glad to weave you a crown, Stevens," she whispered. "And maybe you will give me that bow and arrow one day."

She fluttered about the woods, plucking flowers she saw in purple, pink, and yellow. Then she flew back with a gasp as she neared a cluster of daisies, realizing they were the same ones she had seen the year before when walking with Monte Leblanc. The flowers had grown even bigger now, and their distorted centers peered up at her like maimed yellow eyes.

"It's as if they're trying to pull themselves apart." She dropped the flowers she held in her hand on the grass. "I saw them last year, and they frightened me. They still do."

Stevens' eyes became stormy, and his hands clenched at his side. Then, without warning, he grabbed her hand. His grasp was easy, but determined, and he walked as if his limbs were wood and nails. She realized his face was lucid for the first time since she had seen him.

His enormous feet clumped through the grass, the crumpled leaves bobbing over their heads. They came to a place where the air was damp and filmed with mist. She could feel life forms here, though she couldn't see more than a sliding tail or head disappearing behind trees. The slyness of the animals made her shiver.

A sound buzzed above the quiet, and she realized it was Stevens' voice. He was speaking more coherently. "We took here."

"We? I don't understand," she choked out.

He looked straight ahead into the wall of trees. "Jake. We. Maestro."

"Oh, I see," Vivian said. "You and my brother took Maestro here."

"The frogs. Frightened the frogs."

"Who frightened the frogs?" she asked. "Maestro?"

"Forced." A callousness rang in his voice. "The bushes. Came out — fright!" His voice quivered. "Jake brave. I brutal." The man looked at Vivian with spooked eyes.

"Why was Jake brave?" Vivian asked quietly.

"Soothing," he said. "Knew about me, knew!"

"Who knew what, Stevens?"

"Jake, Jake!"

She waited patiently.

Stevens shut his eyes. "Afraid for the dog." The man covered his face with his hands.

Calmly, she asked, "Why was he afraid?"

She heard a choking sob escape his throat. "Punishment!"

Her gut tightened. "You punished the dog because he was afraid of the frogs?"

"Chain and spikes and—" His hands shook over his eyes.

Vivian tried not to flinch. "Tell me, Stevens. Open the locked door."

"All night out."

"Out where?"

"Woods." The choke sounded again. "Chained to a tree. Frogs about. Just a puppy!"

"Yes," she hissed. "He was just a puppy."

"Howled." Stevens' voice cracked. "Howled, howled, howled!"

Vivian said nothing. She had felt a moment of compassion for the man whose face had been blind with tears. But this was now the beast she remembered, the monster who could be so cruel as to leave a puppy chained to a tree where he had been frightened. Her loathing for him returned.

"We ought to get back," she said coldly.

For the first time, the redhead met her eyes directly. Folds appeared around his mouth and forehead. But a few moments later, the smooth, granite finish returned in his face, and his limbs lay stoic at his side. His head dropped as if there was nothing to hold it. She almost cringed, realizing he had seen the disgust in her eyes.

She took his arm and guided him back toward the path leading to the Waxwoodian. They walked in silence for quite some time, and her revulsion subsided. As they reached the mouth of the clearing, they met with a field of dandelion flowers. Their brilliant yellow shone like small suns. Stevens seemed suddenly caught by them, and, dropping her hand, he knelt down, cupping them with his hands. Something in the tender way his eyes studied the flowers touched her.

"Dandelions are odd flowers," she mused. "They're really weeds, you know."

He let the stems rest between his fingers.

"The seeds disperse in the wind and grow wherever they land," she continued. "They grow into new flowers that disperse their seeds. I've seen them in the cracks of the San Francisco pavement." She gave a rueful laugh. "I always thought how miraculous it was that, despite all the filth and manure, they grow."

A sigh escaped from the man's lips, the large chest heaving through the armor of the vest and coat.

"Rather like the children of South of Market," she said. This made his face relax from its granite pose.

"The first time I went there, a young painter named Christopher Spenlow asked to paint me," she said. "I told him someday."

Stevens' hands were now on his knees, and his head lifted.

"I didn't intend to return," she admitted. "But when I came to live with Nettie, I wanted to know them, these people for whom even a jug of milk was a struggle." She fingered the yellow flowers. "So I went back there. I sat for Mr. Spenlow while he painted me for three weeks. I met others and talked to them. I played with their children."

"Yes." It was a statement.

"They came from violence and poverty just as their grandparents did and their children and children's children would." She glanced at him. "Some were wilted and harsh. But some shone like those dandelions. Do you know why, Stevens?"

His head brushed from side to side.

"A woman there once said to me, 'When one is low, there is only to rise.'" She stood, placing her hand in his. "Do you believe that, Stevens?"

His eyes moved to the dandelions, their spike petals now flapping upward like the flame of a candle. His hand was clammy in hers.

"Do you believe that?" she repeated. But she knew the silent mist that had become his refuge had engulfed him.

"I'll show it to you one day," she said. "Mr. Spenlow's portrait, that is. I don't show it to everyone."

He seemed hardly to breathe as they made their way back to the hotel.

CHAPTER 7

The next day was Sunday, and Mother Nature unleashed a little of her wrath after the serene sunshine the day before. Vivian woke up to a shriek of wind and murky clouds. By the time she and Nettie sat down to breakfast, the threat of rain loomed.

"You're as nervous as a canary in a cage," Nettie remarked as she drizzled maple syrup on her hotcakes.

"An apt description of how I feel," Vivian admitted. "I can't tell you why."

"Perhaps your crusade for this man is caging your soul," Nettie said in a harsh tone.

"His soul is caged, not mine," Vivian said. "But I feel it belongs to me too." She grasped Nettie's wrist. "He spoke to me yesterday. It wasn't gibberish, either."

Nettie sniffed. "Perhaps he was doing all this for attention."

Vivian shook her head. "Stevens isn't that kind."

"Stevens?"

Vivian grimaced. "He always wanted me to call him that. I always insisted on 'Mr. Stevens,' just to annoy him."

Nettie laughed and finished the hotcakes on her plate. "It does a man good for a woman to be formal with him when he least wants it."

"He used to command attention," Vivian continued, leaning back. "He never needed to playact to get it."

"Your visit with him must have been very enlightening," Nettie remarked.

Vivian knew it was her way of opening the conversation about the day before. "We walked in the wax woods."

"A walk is rather harmless," Nettie said.

"He told me about the awful things he did to his dog," said Vivian. "And he was sorry. Truly, Nettie."

"Why shouldn't he be?"

"Because he used his dogs," she said in a ragged tone. "He was proud that he broke Maestro's obstinate will that summer. But yesterday, he was weeping over leaving him chained to a tree all night. He was punishing him for being afraid of frogs."

Nettie flinched. "Which Harland Stevens do you believe is the genuine one?"

Vivian shook her head. "I don't know."

There was a knock on the outside door. Nettie glanced at Vivian with a shrug as she rose to open it. They rarely had visitors in the flat at all, let alone on a Sunday.

Roger stood in a dark sack suit and bowler hat, holding a walking stick by the head. He looked more formal than usual.

"You're dressed in your Sunday best, I see," Nettie remarked.

He tipped his hat to her. "One always wears one's best to church, Miss Grace."

"Church?" She blinked. "I'm afraid we're rather lax about church in these parts."

"Oh?" He stepped into the flat and accepted the cup of coffee she offered him. "I recall Vivian attended regularly during her visits to Waxwood."

Vivian's cheeks grew hot. "I've gotten out of the habit," she mumbled.

"The means of survival clutter our minds, Mr. Howe," Nettie said in a brittle voice. "When Sunday comes, many of us here prefer to spend the hours on our own contemplations and not God's."

Vivian could not look at Roger, as she knew how he felt about "Godless creatures" and how much he valued his religion. It was, she suspected, his only link to his dead mother.

But the blond man accepted this without argument. "I've come to entice Vivian to come with me this morning."

She looked down at the wrinkled dressing gown and suddenly felt self-conscious. "I don't know—"

"We planned on doing some work in the library," Nettie interrupted. "You must appreciate, Mr. Howe, that many of our women have no free time other than the few hours on Sunday when their husbands and children are not demanding their time and full attention. Education requires both." She added this last with a rather rueful glare at the young man.

"I'm sure some of them take the time to pray, even if you don't, Miss Grace." A scant arch of self-righteousness appeared on his brow, though his tone was still light.

"Some do," she agreed. "But we also serve those who don't. We don't judge any woman by her belief in God or anything else."

"I'm sure Vivian will be eager to come with me," he said. "It's not my desire but Harland's."

Vivian stared at him. "He spoke to you too?"

Roger arched his brow. "Then you have made progress."

"Some," she murmured.

"No, I'm afraid Harland still maintains his silence with me," said the young man. "But when I told him I wanted to take him to church—"

"Take *him* to church?" Vivian asked. "I didn't think he ever attended."

Roger grimaced. "He hasn't. I thought perhaps the sanctity of the place would coax his voice." He cleared his throat. "When I told him we were going, he wrote this." He handed her one of the scrawled pages. She read the words *Afraid. Diana.*

"I don't know what he's afraid of," he said with a shrug.

"I do," she said. "He's afraid to go to church." Something about the way the words Stevens had written, more carefully than the others, told her he knew Roger would show them to her. "Aren't you taking advantage of his disposition, dragging him to service when he can't agree or object?"

"I see it as an opportunity to encourage repentance," said the young man curtly. "Harland knows how to resist when he wants to."

"Yes, that's true." Vivian thought of their visit to the farm.

Nettie offered him a cup of coffee and a piece of the coffee cake still on the table. He declined, "Harland is waiting in the car outside. I don't want to leave him alone for too long."

"How did you know 'Diana' referred to me?" Vivian finally found her voice.

"Harland told me, naturally." He played with the edge of his walking stick, stretching it out in front of him as if he were trying to keep someone distant. "He told me a long time ago, of course. He enjoyed casting you as Diana." He rose and took Vivian's hand. "Please come with us."

She wandered to the window. The view was delicate despite the unpolished neighborhood. She could see touches of the wax wood trees mixed with redwoods in the distance. Their tops touched the sky, still a sheet of gray but not so threatened by rain. She remembered the Sunday mornings at church, the serenity of the service and the placidity she had felt when she emerged. She wondered if the redhead might end up feeling the same way.

"I'll go, if Stevens wants me to," she said.

He smiled. "I see you've found your own address with him. 'Call me Stevens, just Stevens,' he used to say." His tone was almost affectionate.

"I can dress in ten minutes."

Roger adjusted his tie. "I shall leave you in privacy, then." He gave her a pointed look. "This means as much to me as it does to Harland. More so, perhaps." With a tip of his hat to Nettie, he left.

"Roger is a firm believer," Vivian said to her friend's questioning eyes. "He has a lovely Bible from his mother. I don't think he ever really knew her."

Nettie started on the breakfast dishes. "I gathered from the conversation that Mr. Stevens isn't as fond of worship as his cousin."

Vivian took her most elegant suit off the peg and held it against her chest. "Roger once insinuated he preferred to be an idol rather than worship a god."

"That's a rather coarse assertion." Nettie turned off the water and looked at her.

Vivian glanced at her. "Nettie, do you believe in God at all?"

The woman looked at her with hurt in her eyes. "Just because one doesn't attend church doesn't mean one doesn't have the same beliefs one doesn't care to hear preached."

As she dressed, Vivian suddenly thought about her meeting with Father Gonzalez the year before: *Do not condemn, and you will not be condemned.* And then she thought of the woman with the crumbled face she had met in the city, and the way she had grasped her hand with her prophecy and the chaplain's words about forgiveness. It made her shiver in the cool morning air.

She expected to see the automobile waiting outside, but she saw Roger sitting behind a carriage with scrolls on the doors and two magnificent black horses. She recognized it as the fancy carriage owned by Mr. Shelley, the town blacksmith.

"I thought it best to make an elegant entrance," Roger said with a brief smile as he helped her in the seat. "One does not come roaring down the road to the house of God."

Stevens sat behind them, facing the rear. He too was dressed in a polished sack suit that fit him very well, though his hat was more of a top hat than a bowler. His eyes glazed, and his pose stiffened with his hands on his knees. He had returned to his safe, silent world.

She greeted him with a "good morning," but he did not turn around. "It's good the church isn't far on a morning like this, though I think it might clear by the time we come out," she remarked.

"We're not going to that church," Roger said. "We're going to Jeremiah."

Her eyes arched. "The church town?"

He laughed as he skillfully guided the horses on the road out of Waxwood. "Goldspur's other side, they say."

"I've never been there," Vivian admitted. "I've heard it has more churches than houses."

"I daresay," he said. "The Church of Saint Peter is one of the largest in town. It's built more like a cathedral, really." He turned a sharp curve. "The reverend lived in England for many years and the churches there so impressed him, he came back and built one like them."

"I hope this one is on a smaller scale than those I saw in Rome," Vivian remarked. She remembered the way the accusatory eyes of the apostles looked down at her from her visits to the Roman cathedrals.

"I assure you it is," he promised. "It only mimics the higher qualities of English cathedrals."

Vivian could see from Stevens' profile that he was inattentive to their talk, though with what thoughts she could not tell. "Roger, what was Stevens' objection to church?"

Roger shrugged. "I don't know that he objects exactly, Vivian. His father regarded the Catholic Church as little more than witchery."

"Catholic?" Vivian stared at him. "I never would have guessed."

The young man grimaced as they eased onto a road along a

thin line of houses. "He walked out one day on one of my great-uncle's sermons, I've been told. Denounced him as a warlock and a thief."

"That's rather brutal," Vivian said.

"My own father had little to do with the Church himself," Roger recalled. "That is, until he met my mother, who was a proper Presbyterian. Then, he became as enlightened as any man ought to be."

"And he enlightened you," she finished, smiling.

"It's been my saving grace." His eyes became a little clouded. "I don't know what I should have become without my faith."

They reached the church, and Vivian could see what Roger meant. The building was hardly bigger than a schoolhouse, but stood tall and majestic with its pointed towers and archways and Gothic etchings. The gray stone gave her a sense of serenity as she walked up the stairs, grasping Stevens on one side while Roger grasped his other arm.

The redhead stopped at the doorway, looking up to the peaked tower with the gleaming blue cross. Vivian saw a moment of terror in his eyes, as if he thought one of the stone angels would crash down and pacify him with a wave of its wings. She whispered, "Don't be afraid. This is a friendly place."

The man sagged a little against her arm, but his steps moved more smoothly, stumbling a little as they passed through the entrance.

The sermon had already begun, so people greeted them with trepidation. An attendant standing near the wall motioned toward an empty back pew. She and Roger sat with Stevens between them. The reverend was a stout man, but what he lacked in stature, he made up for in voice. Vivian had never heard a preacher with such clear, deep vowels, and he read from the scripture as if he were reading poetry. His eyes became wistful, while at others, they darkened with the roaring of his voice.

She could let the reverend's words flow past her, and her eyes wandered to the tall man beside her. She wondered how much of the sermon he was taking in. There was a change in his expression, subtle but visible, like his change of expression the day before in the woods. The eyes of a curious child regarded the stout man at the pulpit, his head bending forward as if he were trying hard to comprehend the sermon.

The preacher was speaking of Joshua's words to the followers of Moses during the exodus to the Promise Land. "'Be strong and courageous. Do not be afraid; do not be discouraged, for the Lord your God will be with you wherever you go.'" The reverend lowered his voice to an almost melodic tone, and the words filled Vivian with comfort.

She realized she missed attending church. She wondered about the chapel attached to Alderdice Hall and regretted she had not asked to see it during her visit. She remembered the story Jake told them when they had come out of mourning about the chapel being haunted: *The face of a vixen appeared in the dust.*

She folded her hands in her lap as the sermon came to a close. The wall behind the pulpit stood in a long arch draped with black velvet. Just then, she thought she saw a glowing apparition appear across the dark fabric, an animal looking at her with sparkling gold eyes. She drew back, and a gasp escaped her lips. Roger glanced at her with questioning eyes, but she could only shake her head. She wondered for a moment whether Stevens had seen it too, as the attentive look changed to alarm.

The sermon was over, and people began filing out of the small church. The blond man put his hand on her arm. "Let's wait until they've gone," he whispered. Leaning back, he asked, "What did you think of the reverend's words about courage and faith?"

"Be strong and courageous," Vivian murmured. "Yes, we must all be. We don't know what's coming, just like the people of Israel didn't know."

"They trusted God with His promise," Roger agreed.

"They were going to the Promise Land," Vivian said. "Perhaps our courage and strength will bring us to a different Promise Land."

She felt Stevens' fingers press into her arm in a way that almost pinched the flesh, and she jumped.

"Perhaps you'll join me now every Sunday," Roger said as the last of the people filed out. "It might be good for you to get back to church, Vivian."

"You sound like a preacher yourself," she snapped, gathering her bag as she rose.

"My mother wanted me to be one," he said. She saw for the first time he had brought his mother's Bible and was holding it in his hands. He had taken it out of its box, and the small, bulky book's gold etchings shone against the glare of the sun through the large windows, polished and new as when his mother must have first received it.

"My father told me that since I was old enough to go with him to church," he continued.

She put down the Bible she had picked up from the pew. "Why aren't you, then?"

He guffawed. "Uncle Joseph had other plans for me." He put the Bible back in its box and shoved it in the inside pocket of his jacket. "It never seemed to matter to him what I wanted. I had an interest in Shakespeare once, too. I remember when I told him they had cast me as Hamlet at the Hale playhouse. He laughed — he has Harland's laugh, so you know what it sounds like and how it echoes — and the next day they duly informed me my services were no longer needed." The biting tone came through in the set of his jaw.

"I'm sorry," said Vivian.

"I'm glad," he said. "He forced me to see what life is about for a young man growing up in the world. I'm no longer a dreamer like my father."

"This would have been a pretty church to serve," she remarked, looking around.

Roger lifted his eyes, and Vivian followed his gaze. Stevens' head tilted in that direction, his eyes gazing like dark glass stones. She noticed for the first time the mural on the archway behind them. She gasped at the magnificent detail.

She heard Roger's voice. "Another characteristic of English cathedrals that the good reverend picked up from his stay there: murals on the archway."

She had seen such murals in the Roman cathedrals, but this one was very different. A bearded man looked harassed and worried while several men, one of them wearing a soldier's helmet, bent toward him, shaking him by the arm. Behind the table, the figure of a woman turned toward them, her face darkened as if the light were away from her, her expression accusatory.

"An excellent likeness," Roger remarked. "Gerald's *The Denial of St. Peter*. You know the story of Jesus' prediction during the Last Supper?"

Vivian nodded. "Saint Peter would deny knowledge of Jesus three times."

He looked at her with gleaming eyes. "No one can deny Jesus was right. Saint Peter was disloyal and betrayed him in the face of fear."

"But he repented afterward," Vivian reminded him.

"'Yea, mine own familiar friend, in whom I trusted, which did eat of my bread, hath lifted up his heel against me.'" Roger sighed. After a pause, he said, "I admire the good reverend."

Vivian took Stevens' arm. "Why does the good reverend arouse your admiration with that mural?" She felt suddenly jumpy.

"It takes true courage to admit one's chosen saint is flawed." Roger gave her a rather insinuating grin.

A Bible fell to the ground, resounding in the now empty church. Even the reverend seemed to have disappeared. Vivian picked it up, recognizing the frayed edge. It was the Bible she had put in Stevens' lap at the start of the service.

The redhead awakened from his hidden world. His eyes widened with fright, like a child who had seen a ghost in the night. His hands rose as if he were pushing back the ghost, and his mouth had dropped open.

"We must get him away from here," she said to Roger in a low voice.

Roger nodded, gathering his gloves and walking stick.

They went out into the sunlight. The blond man stopped to put on his gloves, watching Stevens with a small smile. "Surely you remember, Harland?" Another fearful look appeared on the redhead's face. "My cousin and I once had a fascinating discussion about idols and gods," he explained. "That evening after I met you and Jake in church, in fact."

She recalled the morning when she had first encountered Roger with Jake outside the crisp white church in Waxwood. "You accused my brother of following idols." Her stomach tightened.

"I told Harland about the meeting," said the young man. "We had an argument about false prophets. 'Beware of false prophets, which come to you in sheep's clothing, but inwardly they are ravening wolves.'"

"Yes," Vivian murmured. "I know the passage." Her grandmother's letters eight years ago were now a vague memory, but she could never forget how Grandfather had quoted to Grandmother the same lines when he feared she was being led into the arms of a different sort of wolf than Harland Stevens.

"We would all do well to remember it," Roger continued. "Matthew said we will know the false prophets by the fruit they bear. One who misrepresents a rotting soul as a pure one is just as devious as a bad tree bearing rotten fruit, isn't he?"

A screech rang through the air. Stevens was no longer the stone giant. He was a towering inferno, his full height visible against the bright blue sky. With his finger pointing at Roger, his lips parted, and the terrible noise came out.

"Are you to break your silence with me at last, Harland?" There was a note of mockery in Roger's voice.

But the redhead's gaze remained wild while his tongue neared his lips, silent now.

Roger said lightly, "Shall we invite Vivian to lunch with us?"

Stevens' figure slumped back, and he fumbled in his pocket for his notepad. The message he scrawled was wavier than the one he had written Vivian that morning, but the message was still clear: *Betrayer.*

Roger turned white, the coloring with his blond hair making him look like a corpse. His hands grasped the precious Bible as if he were going to use it as a weapon. But when he spoke, his voice was composed, "I had hoped to show you some of God's grace, Harland. I ought to have known it was a waste of time."

Vivian's hands were shaking. "We must go, Roger."

The young man bowed, taking her hand and almost touching it with his lips. "Forgive me, Vivian. This isn't your squabble."

In the carriage, Roger steadied the horses on the narrow road. Vivian asked the question that had been on her mind since the sermon ended, "Did you bring us here deliberately, Roger?"

"Eh?" He glanced at her.

"I mean, did you know about that mural?"

"I told you, the reverend—"

"I know what you told me," she said. "Did you know about the mural?"

"I knew there was some painting in the church relating to Saint Peter," he admitted. "But I didn't know it was that one."

There was silence as one of the horses cocked its head back, and the young man redirected it on its path. Then Vivian said, "I don't believe you."

She didn't know what she expected, but not the uninhibited laughter that came from the young man's lips. "You are perceptive, Vivian. I knew it was a reproduction of the Gerald painting. But I swear to you, I had no idea Harland would become so violently." He glanced back over his shoulder. Stevens slumped in the seat as if he had fallen asleep. But Vivian knew he was awake, fallen back into his own world.

"No," she mumbled. "You only hoped."

Roger didn't answer, but she felt his eyes on her as she watched the backs of the horses bobbing with the uneven road. The coach lurched sideways, and she grabbed the strap to keep from flinging against the window. Roger steadied the horses until they were back on even ground. "You still don't believe I want the best for my cousin."

"I never said that," Vivian protested.

He smiled. "I have my perceptions too, though I never got much credit for them."

Vivian felt her throat go dry, as if she had breathed in all the dust from the road. "I know you're serious about bringing him out of his silent world, or you never would have asked me. But it was a mistake to bring Stevens to church."

"It wasn't really," Roger insisted. "Uncle Joseph disapproved of my beliefs, but Harland respected my right to have them. He once expressed a curiosity about coming with me one day. I'm merely fulfilling that promise."

"You chose an odd time to do it," Vivian snapped.

"I thought if he saw the painting and knew the story of Saint Peter, I might get him to speak to me. But as you see, I failed."

"And upset your cousin," Vivian added. She threw a look toward the back seat, but Stevens had not moved from his sleeping pose.

"I think Harland has made it quite clear you're the only one he will respond to," said the young man.

Her voice was steady, "Then you won't take Stevens to church again, will you?"

His lips held in a tight line as he pulled into the main road of

Waxwood, easing the pace of the horses as people crossed the street. "I won't, if that's your wish."

They reached the blacksmith's stables. The young man offered to take her to the door of the drugstore, but Vivian refused. "The library is only a short distance. I prefer to walk, if you don't mind." She glanced at the tall figure sitting with his hands in his lap like an obedient schoolboy. "I'd feel much better if we could make it up to him."

"I can't, but *you* can," said the young man. "Come to the hotel tomorrow and take Harland out for a walk on the beach. He's partial to it, you know."

"I didn't know." She tried to imagine the tall, imposing man relaxed in the sand.

"I remember watching him walk down the cliffs of Neart Castle when I was a boy," he said. "He would walk the stretch of beach, back and forth."

"Indeed?" she asked softly.

He leaned his hat back. "He liked to watch the seagulls playing in the sand too." He added in a glib tone, "You know we've both become rather the bird watchers?"

"Have you?" She couldn't help but smile.

"It sounds silly, I know," he said. "A respected architect from San Francisco watching birds! But I enjoy it. I've taken Harland with me to Muir Woods a few times, and he's been quite at ease there."

Vivian raised her parasol against the sun. "It is pleasant in Muir Woods."

"There have been reports of the northern gannet nesting on the eastern cliffs in Waxwood," he said. "I think Harland might like to see them."

"And you?" Vivian regarded him with bright eyes.

"I've other plans tomorrow," he said. "You could take a pleasant stroll. He hasn't seen the beach yet."

"If he's partial to it, why haven't you taken him out?" Vivian asked.

"My, but you suspect me now," he said with amusement. "I haven't had the opportunity. I'm sure, after what happened today, he would much prefer you go with him than I."

"Yes," Vivian agreed. "I think you'd better stay away from him for a while, Roger."

"You're right, of course," he said. "I really didn't mean to upset you or him, Vivian. Please believe that."

Without answering him, she turned to Stevens. "We can go to the beach tomorrow, Stevens, if you care to."

"Yes." It was a faint response, but an assured one, the voice gracious and mild. It almost soothed her.

CHAPTER 8

Vivian had promised to come for Stevens early, but she could not get away until after lunch. A crisis arose with a lady at Mull's Boarding House. Mrs. Mull was a staunch supporter of the Bay Area Women's Social and Political Rights League and knew Nettie when she was once a member. She never approved of Albina Fowler influencing the ladies to throw Nettie out of the league because she had suggested they take their actions further than petitions and letters. Although her social standing matched Vivian's, Mrs. Mull helped at the library when she could and, with Nettie's influence, had turned her boarding house into a shelter for women under dire circumstances.

The crisis involved a young woman who had married a tyrant and was now going to have his child. The tyrant discovered her whereabouts and dragged himself to the house dead drunk, where his threats roared over the street noises. He had thrown his empty whiskey bottle at the window, then tried to get in, only to cut up his hand and arm.

Mrs. Mull had called upon Nettie and Vivian to take away the poor, shaking wife to the basement underneath the library while she called the doctor and the police. It took hours to convince the officer the man ought to be arrested, and only Mrs. Mull's standing in society won their begrudging cooperation. Then there had been the task of dropping in on the ladies she and Nettie could think of who supported their library to see if they could take in the frightened wife or persuade someone else to do so.

In this situation, Vivian was more apt than Nettie. She spent her formative years accompanying her grandmother to such ladies' houses and had watched her weave words and gestures to persuade them to give what they had come for — a donation, an agreement to host this or that charitable event, a promise to use their influence toward a certain purpose. She used those same weapons with as much fervor as her grandmother had, and by lunchtime, they persuaded a Mrs. Riley to arrange for the girl to stay with a relative of hers in Sacramento, provided Vivian and Nettie could get the woman on the train. This they did, pressing what little money they had into the woman's hand and seeing her off on the train as she leaned out the window with her face washed with tears and gratitude, still shaking at the fear of the brute showing up and running after the train.

"A year ago, I never would have taken you for one who could think so quickly on your feet," Nettie remarked as they backed away from the train as it pulled out of the station.

"A year ago, there was nothing for me to think quickly about," Vivian said.

Nettie grinned. "I envy you your dull life then."

"Well, don't!" Vivian grabbed her friend's wrist. "It was all a void."

Nettie nodded. "I've heard such ladies go mad, or think they do. Like that story we read about the wallpaper."

"Gilman wasn't mad," Vivian insisted. "She understood what no one else did."

"Maybe you ought to read that story to your new patient," her friend remarked. "He might understand about woman behind the wallpaper fighting to get out."

"He has the privilege of being a man," Vivian said. "He need not fight his way out. I must coax him out."

"Like a mother bird pushing her baby from the nest so it may fly." Nettie sighed. "It seems a cruel way."

What Nettie said stayed on Vivian's mind as they returned to the flat and had lunch. Soon after, she gathered her things and took the ferry to the hotel.

Roger was in the lobby with his two friends as the last scents of lunch seeped out of the dining room. Stevens sat on a chair in a corner some distance away, staring through the opposite window as people passed by on the boardwalk for their afternoon stroll, the sea itself lying like a carpet beyond.

"Harland's been waiting for you," Roger said in the careless tone she remembered from his college days. "He's been in that chair all day."

"I'm sorry I didn't come in the morning," she lamented.

"Don't apologize." Roger held up his hand. "One charity is as important as another."

Her anger rose. "I don't have charities. I help those who need it when they need it."

"You've made an impression on Harland," said Pete, swatting at a fly with a rolled-up newspaper.

"He said good morning to us," Andy added. "Wouldn't say a word afterward, but at least he didn't look right through us."

"More's the pity," Vivian muttered.

Roger snapped at his friend, "It might have given you some respect if he had." The young man shrank back a little and whistled a tune. "My cousin has said little since yesterday," The blond man lowered his voice. "But he isn't so — stone-like."

The view from the window seemed to engage Stevens' attention fully, but as she approached, he jumped up and bowed. His features were lighter, almost as if he had shed ten years. His eyes rested on her, no longer empty. "Good afternoon." The cracked voice was mild-mannered and pleasant. "You were detained?" He spoke in more complete sentences, though slowly and deliberately.

She perched on the edge of the chair beside him and told him about her morning adventures. He showed much more interest than his cousin had, though his position remained as steady as the closed curve of his lips.

"You help people?" he asked when she finished.

"When I can."

He gave her a weak smile. "No longer hard-hearted?"

She felt a flash of anger as she remembered his accusation against her last year. "I never was, Stevens."

She regretted her words, as it made a little of the blankness come back into his countenance. She fiddled with the pouch hanging from her wrist, speaking in what she hoped was an affable manner. "Roger told me you like the sea."

There was silence, and for a moment, she was afraid she had shut him down completely. But then he answered, "Yes."

"It's the perfect time of day for a walk." She rose and held out her hand. "Shall we go?"

The redhead took hold of her hand as she helped him out of the chair. He was light for such a large man. He seemed to want his hand to remain in hers, so she did not let go of it as they stepped out to the beach.

She cocked her hat forward over her face against the blazing sun and noted that Stevens, after glancing at her, did the same.

He asked, "How is your mother?"

"She's doing well," said Vivian. "She's married again."

"He's good? Your new father?"

"I've no gripes against Bennett." She pulled her jacket closer over her chest. "What little I've seen of him has impressed me favorably."

"And your mother?"

Vivian frowned. "Mother and I are as we always were. We draw, but we don't shoot."

She felt his hand tighten in hers. "You mustn't — mustn't fight."

Vivian smiled. "We don't fight. We're much too civilized for that."

"Civilized." He said the word as if he were turning it around like a rare coin. "Yes. Civilized."

She glanced at him and saw a figure running through the sand toward them, recognizing him as Monte Leblanc. The dragoon mustache was gone, and small wrinkles showed around his cheeks. His sleepy eyes were wide, showing he was genuinely glad to see her.

He pressed her hand warmly. "How are you, my dear?"

"Hello, Monte." The familiarity of his smile comforted her. "May I introduce my friend, Mr. Harland Stevens?"

The redhead gave the man a deep bow in the cordial, if distant, greeting of one older man to another.

Monte's eyebrow immediately jumped. She hid a smile, remembering his jealousy when she had ventured to spend an evening with David Potter and his aunt Leona. "You look marvelous," he continued in his too polite tone.

She thanked him, aware that the blue suit she wore, though one of her most polished, looked a little faded and limp from constant washings and ironings.

"I understand from my wife you've been here all the time." He cleared his throat, and Vivian remembered her mother had told everyone she had left California to recover from the previous year's disappointment.

"Yes," she said. "I never went east. My mother is fond of telling stories about me."

He glanced at the fluttering group a short distance away. Vivian could make out the somewhat erect back of Emile Leblanc, Monte's father, as he held a wineglass in his hand and made animated conversation with the duck-footed Mrs. Sowberry, now Monte's mother-in-law.

"I was right, wasn't I?" she said with a gleam in her eye. "About you and Christina Sowberry."

"We've been very content." He blushed a little. "There is much I have to teach her, as she is so young."

"I'm sure you've taught her how to be a proper wife." She realized her tone was a little too dry, as he looked uncomfortable.

"It's a shame you remained here," he said. "I can't imagine you have much to occupy you."

"You're wrong, Monte," she said. "I'm interested to know what they're saying, though, now that they surely know." She eyed the party. "I told your wife and Amber the truth last month when I came into the city."

He smiled kindly. "You remember what I told you about gossip."

"You never believe in it, and neither does your father." She glanced back at the older man, who looked as if he had aged five years in one. He was now peering over his shoulder, and although he wasn't looking directly at her, she could tell by the sly grin on Mrs. Sowberry's face that he had seen her. "Your father seems to enjoy hearing it, even if he doesn't believe it."

"It's the influence of my mother-in-law," Monte said. "They are rather a pair."

"So I see." She felt uneasy, especially with Stevens standing in attention with his hands behind his back. "We won't disturb you, of course."

"Won't you and your friend come sit with us?" His head tilted toward the redhead. "We've as jolly a party as ever, as you can see."

"Mr. Stevens and I have other plans." She took the redhead's arm.

"A stroll on the beach?" He nodded. "It's rather hot right now for that."

"We're going to see if we can catch sight of the gannets," she said.

His eyebrow went up.

"The northern gannets," she repeated.

"I didn't think they bred this far west."

"They don't," said Vivian. "I believe a colony was sighted on the cliffs."

"I shall tell Tina we must go exploring one morning," he said. "She's as ardent a nature lover as I am."

"Nature and travel?" Vivian eyed him.

"She adores hearing the stories," he said jovially. "When I return from my trips, she is all agog to find out about them."

"I'm sure," Vivian murmured. "Please give her and the others my regards, won't you?"

He glanced again at Stevens, who had remained silent but attentive. Vivian could feel the firm grasp of his arm under her hand.

"Do come and see us when you're in the city, won't you?" Monte added.

"I'm afraid I don't get to the city often," she said. "When I do, I have business to attend to."

"Ah, you're a businesswoman now." He sighed. "I remember you told me you wished to take your freedom, but you didn't know yet how."

"I'm not a businesswoman, Monte." Vivian studied him. "I help other women."

"And *there* your path lies?" he asked, his sleepy eyes wide.

"For now," she said. "But one is always searching, isn't one?"

"Not always," he said. "Some of us find our way quicker than others." He bade her and Stevens goodbye with a bow and returned to the group, lavishing a look of fondness on his young wife.

She couldn't help but feel a little slighted as she and Stevens continued down the sand, though there had been nothing unkind or mean-spirited in the exchange. One of a group of boys playing with a beach ball kicked it in their direction, and it rolled onto the wet sand. Stevens picked it up and threw it at them. Then he asked, "You were engaged to him?"

She glanced at his open face. "How did you know that?"

"His way — speaking intimately."

Vivian held down her hat against the wind. "My mother wanted me to marry him, but we weren't engaged."

"He's not for you!" This came in a growling tone.

"No, he wasn't for me," she agreed. "He always spoke of respect for women, but what he really wanted was a doormat wife." She flung out, "Why is it men say they want one thing when they really desire another?"

A cawing of seagulls accompanied Stevens' laugh. She remembered the deep laugh that sprang out in delightful peals, sweeping in everyone around it. As they passed, two little girls peered up at the giant man with curiosity, as if wondering what he was laughing about. The laugh left a sonorous echo across the stretch of blue water.

"I'm glad I amuse you." Though her tone was dry, she was genuinely glad that, for the moment, his self-imposed prison had melted, and he was part of the world, strolling with confident steps beside her, a vacationer enjoying the beach.

They reached a curve on the eastern side of the shore. It was quieter here, as the bathers had weeded out and the languishers were scarcer. They were heading toward the murkier part of the sea. The cliffs standing before her looked larger than she remembered. The sand was a dark coffee color, different from the pleasant lemon yellow of the stretch they had left behind. A massive hotel stood not far off, built of iron and marble with sharp Gothic towers that reminded her of an abandoned mansion still standing in an enclave of Nob Hill rumored to be haunted. She thought she saw flashes of movement through the windows.

"It's rather eerie here, isn't it?" she ventured.

Stevens did not answer. His chin leveled, and his eyes narrowed, as if he were searching for something in the distance. As they walked along the edge of the curved segment, she followed his pace, fast and wide, and felt breathless. She saw the abandoned cargo ship standing in the shallow waters, a giant mocking the low scenery around it.

"The ghost ship!" The moment she realized what it was, a foreboding air escaped around them, making her shudder.

"The raging giant," the redhead murmured. "Where is it?" His voice was smooth.

She looked up at him, seeing havoc wash over his face, aging him in a few moments. She gently took his arm. "A few more tides, and it will be nothing but a memory, Stevens."

"No, no! The raging giant is gone."

She realized what he meant. The mast once stood tall and flaring out, its levels complete except for the bannister crumbling in spots, and the two chimneys like the throat of canons pointing in the air. The tides had swayed it closer to the cliffs, and now the ship leaned against them for support like a decrepit old man. A storm had collapsed the top level into the lower level, and one chimney was entirely demolished, while the other folded over like a broken wing. The mast, shattered in several places, swung in the wind, ready to fling out to sea at any moment. As she stepped closer to it, she realized the entire front of the ship, visible only if one moved closer to its edge, was cut off.

She felt a heavy breath behind her, "The raging giant has collapsed," she murmured.

The redhead kneaded one hand in the other, looking both

horrified and joyful. The strange combination made his pleasant features leap forward, the brutal contours alarming.

"Its prey has conquered it!" Stevens shouted, raising his hands above his head. "Roger was right. By God, Roger was right!"

She asked gently, "Why was Roger right?"

He looked at her, breathless and grinning like a mad clown. "He said the beast was ready to collapse, and it did."

"The sea, the salt, and the wind," Vivian explained. "It was bound to happen."

The redhead bent forward. "I ought not to have made him do it."

Vivian felt her heart pound as she laid her hand on his shoulder. "Who?"

"Your brother."

Vivian's heart pounded more. "Made my brother do what?"

"Conquer the Trojan horse." The redhead gazed at the ship. "I forgot the horse was hollow inside. Fluted wood." He threw his head back and laughed, loud and deep, making the waves vibrate.

"Yes," Vivian said sharply. "I remember the story." Jake told her about that night when Roger and his friends, drunk on whiskey, challenged him to board the ship, and he had done it, nearly collapsing into the sea along with it.

Stevens examined her with his dark eyes that were no longer vacant behind their wall. He then grasped both her hands. "You know."

"I know."

"It was my fault," he pleaded.

"I should have guessed." Her throat felt parched.

He peered into her eyes. "I made Roger throw down the gauntlet."

She wretched free of his grasp. "Did you think they were the knights of the Round Table?"

He gazed at the decaying ship with wistful eyes. "I said to him, 'Don't let the challenge drop.' I said to him, 'I have faith in you.'"

"Faith!" Tears seeped from her eyes. "The one thing Jake needed, and you knew it."

"Tenacity," Stevens spit out the word with pride. "Courage. The boy had it. He conquered the giant."

"Conquered the giant!" Vivian moaned.

The pride dissipated, and once more deep lines curved around the edges of his mouth. A storm raged in the depths of his deep brown eyes.

"My punishment." He looked down at his hands. "The giant, mirror of my sin. My way was crooked, narrow with a gun and a false move. False prophets…"

His hands were shaking, and his head swung sideways. Alarmed, she tried to take his arm, but he shook her off with an easy violence that made her back away.

"False prophets." He shook a finger at the ship. "You, false prophet! You, the wolf, the hollow horse!" He grabbed a handful of shells lying in the sand and threw them at the ship.

"Stevens!"

"Unmanning Trojan!" he shouted. "Hollow giant!" He picked up anything that came into his hands, throwing it against the ship's belly while wet sand stuck to his jacket.

"You there!" A red-faced man in an ill-fitting blue uniform trudged through the sand. "Stop!"

"Betraying Trojan!" Stevens threw shells and rocks until the man reached him. Though he was not as large as the redhead, he was muscular and clearly used to dealing with odd behavior. He grabbed Stevens' arm, and all at once, the redhead's hand unclenched, letting the shells tumble to the sand. His massive figure grew pliant, his face freed of age lines, and his blazing eyes fell dead of their fire. He was once more the immobile puppet.

"That ain't your property, mister," the man admonished, "It ain't doing you nor anyone else no harm, so leave it alone."

Vivian took Stevens' arm. "He won't do it again."

"Bet your life he won't," the man snarled. "The manager

wouldn't like it, see?" He then examined her with a quick, suspicious eye. "You're not at the hotel, are you?"

"I live in town," said Vivian. "My friend is staying at the Waxwoodian."

The man's lip curled. "Well, you got no cause to be here. This ain't your part of the beach."

"I wasn't aware this was a private beach," Vivian said stiffly.

The man became more amicable. "Well, no, miss, not exactly. But it's sorta understood amongst the proprietors here, if you know what I mean."

"We're leaving," she said. "We only wanted to see the gannets."

"The who?" He squinted.

"The colony sighted on the cliffs." She felt awkward.

"Gannets," he mused. "Birds, right? Well, ain't no birds 'round here, miss. 'Cept for the seagulls, naturally." He grinned.

She felt as if coals burned in her chest. "I see we were misinformed. We won't trouble you anymore."

She led Stevens back around the curving sand, and when they reached the main beach, he seemed to relax, though he remained silent. She didn't speak until they reached the hotel courtyard. Then she turned to him. "You'll be all right?" He nodded. "Stevens, I want to warn you. We've started down a path that may bring anguish to us both. I'm willing, but are you?"

He blinked, his freckled face standing out against the pale light.

"I'll leave it up to you," she said. "You know where to find me."

He tried to smile as he pressed her hand. "Ought to have known."

"Yes," she said. "I ought to have known too." She thought of Roger and the lie he had told her. And she knew why he had told it to her.

～

ivian returned to the flat in the early evening. The sun had set by the time the ferry reached the other side of town, and the sky darkened more with each dragging step. She felt as if she were taking a long road home.

When she arrived, the sound of women's voices greeted her. She recognized the grizzled tone of Odele Redfern. A mild-mannered response came from her friend Lena Hill. Both women sat at the kitchen table, Odele peeling potatoes, and Lena slicing carrots. Sue Bagstock, the third member of the pleasant trio, sifting flour on the counter, looked up at Vivian with a grin.

"We're helping Nettie make the most luscious pot pies you ever tasted," she declared. Only nineteen, she sometimes had the delight of a five-year-old.

Nettie glanced over her shoulder from the stove with a questioning look. In her usual observant manner, she took in Vivian's tired eyes and said, "They're not staying for dinner."

"Of course they'll stay." Vivian unburdened herself of her accessories and put on a housecoat.

"Thank goodness one of you still has her manners," Odele declared. Her guarded suspicion of Vivian and her Nob Hill ways the year before had dissipated into respect when she saw Vivian's sincerity and hard work with building the library.

Vivian smiled. "The company would be grand. I could use it."

Lena eyed her. "Battling the city upstarts, I gather."

"At least we yokels are more inclined to stand by our ways," Sue added, getting flour all over the floor in her effort to keep up with the conversation.

Vivian grinned warily. "City people have their beliefs too, Sue. But, no, I haven't been in the city."

"The beach, then," Odele said shrewdly. "Your shoes left tracks, pet."

Vivian gathered the table settings. "I went for a walk on the beach with a friend." She was aware Nettie was watching her from the stove.

"One of your Tea Cake Sistren?" Odele tossed the skin of the potato in the bowl.

"You know she's had nothing to do with them for a while," Lena insisted.

Vivian thought of Marvina, the blue-stocking of Washington Street who had first introduced her to Nettie. Her heart filled with regret. "The gentleman is a different sort of blue blood."

"The gentleman?" The redheaded woman's eyes jumped like flames.

"Women are allowed gentlemen friends, Odele," Nettie snapped. "It's not as if she's consorting with the enemy."

"I'm not sure they all aren't our enemy, pet," said the Irish woman. "I've seen 'gentlemen' who don't think twice about luring the innocent into crime."

"Surely, you don't mean the compromised widows?" Vivian asked, referring to the woman's crusade last year.

"Odele's through with the widows," Sue said in a breezy voice. "She's bedeviled by their children now."

Her friend shot her a look. "Sue, you look like you've emerged from a dust bowl."

The young woman's face turned scarlet as she looked down at her dress, covered with flour. Nettie laughed and handed her a towel.

The conversation continued as they sat down to the pot pie and a white wine Nettie produced out of nowhere. Odele, with her scraggly voice, dominated the conversation.

"In the Hamilton neighborhood, mothers have their courtyard garden and their sewing circle," she said, her voice growing excited. "They made a little extra last month alongside their day's work."

"Then you haven't abandoned the widows?" Vivian smiled.

"Certainly not!" The woman glared at Sue, who blushed

again as her thin hands struggled with the salad. "But their children play in the streets and are prey to every charlatan and criminal who gives them a penny for any nickel watch they can steal."

Vivian stared at the pie on her plate, her appetite diminished from the events of the afternoon. "Surely there are no Fagins in America."

"Fagin?"

"The miser who teaches children how to be adept pickpockets in Charles Dickens' *Oliver Twist*," Nettie said shortly.

Odele, who ridiculed books, snorted. "They do a lot worse, especially with the young girls. Fine dress, suave manners, and pretty words trap them, and all for one purpose!"

"The wolf in sheep's clothing," Vivian murmured.

"That's it, pet." Odele nodded. "These parasites know where to go. The courts treat these poor mites like miniature adults."

"It's positively barbaric," Lena exclaimed. "They shut them up with murderers!"

"Aren't you painting a rather bleak picture?" Nettie remarked.

Odele leaned forward, the ruffle of her shirtwaist nearly spilling into her pie. "Why do you think I put my efforts in Hamilton? It's right on the doorstep of those crass giants of state politics."

"Perhaps they'll be as numb to your charms as the crass giants of industry," Vivian said with a rueful smile as she recalled Odele's accusation against her the year before for being the granddaughter of one.

"You forget, pet," said the Irishwoman, "some of those crass industrialists responded to the good. I'll eventually reach the ears of the crass politicians." She stopped pounding her fork into the sponge cake Nettie had just served with the coffee and gave Vivian a meaningful look. "I never knew you were so interested in the children."

"Children and young people must be protected from criminals," said Vivian. "They must be protected from those false prophets in sheep's clothing."

"Why, dear," Sue looked at her with wide eyes, "you have as much passion for the subject as Odele."

"I've seen how so-called older and wiser people corrupt younger minds." In a shaking voice, she added, "I've seen it first-hand." She was again aware of Nettie's direct gaze.

"You ought to come down with me to Sacramento next week," said Odele. "See what these youngsters experience in the jails."

"I have no wish to shout into the ears of the crass politicians," Vivian mumbled.

"And what do *you* propose, if I may ask?"

All three women leaned into their coffee cups, the buzz of summer mosquitoes around the lamp above lending a tone of expectation to the quiet evening.

"I don't quite know," she admitted. "But I know education can help them turn their backs on the wolves."

"You'll be stacking your library with grammar books, then?" The redheaded woman eyed her.

"A school would be better," Vivian said. "Young people need guidance, the right kind."

Silence reigned around the table. Lena spoke first, "That would be a rather bold undertaking, don't you think?"

"So was the Waxwood Women's Lending Library and Reading Room, but we did it." She clutched her friend's hand, but it felt clammy in hers.

"What do you know about education?" Odele sneered.

"What one doesn't know, one can learn with will and gumption," Vivian snapped. "I think I've proven I have both."

"So you have." Odele grinned and held up her wineglass, though it was empty.

"You and Nettie could make a go of it," Sue said. "You just go out and do things. Oh, it's noble!"

Nettie poured herself another cup of coffee without answer-

ing. Vivian's waist tightened. "You forget Nettie has her preju-
dices against education institutions."

"They are rather bumpkin," Odele agreed.

"No, they're not." Lena stiffened.

"And how would you know, pet?" Her friend glared at her.

"I took some courses at Mills before I got the job at the mill."
Lena sounded self-conscious. "I would have gone on — never
mind about that. But before I left, I learned all sorts of things."

"Such as?" Nettie asked.

"Oh, botany and things."

"I see," Nettie folded her napkin, "and how does botany help
you now?"

Lena's face turned pale as she pushed away the cake plate.
"Maybe it doesn't, but it makes me feel more intelligent!" All the
women laughed.

Nettie rose. "Isn't it time you got along? You told me you have
an early shift tomorrow."

Odele ignored her. "And will you ask your rich mama for the
money to build this magnificent school of yours?"

"What if she does?" Lena challenged. "It's for a good cause,
isn't it?"

"It's rather simple to do good when one has a purse one can
reach into any time one chooses," her friend snapped.

"I've never asked my mother for a penny since I came here,"
Vivian said in a. Quite quiet voice. "I don't intend to start now."

There was only the buzz of the mosquitoes for a moment. The
three women rose, helping to bring their plates to the sink. Sue's
voice came out a little uneven, "I didn't tell you about the funny
story with Mrs. Sorrel in reading group today, did I, Vivian?"

Her childish way of enlivening an anecdote soon had even
Odele smiling, and the three young women left in good spirits,
Odele promising to return the favor by inviting them to "the best
coddle stew you damn well ever tasted."

The flat was quiet after they had gone, with even the mosquitoes escaping out the door after them. Nettie sat in silence as Vivian began clearing the table. She heard Nettie say, "I thought you were happy with the library."

She glanced at her friend. "I thought you wanted to do more."

"With the library," Nettie said.

Vivian wiped her hands. "I know how you feel about schools—"

"It isn't that," she said. "I'm happy where I am at last. I thought you were too." She played with the salt shaker for a moment. "If you're unhappy, Viv, you ought to open a school."

Vivian laughed. "You forget, I'm no longer an heiress."

"That could be easily remedied," snapped her friend.

Vivian turned toward the dishes and said in a tight voice, "You know me better than that."

She felt her friend's hand on her arm. "I'm sorry."

"And I'm sorry you won't help me," said Vivian. She felt more sad than angry.

"It isn't my fight," said Nettie. "My fight is for the working women. You know that."

"I know," said Vivian softly. "But young people need help in their fight, too."

Her friend eyed her. "You're thinking of someone in particular, aren't you?"

She felt the weight of fatigue on her head and eyes.

"A particular young person captured by a wolf in sheep's clothing," Nettie continued, taking up a towel.

Vivian didn't answer as she felt the warm water lapping her hands.

"A wolf whom you're now helping."

"I'm helping a man who is no longer a wolf," said Vivian. "I saw that today."

"Then something happened." Her friend put down the towel. "I thought it did."

Vivian told her about the walk on the beach. Nettie listened with her usual graceful silence, wiping the dishes with the gentleness one used to put a baby to bed. "So you finally see he's been suffering too," she said when her friend finished.

"I was wrong to think Jake didn't matter to him," said Vivian. "But it isn't only that, Nettie."

"What do you mean?" Her friend hung the towel on the nail.

"Something else happened to him, something that has to do with that summer." She leaned against the stove. "In consequence of it, perhaps."

"You think he's hiding something?"

"Not hiding," said Vivian. "I know how easy it is to turn away from one's ghosts and not face them."

"What makes you think he has ghosts?" asked her friend.

"We all do." Vivian gave her friend a rueful look. "Even you did when I met you."

Nettie glanced down at the table, her hand circling the same spot as if she were not ashamed of the woman she had been, mourning her mother's death for six years, weeds and all. "Are you still going to help him face them?"

"If he wishes it," said Vivian. "I'm waiting to hear from him."

Her friend sighed. "That's that, then."

"He must face them." Vivian looked at her. "Whatever the cost, and the cost will be high."

Nettie watched her as Vivian carefully untied the apron and folded it over the back of one of the kitchen chairs, then finished wiping the kitchen table clean. Those exacting eyes made Vivian prickle. "You don't loathe him anymore, do you?" her friend asked.

Vivian glanced through the kitchen window, steamed up from the evening heat.

That night, she wrote in her diary:

Nettie asked me tonight if I still loathed Stevens. He stirred a tender part in me I thought had died the summer of Grandmother's death. Such a pitiful creature he was today! A child trying to destroy a sand castle. And yet, not far off from Saint Peter when he realized what he had done to Jesus. In that sense, Roger was right. No, I no longer loathe Stevens. But I don't forgive him either.

As Vivian closed the diary with the small key, she couldn't help but think of the old woman she had seen on Washington Street, her words sliding back to her: *In those who have caused you pain, you shall find forgiveness.*

CHAPTER 9

Vivian spent the Fourth of July with Nettie, the trio, and their beaus. She was at ease with these loud but well-meaning young women and men, many of them five or six years younger than she. They looked to her as an older sister, the young ladies often pulling her aside to ask her advice about this or that. Vivian found this a little amusing, considering they had seen more of life than she in her tower of marble and stone on Washington Street. She found herself more of a watcher than a participant in their conversations. Her saturated past life as a Nob Hill debutante had run her tongue dry of witty and flirtatious remarks.

The town council held a picnic and fireworks in the Waxwood city park, and the resort hotel proprietors lobbied for their guests to attend. There were more games, prizes, and food this year, which, Vivian suspected, was the bargain between the council and the prosperous proprietors. She searched for Stevens among the swells who isolated themselves in the choicest spots of the park but did not see him. She even ventured to the croquet lawn on the chance Roger and his two friends might play a game, but she didn't see them either.

After the Fourth, days passed without a word from the redhead. When she and Nettie set up the drugstore every morning, she took the shutters off the windows and peered down the street for the broad-shouldered figure striding with his hands in his pocket and his watch chain swinging from beneath his vest. But only working men passed, if any man passed at all.

On Sunday afternoon, Nettie asked her to accompany her to the lending library. They were rarely together there, but the drugstore was closed, and Nettie wanted to organize a section of books they had been neglecting for some time.

Lena and Sue agreed to mind the desk, the former engrossed in a French novel, the latter struggling over figures from the bookkeeping course she was taking at night school. As two elderly women sat on the couch with the Sunday edition of the *San Francisco Chronicle*, one reading aloud to the other, she and Nettie crouched in the far corner near the window surrounded by piles of books. Nettie went through the list while Vivian searched for the matching book.

The door opened, and Vivian half rose, expecting it to be one of the stooping women who sometimes came in after church to do some reading. Stevens entered alone, ducking through the narrow doorway. He was alone, his gait and smile sanguine.

"Good afternoon." His voice was clearer and less careful than the last time she had seen him.

"Good afternoon," she returned. "I'm glad you've come."

"I didn't intend to come at all."

She rose, aware she was not looking her best with her hair loosely bound, her jacket unbuttoned, and her skirt powdered with the dust. She turned a little away from him and shook off the dirt.

He turned to Nettie and bowed. "I see I'm disturbing you in your work."

Nettie rose and held out her hand, which he shook with gentle vigor. "We were only sorting through some books."

Stevens knelt down and flipped through the pages of a poetry book. He began reading:

Yet the sin is on us both —
Time to dance is not to woo —
Wooer light makes fickle troth —
Scorn of me recoils on you!

Learn to win a lady's faith
Nobly, as the thing is high;
Bravely, as for life and death —
With a loyal gravity.

Vivian bent down. "You're familiar with Elizabeth Barrett Browning?"

His head flicked up, and she realized she had bent down close to him so she could see the smooth lines of his face. "I've read a few poems of hers."

"You chose your passage well." She smiled.

He gave her a keen look. "Because you scorn me, though I do not woo or dance?"

She arranged the book in her hand on the shelf. "I no longer scorn you, Stevens."

"And, yet, the poem gives me advice I would do well to heed." He shut the volume. "That's why I came back." He took her hand. "I must win the lady's faith nobly and bravely."

She felt herself blushing. "I'm no longer a lady," she insisted. "Not that sort of a lady."

"You always will be a lady to me, Vivian," he said. "You'll let me try to win your faith, I hope." This last came with a genuine anxiety in his dark eyes.

The man's eagerness made her calm fade and brought a momentary coldness. She knelt down to the books again.

Nettie, who had been watching in her usual careful way, said, "You may borrow the Barrett Browning if you like, Mr. Stevens."

"Call me Stevens," he said, turning to her. "As Vivian will tell you, I prefer people call me Stevens."

"Of course." Nettie bowed.

"I thank you for your kind offer," he said. "But I came here to offer *you* something."

"Oh?" Vivian glanced at him.

"You asked me — the last time we met." He paused, but when on quickly, "You asked me to introduce you to the lady my cousin referred to who might be interested in your endeavors." He placed the book neatly on the stack, making sure it wouldn't fall. "I would like to take you and Miss — Miss—" His face gathered as he turned to Nettie.

"Nettie," said her friend.

"I'd like to take you and Nettie to meet her." He glanced around the small room. "I think she could help you a great deal."

"It's very kind of you to take an interest in our crusade," Nettie said.

"Is that what it is?" He smiled. "I suppose I never considered it in that light."

"Perhaps because you men don't need crusades," Vivian remarked. "We must go in always with our swords raised."

He let out a rich laugh. The two elderly women buried their heads deeper behind the newspaper. Lena and Sue giggled, their admiration for the tall man obvious in the bright sunlight from the windows.

"You find that amusing?" Vivian stiffened.

"Only the vision of you and Nettie storming the castle with your swords raised," he said with a graceful bow. "I know my Diana would lead the way."

His eyes were warm on her, and she felt a prickling against her skin. "You're too familiar sometimes, Stevens."

"Forgive me." He shifted the walking stick in his hand. "Will you and Nettie allow me to take you to Goldspur to meet my friend? The trip will be well worth it, I assure you."

"Perhaps another time." Vivian turned to the books.

"Those can wait." Nettie's voice was sharp.

"What about the library?" Vivian glanced around. "Others may come later."

"Sue and Lena can watch the place for us." Her friend took her arm.

He grinned. "I'm sure you'll like Juana. She's the lady who had the sauce to point out my flaw."

"What flaw?" Nettie asked.

"My habit of walking into other people's private moments." He glanced at Vivian.

She smiled. "I'd like to meet her, Stevens."

"You'll wait a few moments while we change?" Nettie asked. "We're not quite dressed for calling, are we?"

"In the meantime, I'd like to look at your books," said the redhead with a nod. "If you don't mind a man invading this exclusive women's space, that is."

"Men invade our space all the time," Vivian remarked.

"As do women invade men's spaces," Stevens returned. "You can hardly deny many do so in more artful ways than we would like."

She and Nettie both laughed as they left the library.

They were back in the few minutes they promised in their Sunday best and new hats they had recently received from Odele, who had a knack for rustling up decent cast-offs from the corners of Sacramento. As they walked to the blacksmith, Vivian asked Stevens about the Brata.

"It broke down last year," he said. "I've had no desire to buy another since."

"It was a rather pleasant automobile," Vivian recalled. "Much more so than Roger's hissing vehicle."

Stevens laughed. "It is like a snake, isn't it? He's rather

attached to it, though." His face grew serious. "I'm glad he enjoys it so much. He's been a rock to me, more than I ever deserved."

"He's been terribly anxious about you." Nettie's arm threaded through Vivian's.

"I've known that from the beginning," he said. "It was all strange. My mind was like a screen where everything around me went through it but never clung."

"I only hope Roger isn't too easy with your money," Vivian remarked. "He told me he had that car of his especially made in Chicago."

"If he is, perhaps he has a right," Stevens said.

"One shouldn't pay family for taking care of them during their time of need," Nettie said. "That's their responsibility and, usually, their desire." Vivian knew from the grave look on her friend's face that she was thinking of herself nursing her mother and great-aunt through their difficult illnesses with the willingness and dignity of her character.

Several proprietors stood in the doorways of their shops, giving her and Nettie a nod, while others who didn't approve of their library looked away.

They reached the blacksmith's, which was buzzing with small clusters of people wanting carriages and wagons for Sunday drives. It reminded Vivian of an auction she had once attended, with people flinging their hands up in the air and Mr. Shelley calling out to his son, who was to distribute the vehicles.

"Oh, dear." Nettie looked at the crowd. "I forgot how a pleasant Sunday breeze draws out the leisurely class."

"Perhaps you ought to have kept the Brata," Vivian said dryly. "Even crawling, it would have at least insured us transportation."

"Never fear, Vivian," said Stevens. "I have my ways of procuring us a wagon." He gave her a quick wink.

Vivian caught Roger's eye, Pete and Andy loitering behind. She felt her irritation rise as the young man sauntered toward her, holding Emma on a leash.

He extended his hand. "Harland ought to have told me he was coming to see you."

"Are you his keeper now?" Vivian asked. "Like Cain and Able?"

He blinked with an innocence she knew he did not possess and turned to Stevens. "I don't think you'll get a carriage in this crowd."

"I aim to try," his cousin murmured, disappearing into the throng.

"Out for a Sunday drive like the rest?" Nettie glanced at the two young men behind him.

Roger introduced his friends, who greeted her with the stoic politeness of their breed. "We're going to Goldspur. And are you all out for a Sunday stroll?"

"Your cousin is taking us to meet a friend of his," said Nettie.

Roger's eyebrows jumped. "Miss Juana Swivler?"

"How did you know?" Vivian asked.

"I can't imagine any other friend of Harland's he would wish you to know." Roger's eyes were a little too sly for Vivian's taste.

"Who is she?" Pete asked in a lazy tone.

"A lady friend of Harland's," Roger said.

"Lady friend?" Andy gave him an inquisitive glance.

Stevens returned, and Vivian could see from the fallen expression on his face that the news was not encouraging. "You may have been right about the Brata, Vivian."

"Not a carriage to be had?" Nettie asked.

"Not even a rusty wagon." He sighed. "Not that I would have taken one."

"They can be rough on a lady's skirts," Pete agreed, and Andy chuckled.

"You needn't worry about our delicate health," Nettie said. "Viv and I can withstand the roughest road."

Stevens smiled. "I'm sure of it."

"I'll make a bargain with you, Harland." His cousin leaned

against a post. "You let us come with you, and we can all ride together in my car."

"What do you mean?" Stevens glanced at him.

"We had no definite plans," said Roger. "I'm rather keen on seeing Juana again."

The redhead's face flushed. "I don't think that's wise."

"Because of Juana's profession?" asked his cousin. "Surely, if you're taking your friends there, it must be all right to take mine." He shifted Emma's leash. "Juana is as much my friend as yours. I've been there often enough and left with only the pleasure of the tea."

"Roger!"

The young man's friends, who had heard his remark, blushed and rubbed their heels in the dirt.

"Enough room in the car for all, if you don't mind a bit of a tight ride," his cousin finished.

Vivian turned to her friend. "What do you say, Nettie?"

"There doesn't seem to be any other way to get out of town," said Nettie with a keen eye on Roger. "Truth be told, I'm curious about this snake car of yours. I've never ridden in an automobile."

"That settles it, doesn't it?" Roger took her arm. "I suppose I ought to be offended you refer to it as a snake, but now I'm determined to show you how marvelous a contraption the automobile is."

Vivian stole a glance at Stevens. He slipped his hands into his pockets, trailing after his cousin with his long stride.

Roger explained to Nettie the car's features and insisted she and Vivian ride in the front with him while the others squeezed in the back. His languid attitude annoyed Vivian, and, as they drifted behind other vehicles out of town, she said, "You spoke of the wolf in sheep's clothing several weeks ago, but you forgot about the coyote."

"Eh?" He glanced at her.

"The coyote trickster," she snapped. "Rather fits you well, doesn't it?"

"Does it?" The young man's bouncy mood was gone.

"I'm not fond of coyotes, Roger."

"In what way have I tricked you?" he asked in a quiet voice.

"There was no colony of gannets on the cliffs."

He fiddled with some mechanical thing, clearly stalling for time. His tone sounded almost offhand as he said, "I heard the birds had gone off, but after you and Harland had gone."

"A liar and a trickster!" she snarled. She felt Nettie cast her eye on her.

The man seemed unmoved. "Why would I lie to you about a mundane thing like that?"

"Because you knew what we would find when we reached the cliffs," she said.

He glanced uneasily toward the back of the car, and she lowered her voice. "You knew about the ghost ship and how it would affect him."

"I knew about the ship," the young man admitted. "And perhaps I expected my cousin would respond when he saw it again. That ship brings unpleasant memories for me too."

"It was cruel and unjust!"

His voice was bitter. "That night I thought I was through with Harland. But I suppose one is never through with family, is one?"

Tears threatened to force their way into her eyes. She glanced at the road, pulling out her handkerchief and wiping them. Her voice was steady as she repeated, "It was vicious."

"Perhaps you'll tell me what happened," Roger said.

She told the young man about their encounter with the ship, leaving out no detail. She spoke in a low voice, glancing back a few times to see Stevens was not listening, though there seemed hardly any fear of that, for the two young men, happy their former mentor was with them, were engaged in telling him stories about their business endeavors. Nettie had gone back to staring at the scenery, but her hand grasped Vivian's as she told of Stevens throwing the shells at the ship.

Roger said in a gentle voice, "I'm sorry."

Vivian glanced at him. "For me or for both of us? Or perhaps for yourself?"

He ran over a rocky patch that made everyone jump.

"It won't do to be careless, Roger." Stevens' tone was a little acidic.

"I'm as good a driver as you are," returned his cousin. When the conversation in the back seat resumed, he leaned toward Vivian and asked, "I meant it for both of you. I'm no trickster, Vivian."

Turning so she could see his face clearly, she asked, "What happened last year, after that summer?"

"I told you at the Fourth picnic," he said. "Harland withdrew from us."

She leaned toward him so her cheek was almost touching his. "What else, Roger?"

"I don't know," the young man said. "I started at Vanburgh & Gunn in the fall and took my flat in San Francisco. I didn't see Harland until my uncle's funeral, and he was in his silent state by then." He glanced at her, then turned back, intent on looking at the road. "Why is it so important?"

Vivian sat back. "I think your uncle's death was the beginning of the end."

Nettie leaned over her. "If you're as interested in your cousin's welfare as you say are, you'll trust Viv."

"I do." The earnestness in his tone made the last of her anger disappear.

"Then let me do things in my way," she said. "I mean it, Roger."

"I trust you, but you make it sound as if you don't trust me," he said wryly.

"Perhaps I no longer do," she murmured.

～

*R*oger drove past the seedy main road of Goldspur to a pink and gold house holding steady against the shaking wind of the afternoon. Vivian caught sight of the sign high over the door: *Juana Swivler's Fine Establishment for Gentlemen*. Roger's friends loitered on the grass, glancing away as if they were trying to disassociate themselves from it. Their peach-colored skin flushed red.

Finally, Pete ventured, "Rather bold about her place, this Miss Swivler?"

"Why shouldn't she be?" Nettie asked sharply. "She has a business to run."

"All the same—"

"Pete's embarrassed for you, not for us," Andy put in.

"Don't imagine we haven't seen such women in our work," Vivian said.

Stevens eyed him. "You shouldn't have assumed, Andrew."

"Well, you sure ain't like other ladies I've met," the young man murmured.

"'Do not judge, and you will not be judged,'" Nettie recited.

Vivian's blood froze. "Someone else once said that to me."

Stevens glanced at her.

"A chaplain," she said. "A good friend of Jake's."

The redhead pressed his hands together in front of him as if he were a boy being reprimanded, looking down at the dusty staircase in front of them as Roger bounded up the steps.

A butler answered their knock and led them through the house, as opulent as any Vivian had visited on Nob Hill. When they reached an entranceway with two double doors on each side, Stevens seized control. "These ladies and I have business with Miss Swivler. These gentlemen wish to go into the main parlor."

"Yes, sir."

Roger gave him a questioning look but led his two friends through one of the double doors, where a wave of ladies promptly fell into cooing over Emma. Vivian caught a glimpse of pink and tulle with a stream of bright light making a wavy line on the burgundy floor of the hall as Roger closed the doors.

The butler motioned them inside a small but beautifully furnished parlor.

"Rather like Mrs. Adler's, isn't it?" Nettie remarked.

"Who is Mrs. Adler?" Stevens asked distractedly.

"A woman we used to know," said her friend. "Very rich and very unpleasant."

Stevens gave her a wan smile. "I can imagine what sort of woman she is."

"If she were here, her disapproval would befit a caricature of President McKinley," Vivian said.

A spacious laugh floated into the room. "A splendid way to describe those rather stern eyebrows of his."

Vivian held out her hand, struck by the woman's poise. "Miss. Swivler, I presume? I'm Vivian."

The woman had the self-assurance of one who did not let astringent words rip into her good manners. "I know who you are. Mr. Stevens told me about you some time ago. He said you and I ought to meet."

"I think he was right," said Vivian.

"This is Nettie Grace, Juana." Stevens grasped his hat in his hand as if suddenly intimidated.

Miss Swivler took Nettie's hand. "I've heard of you, Miss Grace."

Stevens cleared his throat. "Nettie and Vivian run a library for women, Juana. I thought you might make a donation."

Miss Swivler's eyes lit up. "If it's books you want, I've a treat for you." She took Vivian's hand in hers and Nettie's in the other. "Tell me about your library, my dears."

Stevens did not come with them as Miss Swivler (who

insisted they call her Juana) led them up several flights of stairs, passing quickly through the first two floors where Vivian could hear the suppressed giggled of young women. A set of double doors faced them on the third floor, opening into a luxurious apartment done in shades of pink and cream.

Nettie, who had been telling Juana about the reading room, stopped, and her face showed a look of awe Vivian had never seen before. "You must like pink," she murmured.

Juana laughed. "Pink is the color of sweetness. Every woman ought to have some sweetness in her life." Her face tightened. "I started out in the gutter. One sees only the foul and the acrid in the Barbary Coast."

"Perhaps we shall see its demise now that reformers are taking hold of the city," Vivian said.

Juana gave a snort. "Nothing but an earthquake could bring the demise of that vile place." There was a momentary silence, and then she said, "But you've come for books, not hear sordid tales."

She led them through the vast apartment to a study. Shelves reached the ceiling, and books lay neatly, one against the other. "These are my private collection," Juana said briefly. She led them to a chest and flung it open to reveal stacks of volumes. "They came to me as a legacy from a gentleman I knew." She chuckled. "A customer of mine from long ago. He thought I needed to educate myself, and I did. So he sent me these. He was an Englishman," she added. "You've no objection to English writers as opposed to American ones?"

"We're grateful for any writers." Nettie was already shifting through the stack.

"Many are translations, I believe." Juana sat on a chair. "French, Russian, Italian. Nothing scandalous, I assure you." There was a twinkle in her eye. "He was a very proper gentleman."

Vivian joined her friend in the inspection, and they were both delighted to see names they knew — Flaubert, Dante, Dostoevsky — along with those they didn't. Her friend blurted out, "Did you ever read any of them?"

The woman threw back her head and laughed. "Bless you, my dear, I never had the patience! My tastes lean more toward *The Saturday Evening Post* and *Peterson's*."

"How odd," Vivian remarked.

"Is it?" the woman murmured. "Perhaps it is." She rose, smoothing down her skirt. "I'll have them delivered to you, if you'll give me your address. Now, shall we join Mr. Stevens for tea?"

As they walked through the apartment, Vivian ventured, "Have you known Mr. Stevens long?"

"You mean as a friend." The woman eyed her.

Vivian blushed. "I'm sorry. It was an impertinent question."

"I would hardly think you capable of impertinence," said the woman. "I expect you were taught to keep your distance and your dignity."

"Yes, that's true," Vivian admitted. "Call it a moment of curiosity, then."

"I've no objection to curiosity." The woman gripped her hand. "If you've no objection to an honest answer."

"None whatever." Vivian stiffened.

"I've known Mr. Stevens since he came of age," said the woman. "He was a wild young man in those days, but he always spoke well and treated my ladies with respect." She peered at Vivian. "It took only a few years for him to tire of sowing those wild oats. He continued to come, but for the company, not the carnal pleasures. Is that what you wanted to know?"

"I didn't want to know anything," Vivian insisted as they clambered down the stairs.

"He was rather a pitiful soul." Juana's voice was wistful. "He once told me I was like the older sister he never had, but I think I'm more like a mother. He didn't have much of one, you see."

"I gathered that." Vivian thought of the jittery woman she had met at Neart Castle two years before.

"Perhaps you won't believe me, but he learned most of his manners within these walls," said Juana. "Though he has a terrible habit of probing into other people's lives."

"You mean walking into other people's private moments?" Vivian asked.

"He told you about that," Juana said with a smile.

"He admitted at the time that a woman had told him that," Vivian remarked. "An experienced and intelligent woman, he said, and one he thought I wouldn't approve of."

"And what did you say, my dear?"

"I said if this woman had the sauce to tell him the truth about himself to his face, I think I should like to meet her."

Juana laughed and pressed her cheek to Vivian's. "I hope neither of you will be strangers."

They entered the room opposite the small parlor. Vivian saw Roger had not exaggerated about the tea. She had been to England only once, but she still remembered the lavish teatime settings. The table was set with tiered serving plates filled with finger sandwiches, small tea cakes, scones and jam as elegant as any she had seen in London. The ladies loitering about the few men there besides their party were all elegant, speaking in low tones and setting their cups delicately in their saucers.

Juana pulled her and Nettie to a window seat where Stevens sat near Emma, who was lapping at a bowl of cream, and insisted on bringing them tea herself.

"What do you think of Juana?" Stevens asked, smiling.

"We're very grateful for the donation," Nettie said.

Juana waved her away. "I tried to give those books to the Goldspur Library, and they turned their noses up."

"They're fools, then."

Vivian took a long sip of her tea, not realizing it was scalding. "You'll come down and see our library sometime, won't you?"

Juana colored. "That would hardly be proper."

"Proper be damned!" Vivian growled. This made Stevens burst out laughing.

"I've always admired your courage, Vivian. And your fierceness." He fixed his eyes on her.

Vivian's gaze wandered to the window which looked toward the back of the house where a weaned garden showed its blooms. "Very gracious of you to say so, Stevens, considering you've been the object of my fierceness many times."

Juana said, "Today ladies must show a little spirit."

"I agree," Stevens said. "Just as a young man must show a little ambition to get anywhere."

Roger, who had been standing with a dark-haired woman, turned around with an interested look. "Only a little, Harland?"

"That rather depends on his opportunities," said his cousin. "And his education."

"That's what college is for, isn't it?" the young man asked in a dull voice.

"I meant guidance from someone older and wiser," said Stevens. "If wiser he is."

The butler slid beside Juana and spoke to her in a low tone. "I'm afraid I must leave you for a moment. Becky and Pat will keep you amused." She motioned toward the ladies as she disappeared out the door. One had brittle features, and the other, a fresh-faced blonde with wide blue eyes, kept staring at Stevens.

"Juana's just told me who you are!" Becky, the first woman, declared.

Vivian blinked as the woman's crushing eyes regarded her with a strange excitement. "You're welcome to come by the library." She glanced at her friend, who nodded in silence.

"I meant your name," said Becky. "It's Alderdice, isn't it?"

"Her name is Mrs. Caulfield," Stevens said.

This seemed to startle the woman for a moment. Then, she said, more cautiously, "You're related to that young man who was here a while back. The shy, gentlemanly boy who took an interest in Geneva."

"So you brought Jake here to get acquainted with these charming ladies?" Roger threw his cousin a mischievous look.

"Oh, you fresh thing!" Pat, the young woman, said with a giggle that sounded a little too much like Fern Tisher's. "Geneva's dead, poor thing."

"I'm sorry to hear that," said Stevens.

"Consumption," said Becky. "You would have thought her young constitution could have withstood it." She sighed.

Vivian clasped the woman's wrist. "You met my brother?"

"Marion and I served him coffee that day, right in this room," said the woman. Her eyes fluttered. "He was such a gentleman. Marian told Geneva it was a lesson to her that not all men are brutes."

"I would hate to think we were!" Roger said with a laugh that seemed awkward in the somber air.

Becky glared at him, then turned to Vivian. "I always thought he ought to know she didn't mean to make such a scene over his paintings. It was just her illness. You'll tell him that, won't you?"

"Paintings?" Vivian's fingers felt icy.

"Why, my sweet, an entire row of them right at your back." And the woman's eyes swept behind her.

Nettie's voice echoed in her ear, "Viv, are you all right?" Another spoke a male voice that sounded like Roger's, "She looks ready to faint." She felt a cool patch against her arm and realized she had tipped her teacup, and the liquid had spilled on her sleeve.

They were all there — the handful of paintings Jake had done of her in the wax woods, with the bright green grass and specks of wildflowers, she looking more like a child than a woman. He said he wanted her to look like a fairy in the woods, another Titania. Stevens insisted she looked more like a huntress and christened her Diana with her crown of thorns.

Voices speaking around her sounded hollow, as if she had entered a dark cave. Becky lamented, "Land sakes, it's jus' like Geneva all over again!" Roger's voice filtered through again, "How did they get here?" Then Juana's deeper tone said with authority, "You ought to have told her, Mr. Stevens." The redhead's mild-mannered tone came last, shrill and confused, "I don't understand! I don't understand!"

The echo disappeared, and she heard the clanking of china, the flutter of skirts, and a general male laughter. Nettie tucked her hand under her arm. She looked at her friend, warmed by the compassion on her face.

"I thought he burned them. He told Mother he burned them." She burst into tears.

Strong hands guided her out of the room, the hollow echo of Emma's bark nipping at her ears. She found herself in the small parlor again. Nettie stayed with her, holding one hand as Vivian let the handkerchief in the other soak up the tears. The room's narrowness made her feel cushioned and comforted. She did not weep for long, and when the doors opened to admit Juana, Roger and Stevens, standing in the doorway, her eyes were dry.

Juana held a cup in her hand. "Better now?"

"It was a damn rotten thing to do, Harland," Roger snarled.

Vivian looked at Stevens. He stood upright, a turbulent look on his face.

"Trickers and false idols," Roger continued with a growl. "Sometimes they are the same."

"That will be enough of that, young man!" Juana snapped without looking at him.

Vivian rose, feeling her feet a little unsteady. "I think I'd like to go home now."

"The car's ready," Roger assured her.

She took the teacup from Juana and drank down the strong liquid. It made her stomach warm and her spirits steady. "Thank you for the books."

"We're taking good care of them, you know," said the woman in a soft voice.

Vivian squeezed her hand, unable to answer.

She took Nettie's arm, and they walked out into the street. The sun was very pale, and the evening was descending like a broken egg. The laughter of the ladies and their guests rang from the window over the scratching crickets.

"I'm sorry, Vivian," Stevens lamented. "I'm sorry."

She did not look or speak to him as they drove home. Roger kept up a steady stream of chatter that competed with the pleasantness of the evening breeze. He didn't seem to mind that she didn't answer him.

CHAPTER 10

She did not see Stevens for several days, and he did not
contact her. The initial devastation she had felt upon
seeing Jake's paintings faded, but the pain and sense of loss still
lingered. She felt as if she had seen the imprint of a loved one
who had recently died.

At the end of the week, she and Nettie found a card under
their door. Vivian recognized Stevens' neat, broad hand. The
message conveyed an invitation to both of them to dine with him
at the Waxwoodian the next evening.

"It sounds very fancy," Nettie remarked.

"It is," said Vivian. "Exactly what you deserve." She smiled at
her friend.

Nettie gave her a shrewd look. "And what about you?"

Vivian arranged the chairs around the small tables near the
soda fountain. "I would just as soon stay here."

"You're angry at him," her friend guessed.

Vivian leaned against a chair. "No, not angry. Unsettled."

"Have you given up your crusade, then?"

"I think it best to stay away for a while," she said.

"You're behaving childishly." Her friend flared.

Vivian rinsed a dishrag in the sink and began wiping down the soda fountain. "It all came back to me when I saw the paintings, Nettie."

"They were his paintings to do with what he liked," her friend shot out. "He's not a young boy anymore, Viv."

The marble counter blurred. She stared down at the zigzag pattern, remembering a game she and Jake used to play in the playroom at Alderdice Hall. They would set up her bisque dolls with their empty eyes and the tin soldiers Grandfather had bought Jake from England around the room in such a pattern and follow the path. The one who ended in a different place than where they began won the game. Jake almost always started at the corner of the room near the sailboat windows and ended up there.

But now, he was in a different place, just as she was. She didn't know where that place was, but his boyish desire for that one place which had defined his idea of security was gone by now, just as hers was. She realized there was no safety in remaining in the same place.

"How old is he now?" she heard Nettie ask in a commanding tone.

"Twenty-three."

"Well!"

"I didn't expect to remember what I lost," she snapped.

Nettie held out her hand, and Vivian took it. "You want to find out about the paintings, don't you?" Vivian nodded. "Stevens can tell you about them. I'll send word we accept his invitation."

Vivian nodded and took up the dishrag again.

When evening came, Nettie could not go. An accident at the mill outside of town left many of the women rushing to their husbands' bedsides, and Lena and Sue needed help caring for the children.

Vivian wanted to help, but her friend wouldn't hear of it. "The moment they saw you, they would know you were a blue blood, even if you came in rags," she declared. "They wouldn't trust us for a moment."

"It hardly feels right," Vivian murmured as she dressed. "Going to a fancy dinner while you and Lena and Sue are trying to get a lot of frightened children fed and bedded."

"Stevens is expecting us," Nettie said. "It's only right at least one of us should go." She cast a knowing gaze on Vivian. "You're the one he really wants to see."

"He has a deep respect for you," Vivian scoffed.

"I think he wanted me there for moral support," Nettie said. "He's afraid of your womanly scorn. Promise me you won't give it to him."

"I'll be as civilized and polite as I know how."

Nettie laughed. "I'm sure the Queen of Denial taught you civility and politeness to perfection!"

As the ferry neared the resort hotels, the Waxwoodian gold lions shining in the moonlight, Vivian saw Stevens waiting at the dock. He was pacing up and down, his shoulders hunched and his gaze preoccupied. As the ferry docked, he rushed forward, holding out his hand to help her.

"You don't despise me?" She shook her head, and he seemed to relax a bit. "Where's Nettie?"

"I'm afraid she had some critical business she had to attend to."

She told him about the crisis, more for something to say to avoid the anxious gaze in his eyes as they entered the lobby. When she had finished, he shook his head in genuine regret. "I'll send money for the families tomorrow. I imagine they won't get a penny from their employer."

"No," said Vivian. "I don't suppose they will."

She shot him a look, but his profile was unmovable, chiseled that evening with the fine cleanliness and dignity of a man of his class. Except for his tallness, he merged with the other men in their crisp evening jackets with the tails swinging back, and their spotless white gloves.

She felt ill at ease. Her best evening dress lacked the graceful silhouette and soft silk of the other ladies' dresses. The sedateness of the dove gray contrasted with the bright colors of the others, and she wore a simple brooch that looked worn against their dazzling jewels. The scene of their strong perfume floated into the lobby, beckoning to her. She almost wished she had coveted a bottle of perfume from the shipment that arrived a few days ago, though she knew its cheap scent could not compete with that of the fine ladies in the lobby.

They followed the waiter to the table waiting for them, and when he slid the chair out for her, Stevens jumped in his place. The gentle ease of his hands pushing the chair in and the lightness of his breath on the back of her neck made her shiver.

"You miss your former life, don't you?"

She grimaced. "You were always bold with your questions, weren't you, Stevens?"

"You were never coy with me," he answered.

"Have you ever been diffident with any lady?" she asked.

He leaned back, laughing. "I suppose I never thought about it in quite that light!"

"Juana implied you sowed plenty of wild oats in your youth." Vivian kept her eyes on the menu.

"As much as any young man," he admitted.

"I suppose it was expected of you," Vivian said. "I know people always found it odd that Jake—" She hesitated.

The waiter came to their table. After they ordered, Stevens leaned back, his hands folded in his lap. "It's all right to mention his name to me now, Vivian."

"People thought it odd Jake never took to such things," Vivian continued. "Oh, I'm sure he had occasional meetings with young ladies and bouts of drinking and whatever else young men do."

"I'm sure," Stevens murmured.

"If he did, Mother and I never knew about it. You know how discreet he was…" Her voice trailed off.

"Yes, your brother was secretive." They were silent for a moment. "I don't want to be secretive with you, Vivian."

"Then tell me what my brother's paintings were doing at Juana's."

"That's exactly why I wanted to see you tonight." He leaned forward. "I told you my memory of what happened that summer is spotty. I didn't remember before, but I do now. Jake wanted to buy a gun, you see—"

"A gun!"

"A hunting gun." His voice was less assured. "He didn't want to ask your mother for the money. So I suggested he sell his paintings to Juana."

"Suggested?" She eyed him.

He sank back into the chair. "Perhaps it was more than a suggestion."

"I see."

"He mentioned giving them to you," he admitted. "I thought it was just a passing whim of his. I had no idea you admired them so much."

"Of course I admired them!" Her throat tightened.

"I ought to have known," he breathed. "Seeing them in such a place as Juana's must have been devastating."

She stared at him. "You think the fact that they were hanging in a house of pleasure upset me?"

"I don't blame you," he said in a soft voice.

"You're wrong, Stevens," she said. "Seeing them again—"

"Reminded you of your brother's lost talent," he guessed.

"They reminded me of all I've lost!" She buried her face in her hands. "I wish he had burned them."

"Do you think I would have let him do such a thing?" he asked.

"Perhaps not, but you exploited them for other purposes." She removed her hands, her lips feeling wooden. "You're the one who persuaded him to buy the gun."

"Yes, I persuaded him," he said. "And I exploited the paintings, and it was wrong. So much of what happened that summer was wrong."

The soup arrived, and she toyed with it, thinking of what he said. His tone was as mellow as it always was, but she detected a note of despair.

"I wanted to tell you I've made amends," he continued.

"Oh?" She blinked.

"I've bought back the paintings from Juana."

Tears washed the corners of her eyes. "You bought back Jake's paintings for me?"

"They're in the hotel storage room," he said. "I'll gladly send them to you tomorrow. I suggest you place them somewhere safe."

The spoon felt heavy in her hand. She dropped it, splattering soup over the white tablecloth. "Give them back to Juana. They mean nothing but pain and remorse to me now." They were silent as she stared down at the soup plate. "I'm truly grateful for your kindness," she added. "But that part of my life is closed."

"Would it help to know Jake sold them willingly and was glad they had ended up there?"

She thought back to her brother's sharp blue eyes and always thoughtful countenance. "Yes, that's just how he would feel." She almost reached her hand to cover Stevens' but caught herself in time and laid it in her lap instead. "Thank you for telling me."

"Then shall we enjoy this lavish dinner and amiable companionship and say no more about it?" He smiled.

"I've very little taste left for lavish dinners," she said with a laugh.

"And the amiable companionship?"

She studied him as he had studied her. "I'm always happy for that." She could see a slight flush under the freckled face as he handed the waiter his empty soup bowl.

Their meal arrived then. Vivian looked down at the rack of lamb and realized how far away she was from the opulence once so much a part of her life. She suddenly felt her stomach churn and pushed the plate away.

She and Stevens sat in silence, neither of them moving while the scent of meat and spices rose from both their plates. Then, he ventured, "There are bitter moments for me sometimes, like that day in the woods."

Vivian stared. "You remember that day?"

He grinned. "My past dour state did not leave me senseless, Vivian."

"Of course not," she said.

"The bitterness running through my blood made me speak that day," he said. "The bitterness of remembering."

She nodded. "One can only get rid of bitterness by speaking of it. Only then can it dissolve into nothingness."

"Then speak of it." He looked at her with his dark eyes.

She picked up her fork but could not eat. She probed at the lamb, watching the meat fall into the butter sauce. "It's as if everything I ever knew has disappeared. There's always that wish to hold on to what you knew just because you know it, isn't there?" There was a stony silence in the room, as if conversation had suddenly stopped. "Isn't there?"

The features of Stevens' face spread out, and his skin looked blanched. "Yes, there is always that wish. Even if what you knew was what you wished you had never known."

"You're speaking of yourself now, aren't you?" This time, she let her hand touch the wide palm lying on the table.

He peered at her. "How do we find that out, Vivian? Where do we go from here, eh?"

The lamb grated against her throat like sandpaper. "We go back."

"Back?"

She put down her fork and knife. "Did Jake tell you I'd been to Waxwood before the summer we met?" He shook his head. "I came here after my grandmother's funeral in 1896 to do what we must do with you now."

He gave her a half-smile. "You're being rather vague."

"It's my habit of speaking in circles," Vivian remarked. "My mother always complained of it."

"Then speak plainly," he said. "There are no secrets between us now, are there?"

"Are there?" She glanced at him.

"I hope there won't be," he said.

"My grandmother's life began here," she said. "The life she never talked about. I had to begin at the beginning, as one says." The food went down easier now.

"So we begin at the beginning, you say?"

"There is no other place," she insisted.

The dining room had gone into one of its strange hushes. People were moving their lips, but she couldn't hear their words. She noted the dining room was more glazed than she remembered it, from the walls to the chandeliers to the glaring white dishes.

Stevens' voice was barely audible, despite the surrounding silence. "And then what, Vivian? Then what?"

"When we get there, we'll know," she said.

He studied her as she ate, his own dinner left half untouched.

"Your habit of staring at people is as bad as your habit of walking into their private moments." Her tone came out harsher than she intended.

His head went quickly down to his dinner. "I'm sorry."

"I didn't mean to sound crude," she said. "I suppose we both have our failings. Mine is dagger-twisting."

Stevens blinked at her, his face a little uneven, and rose. "Shall we have coffee in the parlor?"

"It's getting late." Vivian shifted, feeling the weight of the velvet cushions against her back like an iron ball.

His hand suddenly covered hers. "We mustn't leave things like this."

"All right, if you insist."

"I don't insist." His tone became annoyed. "I've never forced a lady to stay with me if she didn't wish it."

"Neither have I ever let a man force me to stay with him if I didn't wish it," she countered, her eyes sparking.

He leaned his head back and let out the deep laughter that warmed her. "Even in our most heated moments, we seem to understand one another."

She gathered her purse and shawl. "Yes, perhaps we do. In spite of ourselves."

"In spite of yourself, maybe." He helped her out of her chair. "I've always wanted you to understand me."

"Why is that?" She looked at him.

His face turned away as he shrugged. "Oh, perhaps because I've always admired your audacity."

"So you've told me several times," she remarked. "If you believe I have courage, Stevens, your associations with ladies must have been quite pallid!"

He laughed as they threaded between tables to reach the lobby. She heard howls coming from the middle of the dining room and saw Roger and his two friends. She thought of two years before when Roger sat with almost a dozen of his college friends, hooting and roaring and making a public nuisance of himself, but bringing vivacity into the formal air of the place. Now, he and his friends seemed to have forsaken their more sedate personas for their youth again.

The three young men rose and sauntered in her direction. She grasped Stevens' arm, and they passed the last of the tables, reaching the entranceway along with the three young men. Roger greeted her as if she were his cousin instead of Stevens. She recognized the overextended cordialities from Pete and Andy as a sign they had drunk too much wine at dinner.

She had no wish to deal with the over-friendliness of tipsy youth, so she gave Roger a gracious smile and dragged Stevens toward the parlor. But the young man caught hold of her arm, pulling her out of the redhead's grasp. "I wish to speak to you, Vivian," he screeched.

"You may speak to me," she said coolly.

"Alone."

Stevens, clearly irked, but only bowed and withdrew.

Roger squinted. "Are you all right?"

"Why wouldn't I be?"

"Well, at Juana's—"

"That was a misunderstanding," she blurted. "Thank you for asking, but I'm perfectly fine now."

"You needn't go on with that devil, you know." He wobbled a bit and placed his hand against the wall.

She studied him for a few moments. "Roger, why did you ask me to help you?"

"Eh?" He raised one eye.

"Why did you want me to help Stevens get back his speech?"

"He's my cousin!" the young man croaked.

"The cousin you've admitted you despise," she pointed out.

"I don't believe I ever said that," he insisted. "We've had our differences, but a cousin is a cousin."

"Blood is thicker than water?" she asked with some irony.

He gave her a deadpan look. "Sometimes."

"And this was one of them?"

"This was one of them."

Stevens and the other men approached them. The redhead took her hand in his arm. "Pete was just telling me you promised them a roaring good time at Neart Castle next weekend."

"I was going to ask you, of course," said his cousin, his manner reserved. "I haven't forgotten it's your property, Harland."

Stevens' voice softened. "The castle is as much yours as mine."

"All the same, I've no wish to trespass." He bowed. "We'll go only with your consent."

"Naturally, naturally," Stevens mumbled. He led Vivian away, but a group of satin-sheathed ladies blocked their path.

"They're doing a few repairs there now, you know." Roger's voice rose above the sudden flurry of chatter.

"Of course I didn't know," his cousin snapped.

"Uncle Joseph approved it," the young man continued. "Before he died."

There was a pause. "I see. Now, if you'll excuse us—"

"We wouldn't intrude." Roger sounded so extravagantly gallant that his friends chuckled. "We were going to the York to play billiards. You remember how fond we were of the game that summer."

A frightened look appeared on Stevens' face.

"You ought to take Vivian to the castle," Roger continued. "Especially now. I imagine you're going to sell it."

"I haven't thought that far ahead," Stevens murmured.

"It's as medieval as they come," Roger said to Vivian. "All cobblestones and iron. The only thing missing is the moat with the crocodiles."

"I know," she said. "I saw it a few years ago."

The invading silence drew around them. Stevens led Vivian into the hotel library. "Perhaps we should have our coffee here," he suggested. "The parlor might be a little crowded, and I'd rather — I'd rather not see anyone just now." He caught a clerk passing by, and Vivian heard him order the coffee in a dithering tone.

She found a comfortable chair near the bookcases. Stevens seemed much more at ease as he sat on a settee with his legs stretched, their full length visible under the small table between them.

"He wanted to remind you of something." Vivian spoke first, "when he mentioned the billiards."

"Roger's memories are poison!" This shot out like a dart.

Vivian leaned forward. "We must be careful of him, Stevens. Something's happened to him in the last year."

"He's become quite bitter," the redhead agreed. "Being nurse-maid to a relative he never liked isn't exactly in his conscience." He added in a rueful voice, "Bitterness stings all of our tongues sometimes, Vivian."

She picked up a deck of cards left on a small table nearby and began playing with them. "I ought to tell you the whole truth about mine."

"I gathered you were holding something back at dinner."

"I've lost everything, Stevens. That's the bitterness that stings my tongue."

The waiter brought the coffee, and they both remained silent as he served them. When he left, Stevens asked, "What is everything?"

"My family," she said. "Not just Jake. My mother, for one. Oh, I went to see her, but we're strangers."

"Perhaps you always were," he said. "Sometimes, the closer one is to a person, the further away one realizes one is from that person." His eyelid fluttered as if from distraction.

"I suppose it was that way with Mother," Vivian admitted. "And then there were the specters in my life."

"I remember Jake telling me," he said.

She stared at him with alarm, but went on, "I've made my peace with them now, but they've left their mark on me." She put down the coffee and picked up the cards again. "It's like when someone blows out a candle, and the shadow of the flame remains in the dark room."

"But the glow eventually fades away," he reminded her. "So will these specters of yours."

"If I could only believe that!"

"This work you're doing with your friend, for instance," he said. "Or is that her dream and not yours?"

She began sorting the cards. "You've kept a shrewd eye on us."

"I noticed when I came to that library of yours that you don't seem happy, Vivian."

"I'm contented," she insisted.

"That's not the same thing, is it?" he asked.

She spread the cards on her lap and laid her hands on them. A strong breeze shot through the window near them, making the curtain billow and dance. The comfort of those cards reminded her of when her grandparents used to play Écarté after dinner.

"I've my own ideas about what women need now, just as Nettie had her own ideas apart from the Bay Area Women's Social and Political Rights League."

"The what?"

Vivian explained the organization and the disagreements Nettie had with them. As he listened, he sat with his hands in his pockets. Suddenly he pulled a pipe out of one of them. "Good lord!"

Vivian smiled. "I didn't know you smoked."

"I didn't know either." He looked at the pipe as if it were a dead bird.

"You may smoke, if you like," she said. "I like the scent of a good pipe. Perhaps a habit you picked up before your memory faded." She poured herself another cup of coffee.

The heady scent of tobacco filled the small room. "I'd like to hear more about your ideas, Vivian."

"I can't see you interested in women's suffragism, Stevens."

"Only because you judge me ill," he said. "I've always believed women are not the chattel of men."

She felt certain he was thinking about someone in particular, but she didn't question him. "One of Nettie's friends was talking the other night about scoundrels who prey on children."

"Yes, many scoundrels," he mumbled.

"I thought Nettie might help me do something with a school," she sighed. "But she's made it clear to me she's interested in working women, not children."

A strange silence sifted between them. Vivian was keenly aware of the sweet burning scent of the pipe smoke lingering with the scent of lilac from the hallway where two ladies had stopped just outside the open door to whisper between them.

Stevens asked, "Why don't you do it alone, then?"

She chuckled. "It would take money. Perhaps *you've* forgotten I no longer have very much of it."

"No, I haven't forgotten," he said. "But your mother—"

"I won't take money from her," she said bluntly.

He leaned forward with his elbows on his knees. "Vivian, you said before you've made your peace with the dead. Don't you think you must make your peace with the living too?"

She blinked. "Someone said I would."

"Someone?"

"An old woman I passed on the street recently. She said, 'You shall find forgiveness in those who have caused you pain.'"

This seemed to alarm him, as he dropped the pipe on the floor. It lay on its side, staring up at Vivian like an open eye. As she bent down to pick it up, the cards in her lap fell under the table. Both she and Stevens went for them, and as she raised her head, his eyes met hers.

She quickly retrieved most of the cards. One caught her eye. "My old friend, the king of hearts," she remarked.

"Old friend?" He sounded amused.

"The king who put a sword in his head," she said. "They call him the suicide king."

"I never noticed." Stevens took the card in his hand.

"Marvina had a theory about him," said Vivian. "You remember Marvina?"

"Of course."

"He went mad and killed himself," she said. "Like King Charles VII."

"And what's your theory?" He grinned.

"He killed himself for a woman. This woman." She held up the queen of spades. "She persuaded him that his life wasn't worth living, demon that she is."

His look became distant. "Maybe the king of hearts killed himself because he lost everything, like you and I."

The seriousness of his tone alarmed her. "Even with your father dead, Stevens, you're far from losing everything."

"I didn't mean my father." He gave her a wry smile. "I meant my memory. One is lost if one has no memory, Vivian."

"I thought it was only the memory of the past few years."

"It's in those memories I feel lies the key to my life," he murmured. "Don't ask me how, but I know it."

The wind gave a strange cackle, shifting pages of an open book lying on a chair. Conversations in the parlor room near them rose above the ragtime music someone was playing on the piano. A group of men left their sanctuary of cigars and brandy to join the ladies, and she smelled their sour scent in the hallway behind her. She again felt a nostalgia for her former idle days.

Stevens asked, "Why didn't she kill him herself with her spear?"

"What?" She looked at him, startled.

"The queen of spades," he said. "She ought to have killed him with her spear."

Vivian's hands tightened in her lap. "Or a part of him that was no longer his."

He stared down at the king of hearts lying spewed on the table. "If it was no longer his, perhaps he killed himself because he didn't know who he was without that false piece."

"Then she ought to have helped him," Vivian said in a firm voice.

The softness in his eyes showed a light of gratitude. "Thank you for saying that, Vivian."

She felt a prickling sensation in her chest and rose. "I really must get home, Stevens. I don't want Nettie to worry about me."

He rose swiftly and held out his arm. "I'll make sure we don't miss the last ferry."

"There's no need for you to come all that way," she said with a blush. "You won't be able to get back."

He smiled. "I'll get back. I've never let a lady take herself home yet."

As they strolled through the lobby, now partly empty at that late hour, Vivian saw Roger and his two friends sitting on a couch. The young man's eyes followed them as Stevens guided her out the revolving door.

~

They had a pleasant ride on the ferry. A more temperate wind replaced the sharp breeze that had earlier cut into the library curtain. She and Stevens spoke little, both preoccupied by the blackened bay.

When they docked, he insisted on seeing her to her door rather than catch the last ferry across. "There are plenty of taxis here." The year before, some fishermen, hard up in summer, converted their fishing boats into taxis for the young swells who couldn't be bothered with keeping the curfews their parents set for them.

She was glad for the company. Though she felt safe in Waxwood, the major artery of town was deserted of night, and the streetlamps were not very bright. She often wished for the faces she knew, some by sight, others more intimately from errands and Sunday strolls.

Not far away from her flat, Stevens finally spoke, "I see why you left your family and came here."

"I didn't really leave," she said. "I had to find my place by going away from home."

"So you came here."

She shrugged as she fished her key out of her purse. "I had nowhere else. Nettie was kind to me last summer."

"A wise Chinese man once told me we all have one fateful meeting in our lives. Perhaps Nettie is yours."

She paused with her hand on the key she had slipped in the lock. Shadows from the gas lamp hid the crevices of his face. "What was yours? Or is that erased from your mind too?"

He leaned against the banister, looking down at the empty street. She could see a touch of his profile softened with a somber look. "A man I called Allcock. That wasn't his actual name, of course."

"What was his actual name?" Vivian leaned against the door.

"Byrne," he said. "He was my father's rival."

"And your friend?" she asked gently.

"I thought so at one time." His figure was erect. "Now I'm not so sure. I'm not so sure he wasn't the devil in disguise!"

She felt the key, still in the lock, pressing into her back as she leaned against the door. How many times had she felt like that? How many times had she seen the snarling face of Lilith in the innocent countenance of Bertha Ross, the tight features of her daughter Ruth, and the unyielding gaze of Verina Jones? And in the painting of her grandmother, in her rose-colored dress and pearls?

She flung open the door, hoping Nettie would be there at the table or rocking back and forth in the chair reading one of her books. But the flat was dark and empty.

"I see your friend isn't back yet." Stevens peered over her shoulder. "I don't like to leave you alone here, Vivian."

"I'm quite safe," she said briskly as she found a lamp and lit it.

"All the same, I'd like to stay," he said. "We shall leave the door open if you prefer."

She couldn't hold back a smile. "I'm not afraid of you, Stevens. I never was."

"No, fear was never between us," he agreed.

She suddenly felt awkward about the flat. Though not squalid or dirty, old furniture left to Nettie from mother occupied the rooms. Other than a few family heirlooms, the rest was rather cheaply made and threadbare. She chose the largest chair in the room for Stevens, given his broad-shouldered figure, then discreetly placed a pillow on the worn seat where the fibers were showing. But he seemed to pay little attention as he continued to watch her. She went about straightening a few things she and Nettie had left askew.

He said, "You told me once a young man painted your portrait."

She stared at him. "That was on the beach when you were — yes, I told you that."

"May I see it?"

She clasped her hands together. "Sometimes you astound me, Stevens."

He smiled. "You promised you would show it to me."

She went to the bureau near her bed, a large, clunky thing, and found the small lock on the side. It snapped open to reveal a sliver of space. She slid the painting out, covered generously with a velvet drape.

His deep laugh filled the room. "I see why you said you hid it in a safe place!"

She felt her cheeks glowing, though she knew in the milky light he couldn't see them. "I never liked displaying my portrait for all to see. My grandmother never liked hers hung in the parlor, but she had no choice."

"And you have a choice," he guessed.

"I made my choices, Stevens. For better and for worse."

"As it should be," he murmured.

She rested the portrait against one of the kitchen chairs. Stevens bent down and examined it. Vivian, feeling self-conscious, was thankful to discover the lunch dishes still in the sink and began washing them.

When she had finished, Stevens was still in the same kneeling position with his dark eyes intense.

"Who painted it?" he asked.

"A young painter named Christopher Spenlow," she said. "He lived in a converted warehouse with other artists in the South of Market."

"Lived?" He glanced at her.

"He died shortly after he finished the portrait."

Stevens rose. "A pity. The boy had talent, like your brother." He took the chair Vivian had given him, but his eyes continued to gaze at the painting. "He had bold strokes for a sickly young man." He was thoughtful for a moment. "I don't recall a field of dandelions anywhere around San Francisco."

She smiled. "The dandelions were in his imagination. We never left the warehouse."

"Why those flowers?"

It surprised her to see him so disturbed. "They're very picturesque," she pointed out.

"I never liked them!"

She blinked. "Because they're weeds?"

"Because they're parasites," he declared. "We had them all around the garden at Neart Castle. My father used to beat them down with a stick. Days later, there would be new clusters all over the place!"

"That's the way with dandelions," she said, laughing.

"Yes, you told me that, didn't you?" He looked at her with wide eyes. "They grow where they fall." He looked at the painting again. "Rather like some people who have led troubled lives. They appear elsewhere, their morals and hopes tarnished, perhaps, but they go on."

A pain went through her chest. She opened her lips to speak, but just then the door rattled, and Nettie rushed in, holding her cape closed from a gust of wind she brought in with her. She looked from Vivian to Stevens, though her face showed no judgment. Her eyes came to rest on the painting. Vivian placed it in the hidden alcove without a word.

Stevens bowed to Nettie. "You found shelter for the children?"

"Yes, all is well," said the woman with a smile.

"I'd like to send money to you tomorrow," he said. "To the library, if that meets with your approval."

The woman was clearly touched. "You are very generous, Mr. Stevens."

"And what about the men?"

"Three badly injured, six more mildly so. They were lucky."

"Any women hurt?" Vivian asked.

"They were all outside when it happened," said Nettie. "Perhaps the separation of the sexes at the mill was a lucky thing for them after all." She peeled off her cape and brushed a few loose hairs from her face. "Coffee or tea, Mr. Stevens?"

"Neither." He gathered his hat and coat. "I must get back to the hotel."

"Your dinner was a success?" Nettie eyed Vivian.

"Yes, it was very pleasant."

She saw Stevens to the door. Nettie turned the gaslight hovering above the doorway up to its full flame so she could see his face better. He seemed composed and less distressed than he had been before. He bent toward her, and for a moment, she thought he was going to kiss her. But he only smiled and, lowering his voice, asked, "Would you like to see Neart Castle again, as Roger suggested?"

"If you want to see it," she whispered.

"I think I ought to, don't you?" She nodded. "Friday, then."

She stood in the doorway watching him descend the stairs, his feet clomping down on the wooden planks as if he were going to break them. The figure walking away from the pool of yellow light was erect and purposeful.

CHAPTER 11

The week that followed held a sense of doom Vivian could not explain. Her days went on as they always did, except that she accompanied Nettie to the neighborhood near the mill to help with the children. Though some workers were suspicious of her, Nettie reminded them that, were it not for the generous check Vivian's friend had sent, they would all be starving. These people were practical as well as prideful, and they ended up thanking her, many profusely.

Between the children and the drugstore and library, Vivian hardly had time to think about Neart Castle until Thursday night when both she and Nettie settled down to their evening tea. Nettie suddenly asked, "What's the place like?"

"What place?"

"That castle."

Vivian, determined to make herself a shawl, held the knitting needles close to her chest. "Like a Scottish citadel."

"Come, Viv," her friend scolded. "You know I've never been outside Waxwood. I haven't even seen a castle in storybooks."

"Then you ought to pick up a copy of *The Mysteries of Udolpho.* I just put it on the shelf in the library yesterday."

"There must be *something* you can tell me about it!" Her friend was now exasperated.

Vivian stared at the dark window opposite her. She could see an outline of the clouds against a threatening flash of lightning. "All cobblestones and dampness and dogs," she murmured.

"Good heavens!" Nettie put down her knitting. "You make it sound like the Usher house!"

Vivian laughed and poured herself another cup of tea. "In a way, it is. At least it was when I was there last." She sighed. "I wonder what it will be like now."

The image of a gothic castle played in her mind that night, and she dreamed of their approaching the half-circle drive with hounds barking and ghosts peering through the windows with glowing eyes.

On Friday, she arranged to meet Stevens at the blacksmith's establishment, and she arrived early. To her dismay, she saw Roger leaning against an unhitched carriage, Emma in his arms, chatting with Michael Shelley, the blacksmith's son. Both men cut off their conversation in the way men did with manly talk in a woman's presence and took off their hats.

"Good to see you on this fine morning, ma'am," Mr. Shelley greeted her. She had developed a strange alliance with him ever since he had been her driver the previous year on several delicate matters she had undertaken. She always felt a little nervous around him, as if he knew too much about her, the way servants absorbed the strife of the family they served.

"I'm waiting for Mr. Stevens." She nodded at Roger, though she had no wish to converse with him, and petted Emma's head.

"You've become quite friendly with Harland these past few weeks," Roger remarked as Mr. Shelley went to attend to the horses.

She glanced at him. "Have you any objection?"

"None," he said. "I'm merely surprised."

"Stevens is good company," she said.

"I never found him so," Roger chuckled. "I prefer my own friends."

"You mean your past hedonistic life." She gave him a wry look.

He laughed and bowed. "One can be studious for only so long when one is young, Vivian. Surely, you realize that."

"Jake was studious all his life," she said in a soft voice.

"I never denied your brother was a better man than I." The way he said this with a side glance made it hardly a compliment. "He's had privileges I haven't."

"He's also paid for those privileges in a way you haven't," Vivian snapped.

"Forgive me," he said kindly. "I know talking about your brother upsets you."

She stiffened and held her parasol.

"I hope my cousin will take you to Monterey." He glanced past the stable door. "The boat races begin there today."

"He's taking your suggestion," she said. "We're going to Neart Castle."

The mention of the place awakened Roger out of his inertia. "Oh?"

"You were so insistent I see it," she reminded him.

"I'm in no position to insist on anything," said the young man. "I'm a mere spectator, remember?"

"You don't believe your cousin when he says the castle is as much yours as his?"

"You don't know, Vivian," he said briskly.

"I don't know what went on between you before his father died," she agreed. "But he's grateful you took care of him when he needed it."

"A burden I no longer bear, thanks to you." The young man smiled graciously.

"I should think you would want to move on with your life now," she said in a steel tone. "But it seems you've gone back to loafing with your friends."

Roger smiled again, but it was not a pleasant smile this time. "Only for the summer. When we return to the city, we'll all be grindstone workers and virtuous men again, never fear."

"I have no fear of you, Roger," she said. "But I do fear *for* you. So does Stevens. He thinks your memories are poison."

"Does he?" The young man played with his walking stick, grinding it into the soft dirt. "Perhaps some of them are. Or perhaps it's his memories that are poison."

She put her hand on his arm and said lightly, "One can rid oneself of poison if one lets it go."

He looked at her, his face pale, and the trimmed mustache lifted a little with his sneering lips. "Ask Harland to show you the trophy room. It was my uncle's pride and joy, and his too. It would be almost blasphemous not to see it."

Her hand dropped, feeling as if it had been touching a burning log. "I thought you considered your cousin the epitome of blasphemy."

"He and my uncle had their own religion." He placed Emma to the ground. "The religion of Actaeon." He tipped his hat to her and strolled out the stable door with Emma at his heels, leaving Vivian standing there in the dust. Stevens was coming up the drive.

He looked like a country gentleman in his tweed leisure suit and a straw hat that made him seem years younger. His face was more reposed than the last time they met, and he took her gloved hand and kissed it.

"I haven't had my hand kissed like that for a while," she murmured.

"I'm afraid it's going quite out of fashion," said the redhead. "The younger generations are more blasé about such things."

"I've noticed it in Roger and his friends," Vivian remarked.

Steven's smile tightened. "I saw him leave just now."

"I tried to warn him," she said. "About the poisonous memories."

"Warnings don't go far with Roger," said Stevens. "The more one tries to help him, the more obstinate he becomes."

"I'm afraid I can't speak much against obstinacy," Vivian admitted. "I inherited an obstinate streak myself."

He laughed and took her arm. "Such vices are much more flattering in women. They know how to make it a strength, not a weakness."

The younger Mr. Shelley appeared, two combs in his hand filled with horsehair. "Mr. Howe said you're welcome to take the car, sir, you and the young lady."

Vivian felt her hand tighten inside Stevens' arm. He said, "I think we'll take a carriage." He turned to her. "If that meets with your approval."

She smiled with relief. "I don't know that I much like that car of his."

"Darn nuances, these automobiles, if you ask me," muttered Mr. Shelley. "Begging your pardon, ma'am." He tipped his hat.

"Mrs. Caulfield isn't one to shrink from rough language, sir," Stevens reminded him.

"No, sir." The man led them toward the carriages. "Ain't many ladies got the gumption of Mrs. Caulfield."

Vivian's stomach clenched. She knew he was thinking about the time he had taken her to Sitwell.

They set out for Hale County, where Stevens had grown up and where the castle stood on the cliffs. The redhead was usually silent and observant, but during the ride, he blathered on about things that seemed futile to her. She realized he was nervous, as his mild, low tone had a ring of shrillness.

As he turned on an unfamiliar road, easing the horses away from a gutter, she asked, "You're afraid of finding specters when you get to the house, aren't you?"

He blinked away a brush of wind. "What makes you think I'm afraid?"

"You've been chattering like a magpie," she observed.

"I'm trying to entertain you," he said. "I haven't been with a lady for some time, and I know most ladies object to hanging silences."

"I'm not most ladies, Stevens," she reminded him. "I thought you realized that by now."

"I've no fear of ghosts," he said. "The Scotch, they have their superstitions, but my father was a very practical man."

"And a very domineering one," Vivian murmured, remembering her single meeting with Joseph Stevens.

"You rather startled him the last time you were at the castle," he said with a chuckle. "I don't think he ever forgot it."

"It's good for a woman to startle a man from time to time," she said warily.

He laughed and called to the horses.

They entered a valley she had never seen before. Bright shades of green stood against tufts of violet, blue, and yellow. A small lake appeared as they trotted along the dirt path, unworn by carriage wheels. The honking of geese stretched across the water.

He looked at her, wavering from side to side on the unsteady ground. "You remember my talk of my little haven?"

"Wild turkeys, geese, and prairie dogs," she murmured. "I thought at the time it was a strange combination."

"One's kingdom is always idyllic when seen through the imagination of a child," he lamented. "I expect you experienced the same thing."

Vivian nodded. "For Jake and me, our haven was an attic playroom."

"Tin soldiers, a crystal circus, and porcelain dolls," said Stevens with a small smile.

Vivian's cheeks flared. "Jake told you."

"We were all lonely children, all three of us," said Stevens. "One can hide loneliness under a façade of solitariness for only so long."

She settled back in her seat. "Has there ever been another mountain lion here?"

"Eh?" He stared at her.

"You told Jake and me there once was a mountain lion here," she said.

He looked ahead as they rumbled across a stretch of rocky path back to the more stable road. "I don't know. I hadn't much to do with the goings-on here in the last year. Even before my father died."

It took them a short while to reach the castle. Vivian could tell the castle was in terrible shape even before they approached it. The path leading up to it was dark and overgrown. Rust embedded the lettering at the gate, and the red dust of the private road looked washed through with black specks of ash, and the oaks bent over as if heaving a heavy sigh. Their carriage rocked violently with the sea wind.

When they reached the entrance to the drive, she saw the dream she had had of their arrival was little more than a farce. No hounds greeted them, and no glowering eyes of ghosts peered at them through the windows. Only a cumbersome silence pressed against her on all sides. The castle still looked solid with its cobblestone walls, but the windows scraped with sand and black curtains heaved against them.

"I wish Maestro were here." The tone of regret in Stevens' voice made it almost as touching as a little boy's.

"I ought to have brought Pan," Vivian mused.

He drew his hand to help her from the carriage. "Better to hear the echo of reticence than a dog's desperate bark."

She took hold of his arm. "Perhaps you're right. But the place is deserted. I thought Roger said there were workers here."

As they entered, she heard faint knocking and scraping coming from the back end of the house.

"Where shall we go first?" he asked.

Her answer was quick. "The gun room."

"You were frightened of it the last time."

"All the more reason," she insisted.

She noticed Stevens' hand lingered on the room's brass door-knob. His fist tightened and let go of it with agitated uncertainty.

Vivian, feeling she must tread carefully, said, "I thought you liked that room, Stevens."

"Liked!" His dark eyes gleamed like sparkling coals. But, as if seeing the alarm on her face, he relaxed and said, "It's necessary for a man to know these things."

"But not a woman?" she asked with a small smile.

In answer, he twisted the doorknob, and they entered the room.

It looked much the same, only dustier and narrower. The lingering aroma of benzene and flashes of iron made it feel more like a dungeon. But Vivian was not frightened, as she had been the first time. The firearms stood immobile, almost carelessly thrown into their racks or cases, unpolished and unclean. She suddenly saw her grandfather before he died — his fingers bent, his body crooked, and his face washed of all its alarming aloofness. These weapons were just the same — large and dangerous in their youth, but now decrepit and tame.

"You made a few more acquisitions since I last saw it," she remarked.

"Why do you say that?" His voice sounded distant.

"It's more crowded in here," she said.

Her eyes drew to the small display case that had once stood near the door, but now leaned against the wall. Her eyes searched below the glass for the tiny pistol that had caught her eye two years ago, gleaming gold and black pearl. To her astonishment, the red velvet case was empty.

"Where is it?"

Stevens was on the other side of the small room near the rifle rack. He stared at an old cabinet, his hand grasping the doors.

"Where is it?" she repeated.

"Where is what?" the man asked in a vague tone.

"The pistol your father bought your mother," she said. "The one you promised to teach me to shoot."

His eyes were almost like stone. "You remember that?"

"I've changed my mind about it." Her tone sounded bold in the small room. "I should think it would be useful for a woman to know how to shoot a gun."

He looked at her incredulously.

"Why not?" she asked. "For protection only, of course."

The man looked at the floor. "I don't know what happened to it."

"Perhaps your mother took it back," Vivian suggested.

"No!" He glared past the cabinet. "I had it in my hand—" He looked down at his hand as if it were a foreign object.

She neared him. "And what did you do with it, Stevens?"

"I don't know!" He shut his eyes, his breath coming out in gasps. "The sea — I remember the sea. I threw it over the cliff."

"Into the sea?"

"Yes, I threw it into the sea."

"And why did you throw it into the sea?" she asked softly.

He opened his eyes. "I remember looking down at it and thinking how small and lethal it was. And how filthy, like some writhing animal in my hand. I couldn't look at that pistol anymore."

"Of all the weapons here, why that gun?" she asked.

"Isn't it obvious?" He looked at her. "You took an interest in it, and it became all wrong. Every time I came into this room and looked at it, I knew it was wrong!"

His gaze concentrated on her now, the dark eyes so direct she felt as if ants were crawling down her back. "When was this?"

"Last Christmas," he said.

She stared. "Six months ago."

"It was after — after—"

"After what?"

"After." His hand moved to the side of the cabinet. The side flew out to reveal an empty shelf. Stevens stared at it, the tension melting from his face.

"A clever hiding place," she breathed. "Like mine."

"Yes, clever."

"You expected to find something there, didn't you?" she inquired.

He stared at the empty shelf. "Not now."

She took his hand and gently led him away. "I'd like to see your father's study again. May I?"

He looked at her like a bewildered child. "Why do you want to go there?"

"I'm curious to see it again." Then, in a firmer voice, she added, "We must go for your sake, Stevens."

The dust had settled on the high bookshelves in the study as evenly as it had in the gunroom. The leather chairs looked alarmingly tattered, but the moment Stevens parted the curtains to let in the light, she felt it was the same stoic, dark-stained furnished place she remembered. She shivered.

The redhead noticed this and said ruefully, "I always had to dress carefully whenever my father called me into this room when I was a child. My hands froze by the time I emerged."

"I should think you would have appropriated this room just as much as your father did," Vivian said. "It seems to suit you even more so than it suited him."

As he tied back the curtain with a rope, Vivian could see his hands were trembling.

She peered at the books in the bookcase, brushing off dust from the spines with her handkerchief. She tried to understand the titles but couldn't. She did, however, recognize the author's name — Joseph Stevens.

Stevens, seeing her looking at them, said in a wispy voice, "My father's Gaelic translations."

"I remember you told us about them," said Vivian in a soft voice.

"He's done more since then," said the redhead. "It was all he would do once he retired." The man glanced out the window. "That and hunting trips abroad in the season."

She flashed him an ironic smile. "Your father wasn't very fond of change, was he? This room," she added. "It's as if I never left it two years ago."

"He reached a point where change frightened him," Stevens said, hesitating.

"Perhaps we all reach that point." Vivian opened the window, but the room faced the sea, and the wind stabbed her like an icicle. She closed it again and turned around. She was almost behind the imposing desk where a still more imposing man had stood with his faded auburn hair and beard and his pale but astringent countenance. "Strange how a disciplined man can be undisciplined in the quietest corners," she lamented.

"Perhaps I was wrong when I said there were no ghosts here," Stevens said.

"Your father?" she asked.

"The man was a beast!" He hid his face in his hands for a moment. "I don't know why I said that. He was a great man in his own way."

"But not your way?" she ventured.

The redhead stooped over the desk, putting his hands together. He stared into the wall, his eyes empty. The stillness breathed around them, and the book Vivian still held in her hand felt weighted with lead. She returned it to the shelf.

Stevens jumped back, his eyes on the desk. "They ought not to have left it like this," he mused. "My father was as fussy about his quiet corners as he was everything else." With a snicker, he straightened the papers on the desk.

"Perhaps Roger didn't want to touch it, and you were in no position to deal with it," Vivian suggested.

"Yes, perhaps you're right." He sighed. "I hardly think Roger would have cared about proprieties." He laid cream-colored pages in one stack neatly in the corner.

Vivian headed toward the door. "There's one more room I'd like to see, if I may."

"Haven't you seen enough?" His voice rang through the quiet room.

"Perhaps *I* have," she countered. "But you haven't."

His hands jerked over the papers on the desk. "I don't know that I like your way, Vivian."

"You would rather hide your head in the sand, then?" She stared at him. "I took you for a strong-willed man, Stevens."

A crown of light arched over his shoulders. "You're the one with the powerful will."

She let go of the doorknob and leaned against a chair. "I must ask you a question."

He looked at her as a student to a teacher.

"Do you want peace or false forgetfulness?"

He blinked. "I don't understand what you mean."

"Do you recall that night when your cousin brought you to the drugstore, and a rather worn woman named Verina encouraged you to stay in your stupor because it was safe?"

"I don't remember all of it, but I do recall you were quite angry." The edge of his lips curved in a smile.

"I was angry because I know one never really forgets," she said. "One carries the wounds until they split open, if not for you, then for your children or grandchildren or their children." She gave him an exacting look. "Is that what you want to happen?"

He folded his hands in front of him. "You believe it's old wounds I carry?"

"Old or fresh, the pain is just as cutting," she remarked. "That's why you must have courage to follow the path to heal them."

His strong profile illuminated under the window light, making him look like a mature Apollo. "You're madly persistent."

She smiled. "My grandfather once told me to go after what I want and not stop, not even for despair."

"Then neither shall I stop for despair," he said with resolve. His eyes rested on a spewed stack of papers on the desk, and he put them on top of the others. His hand froze, and his eyes stared down at them. A granite pallor showed on his face.

"Is anything wrong?" Vivian ventured.

The redhead stumbled a little as he withdrew from behind the desk and leaned against the side of the nearest bookshelf. "So that's how he knew!"

"Perhaps there's some brandy in the cabinet?" she suggested. As her hand reached for the key inside the lock, his clamped down on it.

She glanced at him, alarmed at the savage look on his face. But when he spoke, his voice was composed. "There's no need. I'm all right now." He let go of her hand. "The trophy room, you said? Yes, I'll show it to you. Yes, we must go there." The last lament faded from his lips as he lurched out the door.

She glanced down at the desk as she passed:

December 8, 1899
San Francisco, CA

Dear Sir,

I thought it best to address you regarding some unnatural business related to your son. I say unnatural because there was involved, I am sorry to say, a crime that, although not intentional, nevertheless laid to rest the body of a person of no consequence to anyone but to those who loved him. I suggest you ask your son about the particulars. Shall we say they involved—

She heard Stevens calling her, and she hurried away, the words ringing in her mind.

CHAPTER 12

Stevens was now more determined, and his stride made her breathless as she followed him outside the castle past a few lower buildings. The cobblestones here were slimy with moss, and a strange mist surrounded them.

"Is it far?" she asked.

"Not far," he answered without turning around. "My father had to hide it away from the rest of the castle. It was the only thing my mother ever insisted upon."

They wound around a path to a small house in back of the buildings. Stevens turned around and took hold of her shoulders. "We moved the trophies here just before my father died. He needed a larger space, you see."

He studied her as she pulled her gloves on tighter. He took one in his own. "Don't be frightened. Nothing bad will happen to you. I'll see to that."

His voice soothed her, but when he pushed open the door, Vivian gasped at the black bear staring down at her. The snarling expression was so real, she shrank back against the doorframe.

"Your brother was appalled when he first saw it too," Stevens said. "I never told him the story of its capture. My father and I advanced alone, leaving the others behind. We found its leg caught under a fallen log. He told me to shoot it. I always obeyed him then. He got drunk that night and boasted about our adventurous chase in the woods after the animal. Tell me, Vivian, how courageous and noble is that?" His voice cracked in the crowded room.

Like the gun room, relics crowded this room. She could hardly count them all. Larger animals stood against the walls or with their heads mounted and hung, while the smaller ones displayed on stands in the center.

"That look of terror—" She could barely speak.

"That was my father's specialty." Stevens' voice grew colder. "It was like an obsession with him. 'You can see the anticipation of death in their eyes,' he said once. The pride in his voice, oh, the pride!"

He walked around the room, reading the plaques. "Harland, age twelve, Death Valley. Harland, Finland, 1888. Harland, Greece, 1895. He stopped putting my age on them when it ceased to impress people." His eyes were glittering. "But there's one missing!"

A draft of icy wind entered the room. His face was as ragged as one who was losing his reason. Vivian wanted to stop him, but she weak and helpless.

"That's what he said that night," the redhead continued, his lips twitching. "'There's one missing, isn't there, Harland? You shall tell me all about it.' 'No, Father, nothing is missing.' 'You tell me about it!'" The roar seemed to bounce off the walls. He had laid his hand on a stand with a tan rabbit, and the creature almost vibrated under the bestial touch, as if it were coming alive. Vivian screamed, her trembling hands covering her mouth.

Stevens shouted, "Beast! Swine! Under the guise of a Teddy Roosevelt, you were another Sawney Beane!" With a push of his large hand, he shoved the rabbit away, and the stand tipped over, rolling to the ground.

Vivian felt her knees folded. She stumbled out the doorway and ran until she reached the horseshoe drive. The lawn lay still with a yew tree overlooking the yellow grass and the few flowers sprouting beneath it. She collapsed underneath its shade, sheltered from the icy wind. Her breathing returned to normal, and the dizziness gave way to a clearer head.

Stevens had followed her and now stood a few feet away at the edge of the grass. His hands swung at his sides, and the thickness of the surrounding shade obliterated the features of his face. She could see his chest rising and falling as if he were gasping for a breath. He tottered toward her, and, at first, she drew back, seeing him as another one of her specters. But as he neared, the depredation on his face that replaced the wild look reminded her of the man she had seen in the wax woods.

"Forgive me. Forgive me."

He collapsed on the grass, laying his head beside her, repeating the choking plea over and over again. Her hand laid on his head, petting it like a soothing mother.

∼

The ride back to Waxwood was at first a silent one. They were subdued, their nerves steady and exhausted. But Vivian's mind was whirling with thoughts. The trophy room — the walk on the beach — the letter on the desk — Roger Howe. His clean-cut face and sandy hair, the mustache that trimmed neatly over his lips, and the penetrating eyes racked her more than the tumbles and starts of the carriage over the rough road out of Hale. Rising above the prickly thorns of the bushes on either side of them was the young man's erect figure, grinning at her like a naughty ghoul.

"Roger," she said aloud.

"Roger!" Stevens echoed over the wheels of the horses. "Yes, Roger."

She glanced at the redhead. "What was that letter about, Stevens?"

"Letter?"

"On your father's desk," she said. "That letter that startled you so."

His features rested uneasily. "I don't know."

"You know," she insisted. "You said, 'So that's how he knew.' What was in that letter, and what was it that your father knew from it?"

"I don't know!" he cried.

"You knew then," she pointed out.

"I don't know now," he said. "I can't explain it, Vivian. Some moments are lucid at one point, but then vanish."

She put her hand on his arm. "It might be the effects of your silent state. The memories are coming back, but some cling and some don't."

He pulled the horses to a stop in the middle of the country road and turned to her. He took both her hands, his touch gentle but persistent. "If I knew, I would tell you. I can't keep anything from you."

"I know," she said kindly. "I think there's a hostile figure in both our lives keeping you from getting at the truth, even as he pretends to push you forward."

"You mean Roger, don't you?" His eyes fell on the road. "He loathes me, Vivian. He always has."

"I know that now," she said. "I know how many lies he's told me." She gently released her hands from his. "He was the one who suggested the walk on the beach."

"For God's sake, why?"

"He knew we would find that ship," she said. "He knew you would remember."

Stevens took the reins, and the horses began again. "I've always known how much he hated me, but I didn't believe he could be that cruel."

"I don't think it was cruelty for cruelty's sake." The coach jumped, nearly knocking her off the seat.

Stevens did not look at her as he said in a watery tone, "You think there was something disingenuous behind it."

"I think Roger's entire manner has been disingenuous," she said.

Stevens did not answer for a while. They rode along the citrus lane, the freshness of oranges enlivening her senses. The late afternoon sun glowed in the blue sky, its heat warming her hands and face.

When they passed into the road that went through Waxwood's main street, Stevens finally spoke. "That letter—" His tone was uncertain. "It was odd."

"Quite odd," she agreed. "I read only a small part of it, but it was very mysterious."

"I didn't mean its contents," he said. "I meant, the way it was written."

"The words, you mean?"

"That," he said. "And the handwriting."

"The handwriting?" She glanced at him.

"The strange way some letters were written — I've seen them before."

Vivian closed her eyes and tried to picture the letter. It was only a flash of smeared black ink on thick paper, but she could see the salutation clearly. The "S" in the word "Sir" had looked more like a scripted "J." She suddenly remembered the note she had received from Roger his first night in Waxwood: *Shall we say eight o'clock?* The "S" in "Shall" had also struck her as more like a "J."

Stevens brought the coach to a stop inside the stable and descended, his hand out ready to help her down. She remained seated for a moment. "Roger wrote that letter."

He did not seem surprised and remained with his hand extended. "How can you be sure?"

She took his hand and climbed out of the coach. "By asking him." They left the stable. "You could ask him, that is. I don't think he would lie to you."

"No, that is his one strength," said Stevens. "He can be brutally honest. So was his father."

They stood on the sidewalk, her arm through his. When she turned toward the flat, he asked, sounding alarmed, "You won't come with me?"

She blinked. "I don't know that I should."

"Please." His arm squeezed her hand. "I don't think I can face him alone."

Vivian wanted nothing more than to retreat to the library where Nettie would still be sorting through the books. But she looked into the black eyes and remembered that morning at the castle and the breakdown she had witnessed. "I'll come."

They took the ferry to the hotel. It was by that time approaching the cocktail hour, when guests had recovered from whatever leisure they had allowed themselves for the day, refreshed for the upcoming measures of the evening. They walked into the crowded lobby, shades of summer colors contrasting with the more somber shades of the lobby furnishings. They both searched for Roger, but there was no sign of the blond young man or his friends.

"He must have gone up to the suite." Stevens headed toward the elevators.

Vivian hesitated. "Do you think I ought to?"

He gave her a crooked smile. "You've told me often enough you no longer adhere to blue blood proprieties."

"But you do," she said sharply.

"I'm as oblivious to them as you are now." He took her hand.

They took the elevator to the top floor, where the doors embossed in gold lions and the hallway adorned in a thick red carpet. She had seen the penthouse suites only once last year, when Mrs. Tisher had organized an evening of theatrics, and she had played the part of a working girl. The Tisher suite had been on the other side of the hotel and looked almost modest compared to the one she now entered. It had felt cozy with its familial atmosphere and knickknacks. But this room was clearly meant for bachelors, and she immediately disliked its marble floor and white walls.

Male voices assaulted them as they entered the parlor, though it seemed almost like a museum. Black leather furniture emphasized the white polished floor and walls even more. Vivian pulled her jacket around her, feeling colder than she had in the castle.

Pete and Andy sat in chairs, their legs crossed in the way of idle young men, but they both stood up and bowed as Vivian entered. Roger was at the bar in the corner of the room and, turning around, a decanter in his hand, grinned. Three large glasses sat on the counter behind him.

"Just in time for a brandy before dinner," he said in a jolly tone. "Vivian, may I pour you a sherry?" He took another glass and a smaller one for the sherry, lining them up with the other three.

"We'd like to talk to you, Roger," Stevens spoke with his usual mild tone. "Alone, if you don't mind."

The young man's mood grew impassive as he glanced at his friends. Without a word, they filed out, their silent obedience reminding Vivian of the days when they were still in college and their soldier-like behavior had been directed at Stevens, its acquiesce unnerving.

When they were gone, Roger put two of the glasses back on the rack. "You'll still have that drink with me, won't you?"

Stevens arranged Vivian on the most comfortable chair with a gentle grace, as one intent on protecting a favorite pet from a storm. Roger poured the brandy and sherry, then filled his own glass with considerably more liquor. "To affections among friends."

Stevens did not drink but looked at his cousin in the attentive way Vivian knew well. Roger drank a little too quickly. "You don't like sherry?" He looked at Vivian, whose glass remained full.

"Your toast was hardly encouraging one to drink, Roger," said his cousin.

"I see you wish to scold me," he remarked with some amusement. "I take it your visit to the castle did not go well. Were the workers in your way? If you had told me earlier you were going today, I would have—"

"Why didn't you put me in that place along with my mother?" Stevens' question darted out.

The young man gawked. "Good Lord, what do you mean?"

"After Mr. Chatham read my father's will," he said, "you took me to that doctor in Sacramento, and he recommended I join my mother for a rest. He thought I would have come out of it on my own, and I believe I would have."

The blood drained from Roger's face. "You couldn't have known any of that."

"I was in the room when you spoke." Stevens' voice grew stronger. "I couldn't speak, but I could hear. And I could understand."

"Well, well," the young man mumbled.

"You could have left me and gone back to San Francisco. Why didn't you?"

Rather than answer his cousin, Roger turned to Vivian. "Would you leave a relative in a place like that? All old people and doctors and nurses?"

"I could if I thought it would help him." Vivian's tone was equally mollified.

"Well, I couldn't!" Roger snarled. "I'm not that heartless."

"I wonder about the twists and turns of your heart," said his cousin.

Anger flared Roger's cheeks a bright red. "That's hardly just. I gave up a lot to care for you."

"You took generous amounts of my inheritance to compensate, I dare say," Stevens remarked. "Not that I begrudge you. My father might have provided more for you."

"I never asked for a cent!" the young man barked.

"No, but you expected it, and why shouldn't you? He'd been like a father to you since you were three years old," said Stevens. "I always meant to do right by you when the time came. You needn't have worried."

The young man looked astonished, his eyes ogling. "What do you mean?"

"I mean," he folded his hands, "you didn't have to take me in so I might give you the fortune you should have received from my father."

Roger went to the bar and poured himself another brandy. "So that's what you think. You think I took on the burden of bringing you back to be rewarded by your altruistic heart later on."

"You should have trusted me," his cousin insisted.

Roger plunked down the empty glass, making it crack against the counter. A roaring laugh escaped him. Vivian's bones shook inside her body. She now knew what twists and turns had taken hold of Roger's heart and what lay beneath the vicious undertones she had heard in his voice. She knew what had made her feel uneasy about his too-cheerful ways and his watchful eyes. And, like a light illuminating a dark corner, she remembered the word Stevens had written when they passed the York: *Amarok*.

"The lone wolf," she murmured.

Both men looked at her.

"You wanted Stevens to gain back his voice," she said. "But not for his sake. For yours."

"Harland was ill after Uncle Joseph died." The young man reached for another brandy. "I had to help him. It was as simple as that."

"Help him?" she asked. "Your guiding hand was in everything

we did. The walk on the beach. The trophy room. You intended it that way."

"You wanted me to suffer!" Stevens' tone reached a thunderous pitch.

"Why wouldn't I?" Roger shouted. "You didn't suffer the first time. I wasn't going to let that go."

"The first time?" Stevens leaned forward.

The young man appealed to Vivian again, his eyes saddened. "I wanted Harland to speak again, I really did. And I knew you could do it when no one else could."

"I don't doubt your actions," she said. "It's your intentions I question."

"My intentions," Roger said. He laughed again. "My intentions. I suppose I do owe you an explanation, Vivian. A confession, so to speak." He took up an empty glass and refilled it with brandy.

"Don't you think you've had enough?" Stevens asked, his voice hollow.

The young man drank the brandy, then turned around with a snarl. He had stood unevenly and, aware of it, held on to the edge of the counter.

"Damn you!" the young man shrieked. "You and Uncle Joseph, always treating my father and me like dogs." He held up his hand. "I take that back. You treated your dogs far better than you treated my father." He looked at Vivian appealingly. "A boy is supposed to be treated better than a man, especially when he's like a son, don't you think?"

"Roger." Stevens' voice came out in a whisper.

"That's how my father said it would be. 'Harland's grown now. A thirty-two-year-old who has done some devious things in his life is no match for a fresh-faced seven-year-old with your potential, Rog.' He called me Rog, yes! The only one whom I ever let call me that."

Vivian asked quietly, "And for that, you sent us to a ghost ship?"

"Oh, that was merely justice!"

"Justice for what?"

"What should have been last year but wasn't," said the young man.

Vivian rose. "Perhaps I ought to leave."

"No, why should you?" Roger grabbed her arm. "You're as much a part of this as we are."

"Not by choice!" She glared at him.

"I want you to stay, Vivian," Stevens said.

She sat down again, feeling the leather crisp against her back.

Stevens crossed his legs. "All right, Roger. If you wish to talk in riddles. What didn't happen last year that should have?"

His cousin looked at him with shimmering eyes. "Your denouncement."

A shadow crossed Stevens' face, and the lines in his forehead deepened. "Is that why you wrote that letter to my father?"

They heard a creak, and Pete and Andy peered in. The former mumbled something about dinner. Roger waved them away, and they dutifully left.

"You found that, did you?" the young man asked.

"Then you wrote that letter," Vivian murmured.

"I wrote two letters," said Roger, snickering.

"Two?" Stevens sat up.

"The other was to the Order of Actaeon."

The redhead's lips went white, and the lines on his forehead disappeared. "How did you find out about that?"

"That's my business," Roger said.

"What — who are they?" Vivian's voice was tiny.

Roger glanced at her. "You mean he never told you about it? But you ought to know! If anyone ought to, you should. Don't you think so, Harland?"

Stevens said faintly, "You'd better tell her, as you seem to be telling all."

"Oh, no, I won't tell all." Roger poured another brandy. "I'll tell only my part of it. That's all I'm interested in."

"Your self-interest has always been so absolute," his cousin snapped.

"I wrote the letter to Uncle Joseph," Roger said, his speech now a little slurred. "I wrote the same letter to the Order. And then I left. I went back to my life in San Francisco."

"Like a skulker!" Stevens growled.

"You don't appreciate good strategy, Harland. You never did." The man regarded him with half-closed eyes. "I went back to San Francisco, expecting to hear a friendly word from my uncle that his precious son had been disinherited, and he wanted me to come back to the castle. I would have come back if he'd asked me." His tone grew a little wistful. "I heard nothing for a month. And when I did, it was the telegram about Uncle Joseph's death."

Vivian looked at Stevens. His head was bent, and his hands pressed against his forehead.

"I came back for the funeral, naturally," Roger continued, looking at Vivian. "For my aunt's sake. I loved her. She tried to be a mother to me. She really tried." His eyes dampened. "The will was read, and Harland got it all. An income for 'the rest of her life' for Aunt Maggie, a 'modest bequest befitting his position' for Cousin Roger, and Harland, 'my beloved son, the rest.'" He scowled. "Odd, isn't it? A puppet becoming a millionaire!"

"That ought to have been vengeance enough," Stevens said. "You couldn't leave well enough alone."

The young man advanced toward him, but the coffee table offered a barrier. He fell against it, grasping it with both hands. "D'you know the funny thing, Harland? I was going to do just that. Then I got curious."

"Curious?" Stevens squinted at him.

"Like Alice," said the young man. "Down I went into the rabbit hole. Only mine was a cellar in a neat little boarding house on Vine Street."

The redhead's lips grew white again, and his face hardened.

"I thought you would recognize the address." Roger gave him an unholy grin. "I found a young man there whom I'd known in college. One of your Youths, I think you call them."

In a low growl, Stevens said, "You devil!"

"He was rather amenable to absinth," the young man continued. "It was one of two things I remembered about him from college. The other was that his tongue loosened when he indulged."

Stevens half rose, his face a mass of rage. Vivian put her hand on his arm, and he sat down again. He asked in a controlled voice, "What did he tell you?"

"All I needed to know," said Roger. "He quenched my curiosity, so to speak, about this sudden silence of yours."

"And you saw a way to take advantage of it," Vivian hissed. "By pulling me into your wretched game."

His face became somber. "I thought you and I were of one mind. You loathed Harland as much as I did. I could see that on the train. I never would have asked you otherwise."

"My loathing does not extend to tormenting people!"

"And yet, I shouldn't wonder that torment has done Harland more good than any doctor could have," said Roger. "I hope you continue, for whatever reasons suit you." He teetered toward the coat rack, where he took down his stick. "I have had my penny's worth, and I shall be contented to go my own way."

"And go your own way you will," Stevens said. "I'll give you what's coming to you, Roger. After that, just as you said to me once, now I'm saying to you — this finishes us for good."

"Amen!" The young man bowed. "I'm not such a fiend as you think, Harland. Now that I know my wish will come true, and not by my own hand, the idea of taking another cent from you or Uncle Joseph makes me want to vomit." His eyes bore into his cousin's. "I'm doing very well at Vanburgh & Gunn, thanks to Uncle Joseph, and now that the burden of pretending to act in your best interests is off my shoulders, I can enjoy life again."

"Will your conscience let you, I wonder?" Vivian murmured.

"You needn't concern yourself about me. I absolve you." He gave Stevens an exaggerated bow. "I'll dine with my friends and return only to pack up my things. They will welcome me with open arms in their suite. Not the penthouse, but ample just the same."

"Goodbye, Roger." It seemed all Stevens could manage.

The young man put down his stick and bent toward Vivian, taking her hand and speaking in an amiable voice, "I hope you'll forgive me. You have an open invitation to come see me in the city whenever you please."

"I don't think I'll be seeing you ever again." She felt resolute rather than angry or disgusted.

"I feel sure once you've had some time to think things over, you won't judge me too harshly." He left, shutting the door quietly behind him.

She expected something from Stevens — an outburst or a response of rage, at the very least. But the man looked as if the life had gone out of him. His face turned away from her, and his figure sagged to half its size. She opened her mouth to speak but realized whatever she could say to him would sound mundane. She rose and, following Roger's footsteps, left the suite.

CHAPTER 13

*V*ivian slept little that night, awakened by dreams of a man wearing a wolf's head, his eyes blood red. Near morning, she woke up screaming, and Nettie had to comfort her with soothing words like a mother to a child.

Just as they opened the drugstore, a small envelope with the Waxwoodian crest appeared under the door with Vivian's name on it. It was from Stevens, asking her to meet him in the lobby after lunch.

"He must be lonely right now," Nettie observed.

"I don't think it's loneliness that makes him call me," she said. "He wants a companion for the journey he must continue."

"Dear God!" Nettie stared at her. "You can't tell me you want to continue now. It will ruin you both, Viv."

"Only if neither of us has the courage," Vivian said. "Last year tested my courage. I think Stevens showed me his last night."

"I can't believe either of you would be willing travelers down that path." Her friend eyed her.

"No one is willing when taking the road through hell." Vivian sighed. "But it does no good to resist. I ought to have learned that by now."

"I should think he would want nothing more than to go back to his old life after what that hellion cousin of his did to him."

Vivian shook her head. "Stevens will be more determined than before."

Her prediction proved correct. As she entered the lobby that afternoon, Stevens was sitting on a couch with a paper in his lap as if nothing had happened the night before. She hurried toward him but was caught by the Tisher party, who were all going to the casino. Their small talk sounded so trite that she could barely be civil to them. She knew they were watching her as she hurried to Stevens, accepting his gracious bow and taking in the way he held both her hands, his pleasure at seeing her apparent. She wondered how long it would take for the meeting to get back to her mother.

"Coffee?" He signaled a clerk.

"Perhaps we shouldn't stay here." She glanced around.

"Your former friends look as if they need somewhere to gorge their magpie eyes," the redhead said with a smile. "High society gossip is amusing when it's so far off the mark."

"I wasn't thinking of them," she said. "I was thinking of Roger."

"You mean of the extreme discomfort that might arise if we were to encounter him?" Stevens moved aside a few magazines as a waiter put down the coffee. "You needn't worry about that. I discovered his two young friends are staying at The Riordan."

"Where?"

"One of the new hotels down at the end of the boardwalk," he sniffed. "They're not likely to come this way."

"You're very calm about it." She eyed him.

"It's been a long time coming, Vivian. Perhaps even since Roger was a child." He looked over her head at the windows behind. "He was right. My father and I never treated him fairly, nor were we very respectful toward his father's memory. We were arrogant fools, both of us." He said the last in a ruffled tone.

"But after all he's done—"

"My suffering so far has done me a lot of good," he insisted. "I couldn't hide in my safe haven forever."

"Is that what you were doing, hiding in your safe haven?" The coffee cup felt heavy in her hand.

He nodded. "I know that now. It was a retreat from the world. Not very noble of me." His face turned a genuine red from embarrassment. "It was only your courage that could have brought me out of it. It's that courage I need now, Vivian."

"That's why you summoned me, isn't it?"

He laughed. "I hope not that! I consider it one friend calling on another." His eyes rose with anxiousness. "I hope you do too."

"I'm not antagonistic toward you, am I?" she pointed out.

He pushed the coffee away. "You deserve to know about the Order of Actaeon. You deserve to know more about my summer with your brother."

She turned away, fussing with the fringes on a cushion lying on the couch.

"Have you lost your fearlessness already?" Stevens peered at her.

She was thinking of the previous year stumbling through her journey, the people she had seen, the words she had read in the journal of a man she never knew, and the name and home she had lost. The specter she had laid to rest now rose, walking into Stevens' dark room.

"I have the fortitude if you do," she said.

He rose. "It means going back."

"To Neart Castle?" She was alarmed.

"To Brandywine."

She stiffened. "You know how I feel about the place."

"That it should stay locked," he said briefly. "I remember. But you can't tell me you believe that now."

"Why go there?" Her voice shook.

"Because my mind is still hazy," he said. "And I must see and feel to remember."

She thought about how she had come back to Alderdice Hall the year before after her visit to Ember Warren and ended up in the room her grandmother had occupied in her better days. She still felt the warmth of that room, the softness of its colors and tall windows where her grandmother had watched the stars. "Yes, I see," she murmured.

As they exited the French doors leading to the boardwalk, she couldn't help but take in the Tisher party, still lingering in the lobby. She noted with some amusement how they all had their eyes on her and Stevens.

As they walked, the sunlight poured over the wooden planks, showing the bright sand and pebbles. She thought of the end of summer and asked, "You'll be leaving here soon, won't you?"

"I don't know."

She glanced at him.

"I've no place to go now," he said. "Going back to the city with Roger is obviously out of the question."

"And the castle?"

His giant frame shuddered, sending waves against her hand as she held his arm. "I never want to see that place again."

"You could do worse than Waxwood," she remarked.

"I already have." The sharpness in his voice made her face turn red.

They came on to the road where a few wagons and carriages were passing by. One held a group of men in work clothes, their darkened skin and scruffy mustaches showing them as laborers. One man tipped his wide-brimmed hat at them. An uneven place in the road jerked the wagon bed to one side, and the man fell down, making his comrades laugh. With a good-natured smile, he raised his hand in salute as if he had fully intended to amuse them.

The dotted trees, neither wax nor redwoods, gave out a fresh scent of green over the powdery sweetness of violets, and the climb was steep with tiered hills. When they passed the first tier, there sat a young man with an easel. His back was toward them, but as they approached, Stevens' foot kicked a rock, and the sound made the young man turn with a startled gaze. He stared at the redhead with pale gray eyes, his lips open underneath a neat mustache. Stevens nodded and led Vivian up the next hill.

"Duff!" The single word bore like a branding into the pale sky that loomed above them.

Stevens turned to look at the young man. A sudden terror rose in his eyes. "Hello, Pines."

"My name's James. James Finley," said the young man. "We need not use those other names now, do we?"

A knowing look passed between them. Vivian leaned on her closed parasol to get a better look at the young man's face.

"Friends call me Jimmy," he went on. "I'd be obliged if you would too, sir."

"You needn't call me 'sir,'" the redhead said.

"Yes, maybe I can," said Jimmy. "We're no longer on those terms, are we?"

To this, Stevens turned a little pale, but his voice was amiable as he said, "Friends call me Stevens." He turned and held out his hand to Vivian. "This is Mrs. Caulfield."

The young man shook her hand with a vigor that warmed her.

"You're a painter now, Jimmy?" the redhead asked in a clipped tone.

"I'm a schoolteacher," he said. "Boy's school. It's nothing fancy." The same knowing look passed between them. "I left, you know."

"I know," said Stevens. "So did I."

"I know."

"Did Smith tell you?" The redhead's eyebrows rose.

"I haven't seen Smith in a long time," said the young man. "We roomed in the same boarding house, you know."

"No, I didn't know."

"Of course you didn't." The young man blushed. "We were forbidden to talk about our personal lives, were we?"

An uneasy silence followed, giving Vivian the impression both men were reminiscing about some shared memory. To break the silence, she asked brightly, "You're a painter, Jimmy?"

"Yes, ma'am," he said. "There might be something in it for me someday, but not just now, if you know what I mean."

"May I see?" she asked. "I'm interested in artists. My brother is one, you see."

"Mrs. Caulfield's brother is Jake Alderdice," Stevens said in a low tone. "Carlyle."

The name altered the young man's mood. He dropped the reserved politeness, and his eyes widened, his hands gesticulating so wildly, Vivian feared he was going into a fit.

"You're the sister!"

"You knew my brother?" She stared at him.

The young man suddenly calmed, folding his hands in front of him. Vivian realized Stevens, who was standing behind her, must have shot him a warning look.

"I knew him a few years ago, ma'am," he said. "We talked about art a lot. I wanted to show him some of my paintings, but he never came back that night—" He stepped back and turned the canvas in her direction. "You're welcome to see it, Mrs. Caulfield. I reckon that's almost as good."

The paintings, though not very original, were well done with color. The brightness of green and violet showed through the distinct lines of scenery the young man was painting.

"I experiment little," he admitted in a sheepish tone. "The art teacher at the school is always admonishing me for it."

"I'm sure many people will appreciate the serenity in the view, especially in these times."

"Yes, it's been rather a jumpy start to a new century, hasn't it?" he asked eagerly. "Those Boxers in China killing all those people and the smallpox in Kentucky. Who knows, there may even be a war in Europe!"

"Fine work, Jimmy," Stevens mumbled as he took Vivian's arm. "We won't disturb you, of course. We were just taking a walk."

"Oh, there's plenty there still," he said, pointing toward the hill. "Most of it is in ruins, of course." He took Vivian's hand. "It was grand meeting you, Mrs. Caulfield. Remind me to your brother when you see him."

This brought a surge of sadness into her heart, and Stevens, as if feeling her pain, quickly led her away up the hill.

"He didn't ask about Jake," she lamented as she held up the edge of her skirt.

"I fancy he would have," said the redhead. "Perhaps I was abrupt, but it's better this way."

"Yes," she breathed. "Thank you."

She was anxious now to reach the top. Their feet hit the gravel with a severe knock, making both she and Stevens breathless. The moment they reached the edge of the hill, she saw a wooden fence and the back end of a few small huts.

She stumbled a little from the path. Pine trees populated both sides, their prickly scent stinging her eyes. She clutched at the edge of the fence.

"I don't know this part of it," she murmured.

"I know it well," he said. "It's mine."

"What do you mean?"

"I bought the land for a purpose."

"What purpose?"

"I'll show you."

There was an opening in the gate, but Stevens, with his large frame, clearly had no intention of going through it. He jumped over the fence and helped Vivian avoid the tangled weeds embedding the floor of Brandywine. They followed a small path between the huts and came out again to what looked like a dead end with a circle of redwoods.

Vivian drew in her breath. The hut at the end had a red roof almost entirely caved in, half-eaten by the elements. "I know that place," she whispered. "My grandmother lived here for a time."

Stevens was hardly listening. He had let go of her arm and stood in the arc of the half-circle. The huts behind him had one front window, though the glass had been broken long ago, and these square spaces stared at him like wide eyes. His own countenance was murky as he spread his arms out.

"I see it now," he whispered. "The men, the fire, the jug of wine."

Vivian knitted her brows. "The colony was disbanded a long time ago."

"Not the colony," he said. "The men. The Order of Actaeon."

The name brought numbness into Vivian's hands. She heard Roger's voice in the hollow woods: *If anyone should know about the Order of Actaeon, you should!*

"Who are they?" she asked.

"I can't tell you."

She grabbed his hand. "Then why bring me here in the first place?"

He looked at her, his eyes half closed. "I mean, I can't tell you details. But I can tell you they're a secret society."

Her hands grew hot, and she wanted to tear off her gloves. "Did Jake know about this secret society?"

"He was a member that summer," Stevens said.

"And this was your meeting place, so to speak?"

He nodded. "We came here often."

"What did you do?" She steeled herself for the answer.

Stevens' features gathered as shards of sunlight filtered through wavering limbs of trees. He walked, and she followed close behind. "There was shame, I know there was. I can't remember what, but it came to me."

She swallowed. "I've heard of those male fraternities."

"It wasn't like that!" He gave her a savage look. "We were kind to one another."

"If it was good, why did that boy leave?" He looked at her. "Jimmy. He left, didn't he?"

Stevens strolled down the path between the main huts, all dilapidated and looking as if they had stories to tell. "He always mistrusted us. An older man pulled him in, just like me."

"You told Roger you left."

"Yes, yes," he said breathlessly. "I left."

"And Jake?"

"Jake left — you know. I left — I don't know why."

"Then perhaps they aren't the martyrs you think they are," she said bluntly. "You always struck me as a man who looked for heroes in the wrong place, Stevens."

"Did I?" He looked at her, then took her hand. "It's odd you should know me better than anyone else. You, who hated me. But you don't hate me anymore, do you?" Before waiting for an answer, he dropped her hand, his face twisting. "But you will when I show you. I know you will."

"Show me what?" she asked.

"I bought this place so the Actaeons could meet. I thought it a lark at the time," he chuckled. "Reviving this artistic place with — with—"

"With what?" She raised her head.

"With what we were."

"I suppose this society was all about carousing and womanizing?" she grumbled.

He looked at her, his face still. Then he burst out laughing. The deep sound rolled through the woods, its pleasant tone bouncing off trees, scattering birds, and coming to rest in the space between them. But then he grew grave. "If I show you, you won't hate me?"

"Show me," she said.

He took her hand and led her back the way they had come. She felt relieved, thinking they were leaving the place, but then he crossed the path into the veil of trees on the other side, shrouded and overgrown. She stumbled a few times across tall grass knotted with twigs. Stevens helped her through some walls of this chaotic overgrowth. She could hear waves in the distance and wondered how close they were to the sea.

She saw a shallow line of water and glistening stones. Across the way stood more trees and a footpath that seemed to lead into an abyss. Stevens' face grew narrower, as if the skin were pressing closer to the bone. His dark eyes shown like onyx.

"This is where the accident happened," he said.

She stared at the shrubs, and the vines threaded together like a tapestry. The dark vegetation served as a canvas for the little she knew—the gun — the echo of a shot — the boy.

"Were you with the others?" she asked softly.

"I woke Jake up just as the sun rose," he murmured. "I wanted — we needed to make amends."

"Amends?"

"I can't explain," he said. "I was thinking about my own position."

"Go on." She pressed her hands together.

"I thought it was a deer," Stevens' voice rose in a shriek. "God help me, I thought it was a deer!"

She felt the man beside her swaying, pulling her along, so she let go of his arm.

"I made him do it." His voice was gasping out the words. "He didn't want to. He was sick of the whole thing. I could see that. But they made me a leader, and I had to make him do it. Shoot, I said. Shoot, shoot, shoot!"

She realized what he was telling her, and her stomach stirred.

Her ankles felt as if they would crack like hollow china, and she tumbled to the ground. But she knew she wouldn't faint. On her hands and knees, she felt the coolness of the ground and the soft flounces of wet grass.

"It was over in a moment," Stevens droned. "I was proud of him. I thought it was a bull's eye. And then when I went to look —" He choked out a sob.

That cry released her. Her ankles felt firm and her stomach still. She rose, steady on her feet, her entire body grounded like an iron statue. "You made him do it, and then you deserted him. You were his guide, and then you flew."

"You promised you wouldn't hate me!" The words ripped out his throat.

"I don't hate you, Stevens." She felt oddly composed, just as she remembered Larissa had been in so many violent situations. "One can only feel pity for a coward and a thief."

"Thief?" His voice shook.

"You rob people of their trust in you." She picked up her parasol and leaned against it for support. "Roger was right. I can't judge him too harshly. You asked him to trust you, but one can't trust a thief and a coward."

"I don't want your pity!"

"No, you wanted my courage," she said. "I've given you all I have."

He looked confused.

She spoke into the darkened scenery, her eyes resting on a crossbow of tree limbs. "I've spent the last year trying to rid myself of scars from the past. My courage is all spent."

"You agreed to undertake this journey with me," he spoke tentatively. "Now you won't see it until the end?"

"I can't, Stevens." Her voice grated as misery rose inside of her.

"You mean you won't."

"Take it as you wish," she threw out. "It's not a companion you want now, but a place to lay to rest your guilt and shame. I can't be that place. I'm the sister of the man you ravaged."

"Ravaged?" he echoed.

"My brother looked up to you, and my mother approved of you."

His gaze lifted above her, almost to the sky.

"You robbed Jake of his trust in you, and our world caved in on us." She sobbed. "I have no more family left."

He tried to reach for her hands, but she drew away from him.

"When Roger came to me, I still hated you," she admitted. "But your plight stirred my compassion. Now even that has gone, and I'm left again with nothing."

"It's becoming clearer," he lamented. "Yes, everything is clear now."

She looked at him for a moment. His voice was barely audible, but she had a feeling he hardly knew she was there.

She straightened her skirt where some leaves had gathered in the folds. "I helped you get your voice back, and I'm glad. But we've no cause to see one another ever again." She began walking back toward the road.

He caught her arm. "Vivian!"

"I mean it, Stevens." The tears slid down her cheeks. She brushed them away with the back of her gloved hand. "Please leave me alone."

"I won't try to defend myself," he said. "Not now." His face fell with humbleness, and, for a moment, she wavered. His tone was stronger as he added, "I only ask you to come with me now."

She glared at him and continued to trample through the grass and twigs. She could see the sky cutting through the edge of the hill. The soft light told of the approaching evening, and Vivian felt suddenly weary. "I only want to go home," she murmured.

"We all want that, don't we?" he asked softly. "But sometimes home is a vile place."

"That's when we must find another," she said. "I have, and I know you will too." She held out her hand. "I'll say goodbye here and wish you the best."

She turned to go down the hill, but his voice stopped her. "There's a letter I think you'll want to read. It's from your brother."

The parasol felt like an anvil, and she let it fall to the grass. She watched with dewy eyes as it rolled down the hill. Stevens rushed to retrieve it and placed it firmly in her shaking hands.

"Why didn't you tell me?" she moaned.

"I didn't remember until now. That's the truth, Vivian." He peered at her. "You want to see it, don't you?"

She glared at him. "You're making a bargain to show it to me if I accompany you?"

"There are some things I need to explain," he said. "The flood of memory — everything is clear now." He grasped her hands. "You said you once had compassion for my plight. Spare me a little more of that compassion, I beg of you."

She was silent as the woods seemed to come alive around her. "I warn you, Stevens, you shall not win my faith nobly nor bravely now."

"I know I've lost that opportunity," he murmured.

She saw for the first time that she had left a trail of damaged lives behind her, and if she were to wrench free from Stevens and rush down the hill, as all her instincts were pushing her to do, she would leave yet another. The shiftless forms of Verina, Ruth, Bertha, and Ember Warren merged into a mass of burning spots like something bursting into flames before her eyes.

CHAPTER 14

Their return to the hotel was so silent that only the sound of their footsteps scraping against the gravel filled the void. The boardwalk yielded more flurry, for it was nearing the hour when everyone returned to the hotels to dress for dinner. Vivian idly observed there were still plenty of swells left, as if they were holding on to the last weeks of summer, and several families had now taken over the beach. The children were running around, filling sand pails with water to wash their feet and destroying sand castles to leave for the next day's creation. Their innocence touched her, and by the time they reached the Waxwoodian, she could walk with a lighter step.

She was aware there were several nods in his direction, people she had met in previous summers. The Tisher party had disappeared, except for Fern Tisher, who nodded as she passed. She felt the young woman's eyes following her and Stevens as they entered the elevator, and the suppositions embedded in them made her want to laugh.

They reached the penthouse suite, even whiter and hollower than it had been the evening before. She vaguely glanced at the door of a room, which was open, noting the empty bed and open closet doors. There was nothing to mark Roger's existence save a brandy glass with only a small pool of brandy in it that undoubtedly some careless maid had forgotten to wash.

"Will you take sherry?" Stevens asked.

"This is not a social call," she reminded him. Then, seeing the hurt look on his face, her tone softened. "Yes, I think a sherry would suit me."

He poured it, she noticed, with an unsteady hand. He reached for the brandy decanter, but stared at it as if it contained poison. Instead, he made himself a whiskey and soda and stood at the bar as he drank it with his back to her.

"I know it hasn't been easy for you," she began.

"I told you once bitterness stings all our tongues," he said. "But we can't let it sting our hearts too."

Her throat was burning, and she set the sherry glass down with a trembling hand. "Perhaps my heart is embittered beyond sweetening."

"Then this will bring you comfort."

The redhead disappeared inside a room and emerged carrying a long envelope. Every muscle in her face tightened as she saw the address: *Sitwell Prison*. He laid it gently in her lap.

She could hardly choke back the tears. "Never a word to Mother or me, but he wrote you."

"Read the letter," was all he said.

She slid out several rough sheets she recognized as the rag paper she had seen in the prison chaplain's office. As she unfolded the pages, her breath caught at the sight of the handwriting she knew so well. It was not the boy's handwriting she remembered with the wide spaces and loops. It was a tighter penmanship, formed with care, and darker, as if Jake had pressed down on the page to make sure all the words were clear.

Stevens,

   "All vows

and oaths,

may they all be permitted

forgiven, eradicated

and nullified."

These words are a prayer said by the Jews on the Day of Atonement, and I felt they were fitting. Perhaps I should have written sooner, as the month of thanksgiving has passed, and this letter is more befitting of that mood. But you will appreciate my circumstances did not leave me the leisure to choose my own time to write.

This is no longer the case. Warden Jenkins has been arousing sympathy for me, and the officials have finally given way. I left Sitwell only a few days ago. Good conduct time, they call it. I am grateful for the people I met, though you may find that difficult to believe. Life in prison was grim, to be sure, especially for one like myself, who hid from all terror, grief, and unpleasantness. If there is one redeeming quality of prison life, it's that there is no hiding — not from the guards nor the other prisoners. Everything is out in the open so that one must look the gorgon in the eye and cut off its head, lest one turn to stone.

When I came here, I was resigned to my punishment and took it gladly. I accepted less the circumstances under which that punishment came. I felt disgrace and humiliation along with animosity and hurt. It's so simple to see a man behind the gorgon's face, a man whose evasive charms slither like the million serpents on the gorgon head. Yes, I blamed you. I know now, and have known for a while, how childish and nonsensical this was. Father Gonzalez, the prison chaplain who was perhaps the truest father in my life, said, "If one member suffers, all suffer together; if one member is honored, all rejoice together." I have spent many solitary nights doing just that.

I accused you that day of being guided by your nemesis because of your own rebellious nature — a nature you were forced to conceal. I understand more about the circumstances that led you to the shameful (let us call it what it is) behavior on the fateful day of our crime (for it belongs to both of us, though it is chiefly mine) from the man who had preached courage to me throughout the summer. Most of all, I forgive you for the suffering you caused me and one whose name we never knew. I have even forgiven the Order for their misguided misanthropy and brutality. All heroes have feet of flesh.

Though you never tried to contact me, I know you have made inquiries. No doubt you are eager to know what has become of me. I have suffered no physical ills in Sitwell except perhaps a want of wandering. I took up my drawing again while in prison. When Culver denounced my paintings as mediocre, I lost the will to put pencil to paper, but the natural agitation of my soul made me want to make art once more. My style now is more idyllic than fantastic, but it suits me for now.

I heard from Father Gonzalez that Vivian did not like my new artistic perspective. She came to see me several months ago. She has since been writing me letters. I warned her I would not answer, but they have not gone unread. I have read every one of them with relish, as my familial disconnect was out of consequence and not desire. As you always revered her, you will be glad to know she has broken free of my mother's shackles at last and moved on to a new life, one with more hardship but also more reward. She is contented.

As for my mother, I have, of course, ceased any direct communication with her, but I know she has remarried a respectable man and is contented as well. A newspaper clipping arrived in the mail announcing the engagement which came, I gathered, from my sister. There was no name or return address on the envelope, and it would be like Vivian, if her whereabouts were uncertain.

As for my future, I am as free as a bird now. I am currently at a boardinghouse, but I shall leave the country soon. Prison life makes one's feet grow wings, and I have always wanted to travel and draw what I see. Father Gonzalez lent me the money for a passage, and I shall work my way to wherever it lands, if need be. A steamship bound for Europe and then Egypt, perhaps, I don't know. Whatever my hands can do to earn my bread, I will do.

You will not hear from me again, or perhaps you'll hear from me

*years from now, when I have my feet on the ground at last. Until then, I
wish you well, and I hope you, too, will find your forgiveness.*

   Jack Albright

   *(I took a new name when I entered Sitwell for the sake of my family,
and I now keep it as the man I have become.)*

Vivian laid down the pages on the coffee table. Her face was
stained with tears. Stevens had wandered to the balcony, but now
he took the grand leather chair across from her.

"Thank you," she said. "I needed to know. When you don't
know what's become of someone you love, you imagine many
horrors."

"I would have shown you much sooner if I had remembered."
He leaned forward with anxious eyes.

"I believe you," she promised. "I would like to know when you
received it."

He rubbed his hands together. "Last year, a little before
Christmas."

Anger flashed in her eyes. "And you never thought to
write us?"

"I was too ashamed."

"But you're not now?"

He sat next to her on the couch, though he kept the
respectable distance. "I thought if you knew your brother had
forgiven me, you might forgive me too."

She turned away. "Jake's heart has always been more merciful
than mine."

"If you knew the circumstances—"

She stood up. "I told you before, you won't win me with false
nobility or bravery!"

"I'm not trying to be brave or noble." He did not look at her.
"I'm trying to be truthful. I know now it all began with that
letter."

She studied him, his back hunched and his hands rubbing

together as if trying to make his panic disappear. She sat down slowly.

"I know you believe I was insensitive to your brother's predicament," he said. "But I suffered as much as your brother in those months that followed."

"But you didn't leave the Order, did you?" Vivian asked. "You as much as told me they had something to do with the accident."

"Only indirectly," he insisted. "I shirk no blame, Vivian."

The room had grown chilly from the wind coming through the open balcony doors. She left the couch and closed them.

"I didn't leave the Order," he admitted. "I threw myself into it. I felt unfit for any company but theirs, and I hardly spoke three words to anyone else. I preferred those men whose values I thought I had absorbed."

"Your long absences from home that Roger told me about last year were because of the Order," she murmured.

"I was building a refuge for young men," he said. "A place they could go for guidance and instruction. I wanted it for all young men, but I was voted down, and they kept the refuge only for the young men of the order." His voice grew grainy. "Roger must have followed me there. I felt a shadow dogging my footsteps several times, but I thought it was only my own imagination."

"You're not one for imagining things, Stevens," she said with a little irony.

He paced the room, then leaned against the balcony doors as he continued, "I had put the refuge in place when Christmas came. I felt it prudent to remain at home. My mother was not well." He took a deep breath before continuing, "Then I received Jake's letter. When I read the words, 'I forgive you,' I broke down like a child. I thought I could begin the new century by making up for my past sins." He gave a snarling laugh. "I did not understand the evil forces at work against me."

"You make it sound like a melodrama," Vivian sniffed.

"I wish it were!" He wrung his hands, "But it was all horrifyingly real." He returned to the couch and looked at her, his expression calm. "I realized yesterday that Roger must have found Jake's letter and guessed something had come between us. My family thought Jake never again came to visit because he was involved in his grandfather's business."

This made Vivian wince and turn away. Stevens was shaken for a moment, then went on. "Roger said he wrote two letters. One was to the Order, no doubt to the clubhouse where he had followed me. The other was to my father."

Vivian stared at him.

"You met my father," he continued. "You know what he was like."

"A spider that corners a fly gives the fly little chance for escape," Vivian remarked a little ruefully. "I read that once."

"Before Christmas, he called me into his study and showed me the letter," Stevens said. "He demanded to know what the writer meant by 'criminal activity.'"

"And you denied it," Vivian guessed.

"Denied it!" He stared at her. "Yes, that's what you would think. But I didn't deny it, Vivian. My conscience broke down. I told him everything. I even told him his enemy brought me into the Order."

Vivian sat back, her head buzzing. "I think I understand now what Jake meant about the hero's feet of flesh. I remember how much you admired your father, and to have the one you most admired denounce you—"

"Denounce me?" The redhead let out a roar. "If he had denounced me, I should have never needed my taciturn shelter."

Vivian was completely astonished. Her parasol, which had been leaning against the side of the couch, slipped to the floor with a loud clamor. She did not rise to retrieve it.

"I told him because I, too, thought he would denounce me," Stevens' voice was weak. "I knew if the word 'coward' came from his lips, I would show my courage for all it was worth. But he betrayed me!"

"Betrayed you?"

"He approved of all I had done, even as far as following Allcock into the Order."

Vivian's bewilderment increased as the man continued, "He even praised my good sense and presence of mind regarding the incident with your brother."

"Your hero showed his fleshed feet at last," Vivian muttered.

"I was horrified and confused," he admitted. "The holiday seemed like something out of a nightmare — my father beaming, my mother attending to things to please him even though she was hardly up to the task, and Roger sullen and watchful."

"I see now you suffered," Vivian said gently.

"After Christmas, my father told me he had arranged for us to go on a hunt in Austria. I think he meant it as a reward for my conduct regarding the affair with your brother."

Vivian's head swarmed. She held her handkerchief to her cheek and closed her eyes. She felt a tiny glass pressed into her hand and held it to her lips, smelling the sweetness of sherry, and when she drank it, her nerves felt steadier. She opened her eyes to find Stevens had taken her hand and was looking at her with a doctor's concern. "I won't go on, if you don't wish it."

"I want to hear the rest of it."

"The idea of going on a hunt with him was as despicable to me as it was just now to you," Stevens continued. "I refused, of course. I wanted the time alone. To think — to consider."

"Consider what?"

"Whether I wanted to remain in my father's house," he said.

Her hands and forehead were clammy now, and she felt the warmth of the cushion underneath her.

"He was disappointed, of course, but he insisted on going himself. He promised friends he would go, and he went."

"And he died?" Vivian asked.

"Afterward, I found out his doctor had told him his heart was growing weak, and he might not withstand the strain of another long hunt," Stevens lamented.

"And you felt responsible?" Vivian watched him.

He shrugged. "I suppose I did. I was the only one my father ever felt was up to his standards, you see. My mother — well, she was superfluous beyond the child she bore. Roger, as you heard from his own lips, was treated no better than the dogs. So I was the one he put all his faith in, and, in his eyes, I could not disappoint him."

"It never occurred to him he might disappoint you," Vivian said with a nod. "Yes, I know what that's like."

"It was part of what made me silent," he said. "I don't know quite how it came about. I only know that, one day I woke up, and I couldn't speak even if I had wanted to."

"Only part of it," Vivian murmured. "And the rest?"

He moved to the balcony doors but did not open them. He glared out into the black sky as he spoke. "I didn't leave the Order Vivian. They repudiated me."

"Because of Roger's letter?"

"Because of what happened two years ago," said the redhead.

"You told them the entire story then." She blinked.

"I would have done so regardless," said Stevens, "even if they hadn't summoned me."

"Summoned you?"

"For a special council meeting. When I got there, I had no idea they had received Roger's letter." He stopped before going on, "They questioned me, just as my father had done. And just as I had done with my father, I told them everything."

"They ordered you out," Vivian guessed.

"They had little concern for my own peace of mind and my wrongs," he said bitterly. "But should my crime come to the attention of the police, it would bring them in and destroy the secrecy to which they were so devoted."

"The heroes' feet of clay," Vivian sighed.

"They promised trustworthiness and solidarity!"

"But withdrew both at the first sign of trouble," Vivian finished.

"When my father died, I was left with no one."

She felt her eyes brim with tears. The center of a blank circle was, she knew, empty on all sides. She had once stood in that circle herself.

He sat on the couch and bent toward her. "I deserved no one. One does not create a silent world unless one is searching for deprivation."

"You've received your punishment, Stevens." She laid her hand in the space between them.

He understood her intention and took her hand. "There is no complete redemption for me unless there is forgiveness."

"You've had that too." She looked at the letter lying on the table.

"I meant from you, Vivian." His eyes became soft. "For years, I was a false man. I was what I thought my father wanted me to be, what the world wanted me to be. Your brother exposed me as a coward and a failure as a leader. I was devastated, but you showed me it was the best thing that could have happened."

"Now, you may reconstruct your life as one builds a house — brick by brick," she said.

"But I can't!" He wrung out the words. "If you leave without forgiving me, my life will remain in shards. So I beg you to forgive me."

Vivian looked at the face twisted with emotion and the dark eyes almost transparent. She felt the gentle grasp of his hand in hers. The night seeped through the balcony glass, melting against the gloss of light floating all around the room. Reflections on the slick white walls merged with white shadows, leaving only her and Stevens' outline.

The words of Father Gonzalez returned: *Forgive, and you will be forgiven.* All the bitterness gathered inside her dissipated, and she could again see the picture her brother had drawn in prison — the family by the lake. Inside that frame, the faces came alive.

"Yes," she whispered. "I forgive you."

He pressed his lips on the back of her hand, then withdrew, collapsing in the leather chair. Vivian wandered to the balcony and opened the doors. The sea breeze was calm with the night. A thread of air wrapped around her and swept out the last of the stinging feeling in her bones.

CHAPTER 15

She returned to the flat in a daze. What happened the rest of that night was equally muddled. She remembered Nettie made her dinner, though she had no recollection of what she ate. She had the sense of complete bewilderment on her friend's face. She knew Nettie was waiting for an explanation for Vivian's stupor after their months of intimate friendship. When none came, she didn't ask questions.

It was only in the first dregs of early morning that Vivian awakened to herself. She dressed and slipped out before Nettie stirred. She walked to the train station and caught the first train to San Francisco.

As she walked up Clay Street, her eyes searched for the beggar woman. The street was empty of people, shades of painted houses giving off a rainbow glare against the fresh blue sky. Just as she stepped past a darkened doorway, she saw the woman, sitting in her enchanting repose. Vivian extracted money from her reticule and dropped it in the tin can the woman had placed in front of her. The beggar murmured her blessings.

"You were right." Vivian bent toward her.

"Ma'am?"

"You prophesied I would find forgiveness in those who had harmed me," she said. "I have."

"I ain't no charlatan, ma'am!" the woman insisted.

"When one finds forgiveness, one must pass it on to others," Vivian remarked.

The beggar laughed, deep and rigorous. "That we must, ma'am, that we must!"

Vivian reached Alderdice Hall with the still breath of one who had just climbed a mountain.

Basset let her in, his expression astounded for once. "Why, madame, we weren't expecting you!"

Vivian deposited her gloves and parasol on the bench in the hall. "Is my mother awake?"

"Mr. and Mrs. Blackwell are on the veranda," he said.

This time, she didn't wait for Basset to announce her. She strolled through the hallway she had known so well to the porch where the scent of lavender curled around the strong roast of the coffee. Her stepfather hid behind his newspaper, and Larissa had just taken another sliver of toast, which she dropped on the table when she saw Vivian.

Her mother recovered with her usual grace and gave her a warm smile. "You ought to have told us you were coming into the city."

"Good to see you, Vivian," Bennett murmured from behind his paper.

"You haven't had breakfast, have you?" Larissa nodded at one of the iron chairs. "You're still looking too peaked for my taste."

Vivian sat down, her hands pressing in her lap. "Mother, I want to apologize."

"Apologize?" Her mother blinked. "What on earth for?"

"I've been punishing you," she said. "For — well, everything."

"If you've been punishing me, I didn't feel it," her mother said warily as she motioned for Basset to bring an extra place setting.

"But I have," said Vivian. "I've neglected to visit you because I was — well, ravaged."

"I see you haven't given up your habit of circle talk," her mother remarked. "Perhaps some breakfast will give you more sense."

"I don't need sense, and I don't want breakfast!" Vivian took a breath. "Last year was the end of so many things. We know that."

Her mother's mild manner faded, and her eyes pierced like pins. "I don't want to talk about last year."

"I don't want to talk about it either," Vivian agreed. "I only came to say two things. One is, I didn't realize how much I had to forgive until now. I forgive the past. I forgive you."

"I'm grateful." Larissa's tone was dry. "May I ask exactly of what am I being forgiven?"

"Be kind, Rissa," Bennett mumbled.

"Everything!" Vivian answered. "The lies, the evasions, the demands. Everything that's happened, really."

"What 'happened' resulted from your own prodding and probing, Vivian," said her mother in a severe tone. "I never had a hand in it."

"No, not directly," Vivian agreed. "But I wouldn't have had to prod and probe if we had been a family who valued the truth. And it began with you, didn't it, Mother?"

Larissa's blue eyes turned an icy shade. Even Bennett, who had now folded his newspaper, seemed apprehensive about what would happen next. Vivian guessed he had never seen her mother angry.

But Larissa's anger vanished inside a wave of composure and regality. She finished her toast and motioned for Basset to bring a fresh pot of coffee. Only then did she speak, and her voice was steady. "I assume you had some startling revelation that urged you to come home?"

"In fact, it was," said Vivian. "I've heard from Jake."

The coffee pot Larissa had just picked up almost wrenched

out of her grasp. Bennett caught it in time and poured the coffee for her, then a cup for himself.

"He said he wouldn't write," said her mother quietly.

"He didn't write me," Vivian said. "He wrote Stevens. You remember Harland Stevens, don't you?"

"I remember Harland Stevens."

"I've heard of the Stevens Canneries," Bennett offered.

"Stevens is now the heir." Vivian nodded. "His father died earlier this year." She studied her mother's face. "You want to hear about Jake, don't you, Mother?"

Larissa stared out into the garden at the purple and yellow blooms and the gazebo with its fine wall of ivy. "Yes, I want to hear about Jake."

"He's out now," she said. "He knows about me. He knows about you too."

"About me?" Her mother glanced at her.

"About your marriage," said Vivian. "He received the newspaper clipping you sent him."

"What clipping?"

Vivian blinked. "He thought it was me who sent it, but it was you, wasn't it?"

"I don't know what you're talking about, Vivian." Her mother's voice was jagged. "Your brother asked us not to communicate with him. *I* kept that promise." She looked pointedly at her.

"I sent him the clipping."

Both she and her mother stared at Bennett. He put a few lumps of sugar in his coffee and stirred it with the earnestness with which he handled most things. His heavy brows remained even, but his expression was more resolute than Vivian had ever seen.

"You, dear?" Larissa echoed.

"I knew how you felt, Rissa," he said. "I also knew you wouldn't tell him, so I thought it best to send it anonymously. It didn't seem right, a son not knowing about his mother's remarriage."

Her mother turned away, her gaze on the garden again. Vivian felt the tears in her own eyes as she regretted telling Nettie that Bennett was a milksop. She took his arm. "That was very gallant of you, Bennett."

He looked at her. "I did right, then?"

"You did right," Vivian said. "Now we know he has a place in his heart for us just as we have for him." From the corner of her eye, Vivian caught her mother lifting her handkerchief to her face. She continued in a more forceful tone. "I said I came for two reasons. The first was to forgive you. The second was to ask for money."

"You're welcome to that, of course," said Larissa. "I've always told you."

"Perhaps you won't be so generous when you hear what I want the money for," Vivian said ruefully. "I want to bring Jake home."

Her mother's cup dropped inside the saucer with a clatter.

"He said he was going away in the letter," Vivian continued. "I want to go abroad to find him and bring him home."

"Where abroad?" Bennett inquired.

"He didn't say exactly."

"So you intend to roam the world looking for him?" Larissa asked in a tense voice. "It's not very practical, is it, dear?"

"I know where to start," said Vivian. "Egypt."

"What makes you think he's there?"

"I know he's there, or he was there," Vivian said. "It was a game we played when we were children. I shall start in Egypt. If he's not there, I'll make inquiries. So I'll need an open purse." She looked at her mother.

Bennett cleared his throat. "I admire your gumption, Vivian, but I hardly relish the idea of you traveling alone."

"I've been alone most of my life, Bennett," she said wryly.

Larissa studied her. "What makes you think Jake will want to see you?"

"I don't know," said Vivian. "But I need to see him, as much as I need to see you. I know that now."

"You may not find him at all," her mother reminded her.

"Perhaps, but I shall have no peace of mind unless I *try*." Vivian put her hand over her mother's. "I think you won't either, Mother."

They were silent for a time as a pair of bluebirds perched on the veranda rail sang a morning song. A wave of nostalgia overcame Vivian, and she almost felt like a debutante again, lingering in the last summer months until fall, with its balls, parties, and soirees fell upon her. The memory remained like an imprint of what was unhindered with the sadness of a few months before.

Her mother rose and retreated into the house. She emerged a few moments later with a check in her hand that she handed to Vivian. Vivian saw the check was blank.

"When will you leave?" Larissa asked, her tone quiet.

"The first steamer I can catch." Vivian pushed her chair back.

"You'll let us know which one," said Bennett. "So we can come and see you off."

Touched, she bent down and kissed his cheek.

"You'll write us?" Larissa asked, grasping her hand.

"If I need more money."

"I didn't mean that," said her mother. "Let us know how you're doing and if — if you've found him."

Vivian pressed her mother's hand. "Of course I will." She took a last look at the garden, now invaded by an aromatic scent of roses. It made her think of the rose-colored handkerchief in her grandmother's hand on her debutante portrait. "May I have the key to Ancestor Hall?" she asked.

Her mother jumped. "Why do you want to go there?"

"I want to see Grandmother's portrait," said Vivian. "The one of her before her coming out ball."

"What do you want it for?"

"To take it with me," she said. "It doesn't belong there now."

Her mother's hands wavered over a slice of toast. Then, she put it down. "The key is in my jewelry box. You know where."

Vivian found the key and crossed into the hollow hallway where the floor turned from wood to marble. The large doors with their ring handles gazed down at her with menace as she unlocked them and stepped in. The room had the musty odor of abandonment.

She found her grandmother's portrait hung a little apart from the others. The steady smile illuminated the gazing eyes. Vivian realized they looked as her brother had once told her — unhappy and restricted. The picture was lighter in her hands than she thought it would be. She fetched some canvas sacks from Missy, the scullery maid, and wrapped the painting as if she was wrapping a baby against the winter cold.

~

She arrived in Waxwood before lunchtime. Wealthy families returning to their city life crowded the station, their suitcases taking up much of the platform. Vivian threaded her way around them, holding the wrapped portrait close to her chest so it wouldn't scrape against any of the baggage. She breathed easier when she reached the main road and turned into the small street where the *Nettie's Drugstore* sign flapped in the wind. Her step was light as she trudged up the stairs to the flat.

Her friend was there, her eyes seething. "You ran off in a hurry this morning."

Vivian sat down with a sigh in the rocking chair. "I had some family business."

"Don't tell me you went to see the Queen of Denial," her friend scoffed.

"I think she's ready to shed some of that denial, Nettie," said Vivian. "Forgiveness has its rewards."

"Forgiveness?" Her friend peered at her.

"When one has it, one must pass it on to someone else," she repeated.

Nettie put on an apron. "You make it sound like a virus."

"The past was just that to me until a few months ago," said Vivian. "I couldn't see through my grief and bitterness."

"And now you're no longer grieving and bitter?"

"So much has happened." Vivian told her friend about the events of the previous day and that morning.

Her friend was thoughtful when she finished. "You're really going to Egypt to find Jake?"

"I must," she said. "I must try to put back the pieces of the fragile puzzle that was the Alderdice family."

"You've told me repeatedly you had no family."

Vivian leaned forward. "I was wrong. Now that all the lies and half-truths are exposed, there is perhaps only the skeleton. But one can make something of a skeleton."

Pan trotted up to her, his tail swinging from side to side, looking at her with his thoughtful eyes.

"You'll take care of Pan for me while I'm gone, won't you?" She asked, absently patting the dog's head.

"Of course." Her friend put her hands on her shoulders. "We'll both be waiting here when you return."

Vivian was silent for a moment, looking through the high window. "I don't think I'll be coming back here."

"Oh!" Her friend was clearly alarmed.

"I'll be coming back to Waxwood," she promised. "But not to the library." She glanced at the woman. "It was your dream, dear, and I'm happy to have helped you make it come true. But it's *yours*, Nettie, not mine."

Her friend's face was stiff as she turned to the pot on the stove. "You're going to do something with the children."

"I was thinking about it on the train," Vivian said. "A school for young women."

"Not children?"

"Young women at the age between girlhood and womanhood," said Vivian. "When they're the most vulnerable."

"It's a vast undertaking, Viv." Her friend sighed.

"I realize that." She stiffened. "I also realize I'll need money. Lots of it."

"Surely, your mother—"

"I've already asked her for money for this trip," said Vivian. "I can't ask her for more." She leaned her head back and rocked. "I don't know how, but I'll get it."

"I'll help all I can," her friend promised. "Now, come to lunch."

As Vivian rose, her eyes fell on the portrait. She unwrapped it carefully and laid it on the bed.

"Your grandmother, isn't it?" Nettie asked. "How regal she was!"

"In this portrait, perhaps," said Vivian. "In another, she was a rebel. I know all about it now."

"I don't see where we have to put it," her friend said, glancing around. "It's much too fine for the Waxwood dust."

"I don't intend to hang it," said Vivian.

"Not hang it?" Nettie stared at her.

She sprang open the trap door to the cupboard and slid the portrait next to the one Spenlow had done of her.

"Isn't that rather a shame?" Nettie asked.

Vivian closed the door firmly. "A shame for Penelope Alderdice. But Grace Carlyle would have wanted it that way."

CHAPTER 16

It was one of those grand mornings in San Francisco where majestic buildings shot up through the bright blue sky, and seagulls flew over the bay, their cries enshrouded in the morning air over Nob Hill. Vivian awakened to the sound of the birds, unused to the perpetual darkness enveloping Alderdice Hall. She had been staying only a few days until her steamship was to depart, in the pleasant position of a guest who felt at home in her surroundings. The opulence of the room she had chosen on the first floor, far away from her old room, had little effect upon her. She saw the satins and the velvets and gold trims as a stamp of another era, one she had left behind long ago.

She had time before breakfast to linger on the veranda in the warm September air and write in her diary:

> *I sail today, taking the long journey to Europe and Alexandria to catch a boat to Egypt. I always hate that point when the water lies like a field of shimmering aqua velvet and one cannot see land. But this time, I shall be glad to be heading toward the unknown. Funny how I've always been afraid of the unknown. Perhaps I've finally realized the known can be just as frightening. I wonder if Jake knows this too.*

Larissa behaved through the morning in a maternal way Vivian had never seen. She fussed and rushed about, overseeing servants through the packing, pushing new silk gloves or scarves at Vivian, even though they were all far too fine for the more practical clothes Vivian was taking.

"Leave the girl alone, Rissa." Bennett stood in the doorway, watching with male amusement. "She knows what she wants."

"That's the trouble, dear," said her mother, distracted by several coats lying on the bed. "Vivian's decisions are apt to be far from her best interests at times."

"As are yours, Mother," Vivian remarked. "At times."

She and her mother were on amiable terms once the carriage arrived at port, though Larissa still delivered words of caution useful to young women ten years ago but obsolete in the new era. Vivian caught sight of Nettie's bright red hat and embraced her with a tight grip.

"I wanted to see you before you left." Her friend's voice sounded muffled in the throng. "The flat is always open to you, Viv. And to Jake, if he wishes it."

"I don't know what we'll do," she said. "He may not even want to come to Waxwood. It holds sad memories for him."

"Then we shall make them happy ones, just as we have yours." Nettie put her arm around her.

"We must hurry with your baggage, dear," her mother reminded her.

Vivian lifted one of her suitcases. A large hand clasped over hers, and she looked up to see Stevens' broad frame before her.

"I thought you went back to the castle!"

"I told you I would never go back there again," he reminded her. "I'm having an agent handle the sale." He forced her to put the suitcase down and took both her hands. "How are you, Vivian?"

She was grateful Nettie was leading her mother and stepfather away. "Nervous," she said truthfully. "Mother reminded me just this morning that Jake might not want to see me, even if I find him."

"He'll want to see you," he insisted. "No one gives up their childhood companion so easily."

"Even when one is no longer a child?" She eyed him with a smile.

"Especially when one is no longer a child."

"It was good of you to come see me off, Stevens," she said. "Nettie told you when I was sailing?"

"She told me everything," he said. "I came yesterday to look for you at the drugstore. I ought to have told you that night—"

"Tell me now, then."

"I mean to make things right," he said. "For Jake, I mean. I intend to do what I should have done two years ago."

"And that is?"

"Go to the police." He was adamant. "If I came forward with the truth, it would clear your brother's public record."

"Then it wouldn't matter to Mother or the Washington Street blue bloods if he was in jail, would it?" Vivian murmured.

"Not if I know blue bloods, it won't!" Stevens laughed. "There are too many who ought to be in jail for worse."

"I'm glad, Stevens," she said. "Jake will be grateful."

"I wish you'd let me come with you."

"To Egypt?" she asked, surprised.

"You may have to travel for quite a while," he said.

Her throat felt scratched with tears. "I need my brother, Stevens. I'll find him."

He leaned forward, and she could see the clear rim around his dark eyes. Her hands in his felt warm and comforted. "I know you will, Vivian. But what about afterward?"

"Afterward?"

"When you come home. With or without Jake."

"I don't know," she said. "I have some ideas—"

"I know," he said. "Nettie told me. You want to build a school."

"If I can raise the money and find a place," she said.

"I can offer you both," he said.

She glanced at him. "What do you mean?"

He slipped out of his breast pocket a sheet of parchment that he handed to her. It was a legal document, and although she was too distracted to read it, the word "Brandywine" stood out.

"The deed to the place," he said. "I'm giving it to you. Perhaps it will bring you better luck than it has me."

"For the school?" She stared at him.

He nodded. "Whatever money you need to build it, you have only to ask."

She blinked through a vale of tears. "I'll accept it only if you help me, Stevens."

"I'll do whatever you say," he said.

A woman who held a basket overflowing with bouquets of wildflowers jolted them. The woman was profuse with apologies, lamenting about "all the teeterin' ladies, you'd've thought it was a garden party!" in a charming Scotch brogue. Stevens grabbed a bouquet and slipped a few bills in her basket while the woman bowed her thanks. He put the flowers in Vivian's hands.

"A rather odd place to sell wildflowers," he remarked.

She looked over the glaring shades of pink, purple, and white and, spotting the yellow dandelion, slipped it out of the bouquet.

"The little nuisance," Stevens remarked good-naturedly.

"The little survivor," she murmured. "When I reach land, I shall plant it somewhere."

"It would hardly be more than a wilted mass by then," he reminded her.

"Perhaps," she said. "But it will grow. They always do."

~~~~~

Author's Note

Hi, reader! I'm so glad you got to the last book of this series. I
~~~~~

hope you found the relationship between Vivian and her nemesis Stevens intriguing.

When I first conceived of the Alderdice family saga, I only had three books in mind. Actually the series was originally a novel told in three voices with three different coming-of-age stories that I wrote back in 2014 during a difficult time in my life. The novel morphed into a series where only two of the voices remain here (Vivian's and Jake's). Originally, I was going to end with Book 3 (and if you haven't read it yet, I highly encourage you to check it out, as it's a pretty potent story of Vivian's journey to discovering her own identity in the midst of uncovering more family secrets and lies).

So why did I add Book 4? Quite simply, because when I wrote Book 2, the character of Harland Stevens absolutely fascinated me. There were things about his character I knew were hidden (though I didn't know what they were at the time — contrary to what you might think, writers don't know absolutely everything about their characters!). The adversarial relationship Vivian has with him in that book felt unfinished. Like many writers, I started to play the "what if?" game. What if someone who was supposed to be your nemesis becomes, through circumstances, your friend? What if Vivian were faced with helping Stevens uncover his own family secrets? I couldn't resist the temptation to write their story.

Many readers have told me they loved this book best of all the books in the series and they even wanted a sequel. If you'd like to see a sequel, feel free to say so in your review or email me at tammay70@tammayauthor.com.

. . .

So, what next? How about a short story collection that tells five different stories of women at the dawn of the women's movement? Read on to find out more!

Happy reading!
Tam

Women in post-war America had it all: generous husbands with great jobs, comfortable suburban homes with nice yards and a two-car garage, and all the latest gadgets to make their housework easier.

It was a perfect recipe for happiness and fulfillment. The women's magazines told them so. Advertisements told them so. Doctors told them so.

They were sold a bill of goods about post-war life. Some bought it and some didn't. This book is about the women who didn't.

Five stories. Five women. Five journeys of self-discovery.

"Great short stories that really do speak to what women had to face mid 20th century."

Read on for an excerpt from this book!

"You're headstrong too," Rachel mused. "Dad always said I take after you."

A shadow appeared around her crow's feet eyes. "That was my undoing. Don't let it be yours."

"What do you mean by 'undoing'?"

Her aunt set the game down near the bed with care, as if afraid to upset the pieces inside. "You must believe me when I tell you I thought I was doing the right thing."

Rachel nodded. "It was wrong of me to say you were selfish."

"I don't deny I was selfish," said Amelia. "I didn't see it that way at the time." She turned to her niece. "You see, dear, I was always led to believe you took care of a child so he would take care of you when you got old."

"That's a pretty unfair burden to put on kids, don't you think?"

"Your grandfather didn't think so."

"Grandfather?" Rachel had a flash of the faded photo on her father's desk of the man dressed in a striped, baggy suit with a straw hat who looked very much like him, a man who had died before she was born.

"We were very close," Amelia murmured. "I always believed everything he told me. It never occurred to me he could be wrong."

Rachel took her hand. "No one has to be right or wrong."

"I *was* keeping Donny in a crucible." Her aunt sighed. "A child can only stay locked up for so long before he starts to look for the key."

"All children look for the key when they grow up," Rachel insisted.

Her aunt gave a wry smile. "You were perfectly willing to blame me earlier, and now you're making excuses for me."

"I wasn't blaming," Rachel said. "I was trying to make you see things from Don's point of view."

"I wanted so much for him." Amelia's globe eyes turned almost a pale peach under the lights above the bed. "It isn't about what the parent wants. It's about what the child wants when he grows up, isn't it?"

Rachel rose. "Let's go back to the party. Dad said he wants to dance a waltz with you, remember?"

But her aunt remained seated on the bed. "You don't hate me anymore?"

Rachel's eyes filled with tears. "I never hated you, Aunt Amelia. And neither does Don."

"I know Warren always said I was too overprotective," Amelia said. "In his way of thinking, a parent doesn't hover over a child. Your mother and father didn't hover. Maybe because they had each other."

"You might have married again," Rachel mused.

"Don't think I didn't have my opportunities!" Her aunt leaned her head back, a little of her old twinkle back in her eyes. "But a husband isn't always the answer, Rachel. I never liked being told what to do."

"Because you're headstrong." Rachel smiled.

Her aunt grabbed both her hands. "That might be your downfall, dear. Or your salvation."

Will Rachel's strong will be her downfall or her salvation? You can find out by purchasing a copy of *Lessons From My Mother's Life* at your favorite online bookstore at this link: https://tammayauthor.com/books-2/lessons-from-my-mothers-life .

How about that cool freebie I promised you? If you're into historical cozy mysteries featuring strong women who don't let society's rules about female behavior stop them from doing what they want, I urge you to check out the Adele Gossling Mysteries! Read on for how to get hold of the series' free novella, *The Missing Ruby Necklace*.

When a jewel and a girl go missing on New Year's Eve...

Eleanor McCarthy, a lovely though somewhat flighty debutante, has graced the tiny town of Arrojo, California, with her presence. One of Arrojo's prominent ladies throws a New Year's Eve shindig to introduce her to Arrojo's high society — whatever little of it there is. Naturally, the daughter and son of one of San

Francisco's influential lawyers, Adele and Jackson Gossling, are invited.

But screams replace popping champagne corks when Eleanor's priceless ruby necklace is discovered missing. And soon, so is Eleanor!

In this historical cozy mystery set in the early 20th century, follow Adele Gossling, stationary store owner and amateur sleuth, and her clairvoyant sidekick Nin Branch as they search for a ruby necklace that may or may not have been stolen and a young woman who may or may not have run away.

Want to read an excerpt from this book? I got you covered! Turn the page.

"Coffee!" Miss McCarthy laughed. "Heavens, no! I haven't had my first taste of champagne yet." She flung her hand out to her brother. "Bring me a bottle of champagne, my good man."

"I don't mind," he said.

Before he could saunter out the door, Mrs. Abberton jumped up. "I'll get it."

"I really think we ought to get coffee," Mr. Abberton mumbled.

"She wants champagne," Mrs. Abberton was almost stern. "It's a celebration, after all!" She practically fled from the room.

Adele followed her and caught her arm. She spoke in a soft tone. "Mrs. Abberton, why did Miss McCarthy faint?"

"She just told you, didn't she?" The woman gave a shrill laugh. "Albert said we ought to open some windows, but it was such a windy night, I —"

"It wasn't the windows," said Adele. "Or the corset."

"Of course it was!" The woman examined some bottles on the floor. "I never could read these labels."

"You were staring at Miss McCarthy as if something that wasn't there."

"What an imagination you have, dear." The woman said.

"Miss McCarthy had her hands on her throat when she fell," Adele continued. "You kept looking at her throat."

"Nonsense," the woman hissed.

"Miss McCarthy wasn't wearing her ruby necklace," Adele declared.

Mrs. Abberton tore through a row of bottles lying on a table. One rolled onto the floor with a crack and the bubbly drink spilled across the marble. She sunk into one of the chairs. "You're too observant, Miss Gossling."

"You saw it too."

"Just before the lights went out," she said. "But Eleanor is one of those girls who gets easily flustered with her jewelry. She says it weighs her down."

"If that's true, why were you so alarmed just now?" Adele said.

"I wasn't," the woman insisted. "She locks that necklace in a box. Albert tried to persuade her to put it in our safe at the finance company, but she refused."

"That's rather unusual," Adele said.

"Eleanor's a lovely girl, but rather flighty," The woman said in a harsh tone. "I expect Celestine spoils her."

"If the necklace is missing, there might be a theft involved," Adele suggested.

Jewelry goes missing all the time. But does that mean theft? And why is Mrs. Abberton so nervous?

How can you get your hands on a copy of *The Missing Ruby Necklace*, not available in any bookstore? Simple. Go to this link: https://landing.mailerlite.com/webforms/landing/ l2u0c3. What else will you get when you get this novella? How about fun facts about women in history and true crime classic mysteries, which are just as fascinating, if not more so, as contemporary true crimes?

ABOUT THE AUTHOR

Writing has been Tam May's voice since the age of fourteen. She writes stories about powerful women set in the past. Her fiction gives readers a sense of justice for women, both the living and the dead. Tam's stories are set mostly around the Bay Area because she adores sourdough bread, Ghirardelli chocolate, and San Francisco history.

Tam is the author of the Adele Gossling Mysteries which take place in the early 20th century and features sassy suffragist and epistolary expert Adele Gossling whose talent for solving crimes doesn't sit well with the ideas of some people around her about women's place. Tam has also written historical fiction about women breaking loose from the confinements of their era.

Although Tam left her heart in San Francisco, she lives in the Midwest because it's cheaper. When she's not writing, she's devouring everything classic (books, films, art, music) and concocting yummy vegan dishes.

Tam May can be reached at:
WEBSITE: http://tammayauthor.com/
EMAIL: tammay70@tammayauthor.com
FACEBOOK: https://www.facebook.com/tammayauthor
INSTAGRAM: https://www.instagram.com/tammayauthor/
PINTEREST: https://www.pinterest.com/tammayauthor/

www.ingramcontent.com/pod-product-compliance
Lightning Source LLC
Chambersburg PA
CBHW021648110726
47902CB00007B/1872